Cal raked his fingers through his long hair. "Are you moving back in here? Your dad is a maniac."

"You heard him. I don't have a choice. Debby will have her baby in a couple weeks, and I have nowhere to go."

"You can live with me. My place is small, but we could make it work."

I didn't know him well. What if we didn't get along after I went with him? Besides, Dad would call the law on us.

The door rattled, and my heart thumped when it flew open.

"You know boys aren't allowed in here," Dad said.

"Dad, we're just talking—"

"Shut your mouth, or I'll shut it for you." His posture stiffened.

We had to get out of here. Dad blocked the exit. Rather than challenging him, I stayed put. I could hear Cal breathing. He was no match for my father.

Dad glared at both of us. "Cal it's time to say goodbye." He stomped away.

I exhaled. It was safer with Cal here. Any other time, Dad would've stripped off his belt and whipped me. There was a five-minute window for Cal to leave before Dad threw him out and came after me next.

"He's crazy. Come with me." Cal sat on the bed's edge, one leg dangling, ready to stand.

Praise for Ellen Y. Mueller

"Ellen is a wonderful storyteller. I have had the privilege of reading some of her works in progress and cannot wait for the release of her YA novel. She's not afraid to let the characters run off the pages and come to life within the reader's mind. Her attention to detail can easily have the reader forgetting they are reading rather than watching a story play out on a film."

~Nicole Donoho, Author

Run Girl Run

by

Ellen Y. Mueller

Run Girl Run

Cover Art by *Kristian Norris*

The Wild Rose Press, Inc.
PO Box 708
Adams Basin, NY 14410-0708
Visit us at www.thewildrosepress.com

Publishing History
First Edition, 2022
Trade Paperback ISBN 978-1-5092-4490-4
Digital ISBN 978-1-5092-4491-1

Published in the United States of America

Dedication

For Victor, who encouraged me and was always in my corner.

Chapter 1

I started the trouble. If Dad were here, he'd say, "Tracie, you did it again." That's how it was, but I couldn't help it. One day, Dad pushed me too far. When I toppled over the edge, it caused a domino effect. In the end, we all paid for my mistakes.

My problems surfaced on a typical Friday afternoon. Fridays sucked. Once the last school bell rang, I went home and spent the weekend with my parents. Only my little brother and our dog made it tolerable. While other moms picked up their kids or allowed them to drive their own cars, I walked. They were lucky. Their smiling mothers hugged them and asked them about their day. Good for them. I knew I was in for a rotten evening when I reached my house. I had one hand on the door, with a storm raging inside.

"Why, Mom?" Jason, my eleven-year-old brother, was normally a quiet boy except when he played video games, not the screaming banshee beyond the front door.

"Because you didn't listen."

Going in there, unsure if I was in trouble or not, made me queasy. Still, I didn't have a choice but to step inside. I couldn't stay in the yard all night.

Mom leaned over kitchen the sink, peeling potatoes with a paring knife. No smile for me. Instead, she offered down-turned lips and squinty eyes with crow's feet marching into her hairline. Her nasty scowl matched the smell in the house.

Liver and onions again? Yuck. Though feeding Dad his favorite dish put him in a better mood.

Jason wiped his eyes with a paper towel. Few things reduced my brother to crying. Dad. It must've involved Dad. Only he was at work, along with his whipping belt.

I let my backpack slide off my shoulder but held onto the strap. "Hey, what's going on?"

"Dad gave our dog away."

Mom's blank expression said, "Don't blame me. I had nothing to do with it."

"Why?" I dropped the bag.

Mom turned and shook the knife at us. "He dug up the yard. I told you two to fill in the holes." Unlike Dad, who hit us, she took her anger out on the potato, stabbing it. When she yanked the blade free, she sliced her finger.

"Ow! Look what you made me do." Blood poured into her cupped hand.

I grabbed a dishtowel. "Here."

In her panic, she snatched the cloth and popped me hard on the nose.

"Mom."

"Don't Mom me." The red seeped out. She uncovered it, exposing a gaping wound. "I might need stitches. Tracie, finish cooking dinner. Dad is on his way." With her good hand, she scooped up her purse and wrangled it onto her shoulder.

Slow to change with the times, we still had a landline telephone for emergencies. "Shouldn't I call him?"

"No, cook dinner." She sprinted across the street to the neighbor's house. Her car was in the shop, and she ran like she didn't want to deal with Dad, either. She let me off the hook by not involving him just yet.

Jason blew his nose. "I wish she was dead. And Dad, too."

"You don't mean it." With a wet washcloth, I swiped the blood splatter. It smeared over the white counter, making it look like a crime scene. A squirt of Lysol and a few more passes had it clean again.

"If they were gone, we could get Tigger back and live with Mimi."

Careful not to cut myself, I peeled the potatoes. "Mimi doesn't want us. But if we had Dad's money, we could live here by ourselves."

"And Tigger. Don't forget him." His moist eyes sparkled, and for a split second, we must've shared the same dream. But the chance of getting rid of both our parents was nil.

"Someday, when I'm older, I'll find us a place. We'll take care of each other," I said, meaning every word. Jason was my favorite person in the world.

"By then, Tigger will be dead. Dad gave him to the Thompsons. They tie their dogs to trees."

Poor Tigger. No more belly rubs. No more wagging tail when we got home from school. A chain on his neck would break his spirit.

My eyes watered, but there wasn't time to think about it. Dad was coming. With Mom gone, we were on our own, not that she cared to protect us from him.

I scraped up the peelings stuck to the sink and dumped them in the trash can.

"Do you see it?" Jason asked, pointing to the garbage spilling out of the waste bin.

"Yeah, it's stuffed to the gills. Do you mind taking it outside?"

Jason pointed to something under a milk carton. "Those shiny boxes."

"What boxes?"

He pulled them free. The window's light washed over the metallic wrappers. They glistened as if to say, "We're special. We're not trash."

"I searched for those but thought they were gone."

Mimi, our grandmother, had mailed them to us, but Mom took them away. 'You don't need it,' she said and stomped off to her room. She got on the phone. 'Mother, what the hell are you trying to do? Stay out of our business.'

Weeks passed, and Mimi never called us again. No amount of snooping turned up the gifts, not until today.

Jason's nose trumpeted into a clean paper towel and jarred me from the memory. "Dad's coming."

A car door slammed, and a key fob chirped.

Damn.

I gave the liver and onions a stir and dialed up the heat under a pot of water.

Jason skittered to his room with the packages. No doubt he would stow them under the bed or in a jacket pocket in his closet.

Dad lumbered my way.

Potatoes. Chop, chop. My heart raced. Dad was a man who demanded his dinner on time.

"Hi, Tracie. It smells good… Julie, I'm home." He removed his shoes and placed them neatly against the wall. It took him only a second to notice mine. "I told you not to wear shoes in the house."

I set the knife down and took off my sneakers and lined them up against the wall next to his and Jason's. "I'm sorry. Mom was hurt, and I forgot."

He scratched his chin. "What happened?"

"She cut her finger, bad. Said she might need stitches—"

"Great. Another bill." He leaned back and kicked the shoe across the kitchen floor.

"She didn't mean to—"

"Where's your brother?"

Mom made him mad, and he started in on Jason. But not if I could help it.

"I think he's shooting hoops at Rick's house." Jason was smart enough to stay quiet until dinner. Maybe by then Dad would calm down.

"Jason," he called.

Damn. Something in my voice tipped Dad off to my lie. I never was a good liar.

I chopped the potatoes as fast as I could and dropped them into the boiling pot.

Little feet pattered down the hall and stopped at the doorway. "Yes, sir."

"The backyard is full of holes. Get the shovel and fill them."

"Yes, sir."

"The dog had to go. I twisted my ankle while mowing."

"I can train him not to dig."

"It's too late. It's a done deal."

Jason inched into the kitchen and grabbed his shoes. "You can't give our dog away. He's family."

"Don't you sass me, boy. We've got bigger problems than a dirty mutt. You should've named him Digger instead of Tigger. Now he won't have a choice but to behave. Red Thompson won't put up with that nonsense."

Jason slipped his foot into a sneaker. "It's not fair."

I held my breath. Jason, please go. Don't push him.

"Life's not fair, son."

Jason's foot slid into the other one.

Oh God. Hurry up and go outside. Don't argue with Dad.

The phone rang, and I exhaled.

With Dad's back turned, Jason headed outside.

On the second ring, Dad answered. "Hello, Julie?"

It couldn't be her. Mom didn't have a cellphone. If she went to urgent care or to the hospital, it was too soon for her to call. But on second thought, the neighbor lady, Kristy, did have a phone.

"No, Cal, you can't talk to her. Stop calling." He set the receiver on the hook. "I want you to discourage *Lover Boy*."

"He's not my boyfriend." I covered the liver so I didn't have to see it and to keep it warm. Besides, it gave me an excuse not to look at Dad. He had those accusing eyes, and the things he said about Cal made it hard to keep my mouth shut.

"He's too old for you. I thought when we left Texas, he'd forget about you. But since he hasn't, I know something went on with you two."

"We're just friends." It wasn't like I had many in Arkansas. If *Dad* hadn't waited until March to move us, I might've fit in better at school. It sucked to be the new girl when the other kids had all the friends they wanted. In Texas, I knew lots of people.

"Tracie, men and women can't be friends. It doesn't work that way."

He had this sick idea all guys had one agenda. Sex.

I picked up a fork and poked a potato. They were

half done, like his lecture. Cal Russo was my last tie to Texas. My other friends moved on after I left. Oh, how I wanted to go back. If I could, I'd pack up my stuff and take Jason and Tigger with me.

"Did you hear me?" he said.

"Yes, sir." I dropped my gaze. Dad had a way of staring at me until I buckled under pressure.

Hurry up, Mom. She had to come home so he'd have someone to talk to. Someone other than me. Dad never let me have my own opinion. It came down to control. He was the big boss, Brent Bigelow, like he was at work. Only he probably treated his employees better than he treated us. If only I could run my own life, I'd be happy.

"Next time Cal calls, you say you can't talk to him anymore. Tell him you have a boyfriend. Anything."

I nodded, though I'd never tell Cal such a thing. It was none of Dad's business. His rules made me want to call Cal and talk all night. But Dad confiscated my cellphone a week ago. When my parents weren't home, I called him from the landline telephone. I told Cal I broke the cellphone.

****

After a painful dinner, without Mom present, Jason and I escaped to his room.

"Ready to do this?" I booted up the laptop.

Jason's heart must've been pounding since he kept glancing at the door like he expected Dad to barge in and catch us.

"Dad doesn't know about these. He's watching television or checking on Mom," I said, knowing if he ate dinner without calling the neighbor lady, he didn't care.

He dug inside his pillowcase and pulled out the

shiny boxes. "What are they for?" An eleven-year-old boy had no idea about such things.

"It's one of those kits like on television. You know, DNA to learn about your ancestors." I ripped into the wrapper. "We have to register ourselves online, spit in the tube, and mail it back. The MyDNA people will send us the results by email." I found a pen in my backpack and filled out the form.

"Why did Mimi send these?" He unboxed the items, lining them up on the bed.

"I don't know. Maybe she thought we'd think it was fun. Who knows? Maybe we have other siblings. Mom might've had a baby before us and put it up for adoption. Something's going on, because she chewed Mimi out for sending these."

He labeled his tube and spat into it, filling it to the marked line.

"You can't let Mom know, even after we get the result. Understand?" I said.

"Yeah, but if we have a brother or sister, are we going to meet them?"

Another sibling would be older than us. If they accepted us and had their act together, they might let us live with them. The endless possibilities ran through my mind.

"I don't know… I guess." I had barely finished the forms on the MyDNA website when Mom's faint voice filtered through the wall. "Oh, crap. She's home."

"Tracie, where are you?" Mom called.

"Coming," I said. "Hide it, just in case." I met her in the hallway. Her smudged mascara made her look like an angry raccoon in a dark alley. "How's your finger?"

A gauze wrap covered her hand, much like a white

oven mitt. "Kristy said it didn't need stitches and patched me up. It's not bleeding."

The neighbor lady worked as a nurse, and it was nice of her to take care of Mom.

"Sorry, Mom."

"Why didn't you clean the kitchen? Did you think I'd come home and work like Merry Maids? Don't you ever think about anyone but yourself?"

"I was going to do it after you ate."

"I ate already. Get busy before your dad complains. Until my finger heals, you have to take on more responsibility."

"Yes, ma'am."

"Julie, is Tracie giving you trouble?" Dad asked, nosing into our business.

"No, everything is under control."

With one word, she had the power to sic him on me. Washing dishes didn't bother me. It was the way she and Dad assumed I was lazy that pissed me off. As if that wasn't enough, the evening got worse.

When the phone rang again, I had my hands in hot, sudsy water. Of course, Dad strolled in with an empty glass and answered before I could pick up.

"Cal, I told you not to call here. No, she can't." Dad shook his head. "Tell him," he said to me.

I dried my hands and took the phone. "I'm sorry, I can't talk right now."

As I tried to end the call, Dad grabbed my wrist. "Tell him why."

"I'm cleaning the kitchen, bye." I almost had the phone on the hook, but he'd have none of it. He forced it to my ear and mouth.

"Tell *Lover Boy*." Dad had the 'don't test me' look

in his eye.

"Bye, Cal," I said, and the phone clicked on Cal's end.

Dad's heavy breathing made my heart pound like it could break my ribs. His reaction was one I knew all too well. I wasn't sure if I could talk my way out of trouble, but it was worth a try.

"Cal's a good friend. I don't want to hurt his feelings." I retreated to the sink and rinsed the final dish.

"You don't make the rules." He unclasped his belt buckle. The sound of stiff leather rubbing against his khaki pants came next. "Bend over."

I dodged him. "No, you can't tell me who I can be friends with."

In a swifter move, he clenched my arm. Each finger dug into my flesh, locking me within his reach. A doubled over belt whacked me, each hit stinging more than the last.

"Ow, stop! I'm sixteen, too old to spank."

"Yeah, and you still need a whipping like a little kid. You're going to mind me, or I'll make you mind."

The leather slapped me hard. While it burned, the shame was the worst. Tears streamed down my cheeks. Technically, I became a woman three years ago. Mom said so. He had no right to hit me.

"Stop it."

"Only if you call Cal and tell him." He planned to break me like he broke Tigger. Big Brent Bigelow had to be a bully, and the sooner he thought I submitted, the sooner I could escape.

"Okay," I said in a shaky voice and picked up the phone.

Dad kept the belt in his hand, ready to punish me

again if I didn't do as told.

Cal's number was committed to my memory. Punching in the Texas area code and the following digits convinced Dad I called him. A male answered on the other end. Dad didn't know the last number I pressed rang a stranger.

"Cal, I have a boyfriend. You can't call me anymore," I said between sobs and slammed the phone on its hook before the man could blurt out, 'Sorry, you have the wrong number.'

"That's more like it," Dad said.

As far as he knew, Cal and I would never talk again. My plentiful tears and snotty nose convinced Dad I learned my lesson. And I did. But it wasn't the lesson he thought.

Chapter 2

I couldn't wait for morning to set my plan in motion. With a screwdriver, I popped off my window screen and slid it under my bed. No one would stop me, not my parents who retired to their bedroom with a television droning until it lulled them to sleep.

A soft glowing moon and neighborhood streetlamps lit the way to my best friend's house.

Was she awake? If so, what would Bobby, her husband, say?

Six blocks later, I knocked on her door. The excitement had me breathing hard.

After another few taps, the porch light blinded me.

"Who is it?" Debby asked in a whisper.

"It's me, Tracie."

The door creaked open, and she stood before me, her huge pregnant stomach draped in a robe. "What's wrong?"

"I need to place to stay."

"Shh, Bobby's sleeping. Come in and tell me what's going on."

Once inside, I pulled down my britches enough to expose Dad's latest handiwork.

"Oh, Tracie, you're covered in bruises. Who did it, your dad?"

I tugged my pants into place. "Yep. He won't let me talk to my friends in Texas. Got mad as hell about this guy, Cal. I swear, Dad's crazy." My voice cracked, and I trembled like I was going to lose it. Not what I intended when I woke her.

She took me by the arm and led me to the sofa. "I can't believe your mom lets him get away with this. I should report him to the police or whoever stops this crap."

"No, please don't. He'll talk his way out of it. He'll call me a liar. Then I'll get another beating."

"Deb, where'd you go?" Bobby called from the bedroom.

Oh great. He's awake.

"I'm getting a drink of water. Be there in a minute," she said in his direction. "I'd let you sleep over, but I don't want to upset Bobby. But tomorrow you can move into our spare bedroom."

"Do you think he'll care?"

"Yeah, but I can handle him." She patted her enormous belly. "With the baby coming, he gives me my way. Besides, it's a great tradeoff for him. You can sand and stain cabinets in his shop. I can't do it anymore."

"You sure it's okay?"

"Yes, absolutely… Your dad still goes golfing on Saturday, right?"

"Yeah."

"Pack your stuff. I'll come by with my truck, say ten."

Moving out. Me. Mom will shit a biscuit.

"What about later? After you have the baby?" People changed after they had kids. Mom had said so.

"That's the best part. I need help with the baby. It'll be great." She leaned in and hugged me. She was warm, and the baby kicked through her robe.

"Deb, honey, come to bed," Bobby said.

As much as I wanted to savor the love she and her little one gave me, I knew it was time to leave. "See you tomorrow."

****

My sheets were twisted from tossing and turning all night long. I stayed in bed while Dad took his shower. It wouldn't be long. He usually grabbed a bite to eat at the club with his friends while Mom slept in. Pretty soon, Jason would stir in the kitchen. He'd eat a bowl of cereal in front of the television.

No one expected me to wake up early. Once Dad's car rumbled away, I'd check the garage. Boxes. I needed three or four. The clothes on hangers could stay on hangers. There wasn't much to pack: underwear, pajamas, books, makeup, and toiletries.

By nine thirty, I stuffed everything into trash bags. Dad threw away all the empty boxes. Why shouldn't he? He'd never expect me to use them. One by one, I carried them outside before Mom finished her shower.

My stomach knotted when I stepped inside the house a second time to get my Fender acoustic guitar.

Mom was in the kitchen. "What are you doing?"

A wave of guilt hit me. Her bandaged hand hurt. She only had Jason to help, and he couldn't do much for her.

"I'm moving in with Debby."

My new best friend graduated high school two years ago. I met her while walking home from school, and we hit it off. We liked the same music, television shows, and stores. Our favorite pastime, playing guitar together.

In the living room, the sound of guns blasted, while Jason's thumbs pounded the controls. Leaving him here was my only concern. Later, Dad would forbid him to see me.

Mom glanced at me, then back at her coffee cup. She didn't yell, scowl, or frown. Instead, she dumped cream into her drink without showing a bit of sadness, worry, or anger in her hazel eyes.

"I'll tell your dad you're spending the night with Debby. When you get over being mad at us, come home. But don't stay too long—"

"Don't you get it—"

"You're spoiled. Go, go to Debby's house. I guarantee they have rules there too." She picked up the cup and blew the steam away.

I wanted to tell her I was more than angry. It was Dad's temper I couldn't tolerate. Who cared about doing chores? Not me. I could do them all day if they'd treat me like an adult. They expected me to work like one and treated me like a little kid.

Debby's truck rolled into our driveway. "Whatever, Mom. I have to go."

Chapter 3

Mom could've warned me. It was Sunday morning when Cal blew into Bobby's cabinet shop. I was alone, staining the wood while Bobby ran an errand.

The front door flew open, and Cal stepped inside. "Tracie." He ran a hand through his dark shaggy hair.

"Hey, Cal...what are you doing here?" I dropped the paint brush, splattering cherry stain onto the floor.

"Is that all you have for a guy who drove from Texas to see you?"

I hadn't seen him since moving to Arkansas. He walked toward me in the flesh. I hopped up and closed in for a hug.

Cal wrapped his arms around me. "I called yesterday. When your mama said you were staying with Debby, I had to come. I had a feeling something bad happened." He let go, allowing me to catch my breath.

"She told you where to find me?" It wasn't like Mom. She despised Cal and his roaring motorcycle. She hated his New England accent. 'Those east coast people don't pronounce their Rs correctly,' she said. She'd go on to imitate him. 'Pahk the cah,' she said.

"Heck no. Your mother wouldn't tell me where she lived. I googled for cabinet shops. There's only one in this dinky town."

"I'm glad you found me. Hey, I want you to meet her. She's my new best friend." I took his hand and led him to the house in front of the shop. "Wait here a second."

Cal stood on the porch while I went inside.

"Debby."

Debby waddled out of the hallway. "What?"

"My friend, Cal Russo, is visiting from Texas. I want you to meet him," I said.

Debby picked up a couple of empty glasses. "Where?"

"Outside."

"Don't let him in. The house is a mess." She carried the tumblers to the kitchen, stopping to grab a bowl from the coffee table.

A half-full basket of clean laundry sat on the floor along with dirty socks and two pair of Bobby's shoes.

"Cal doesn't care," I said.

She set the dishes down, dropping a plastic tumbler. The grape Kool-Aid spilled on the linoleum. "He can't come in. Can you help me?"

Gee, I live here too. I have a right to have people over. It's not like I haven't been slaving away in the shop all morning. I do everything: sand the wood, stain the wood, lacquer the wood.

With a few paper towels from the kitchen, I mopped up the spill. Bobby and Cal's voices filtered from outside.

"I'll meet him on the porch, if you can find my shoes," Debby said.

"Yeah, sure." Her blue clogs, the ones she could slide her swollen feet into, stuck out from under the sofa. I pried them free.

The front door opened, and Bobby entered, leaving Cal standing alone. "Debby, we need to talk."

"Okay, let me get my shoes on." She wiggled her foot halfway inside.

"Now." Bobby looked over to me. "Did you finish the cabinet?"

"Not yet."

"Get busy. The order is due next week."

Debby followed Bobby into the hallway, and the two of them disappeared into their bedroom.

Bobby grumbled behind the wall.

I went outside to check on Cal.

"Where's your friend?"

"She's not feeling well. She's pregnant."

"Her husband's not very nice." Cal pulled a strand of frayed denim from his jeans. Loose threads hung across his knee. He was the opposite of Bobby who never wore faded T-shirts and scuffed boots, let alone holey jeans.

"Bobby's in a bad mood. He wants me to finish my work."

"What? I drove most of the night. When I started seeing cows in the road, I pulled over and slept a couple hours."

"I don't want to work, but I don't want to make him mad."

"Let me help. We'll get it done faster," Cal said.

Together, we went to the shop. The paint brush I used earlier had stiffened. I threw it into the trash and found two more. Cal and I stained the cabinet until Bobby barged in on us.

"Tracie." Bobby scowled from the doorway.

"Yeah."

"Come here." He led me into the yard. "You can't bring people into my shop."

"Why not? People come here all the time."

"Customers are welcome. You can't invite friends in here or in my house… Tracie, this arrangement won't work. Debby wants you to stay, but after the baby comes, you have to go home."

Oh my gosh. No. Debby wouldn't let him kick me out. She told me I had to get away from Dad. I can't crawl home.

"I'm sorry, I didn't plan this. Cal showed up unexpected," I said. "He only wanted to help me stain the cabinet so we can visit. I promise, it won't happen again. Don't make me leave."

He looked back at his house and frowned. "It's not going to work. Now get that guy out of my shop." Bobby stomped away. A curtain in the window fluttered as he headed home.

Inside, Cal flushed the brushes with paint thinner. "What happened?"

"Bobby's mad at me. You can't be here." I picked up the lid to the stain and pressed it onto the container.

Cal stood the brushes on their wooden handles and washed his hands in the utility sink. "Is he paying you?"

"Sort of."

"Either he is, or he isn't," Cal said.

"He's letting me stay at his house until Debby has her baby." I washed my hands and wiped them on my jeans.

"Why did you move here?"

I didn't want to tell him my dad knocked me around. How do you say that to a guy you barely know? My face warmed while thinking about it, and I couldn't look him in the eye.

"I'm hungry. Let's get a bite, and you can explain

what happened."

****

Cal and I finished lunch at Bob's Burgers, and he pulled up to Debby's house.

"Is thirty minutes long enough?" he asked.

"Yeah." I hopped out of his truck. He was being a good sport, giving me time to talk to Debby considering he had to leave tomorrow. Maybe she could change Bobby's mind. If not, I'd go home before Dad realized I moved.

Cal put the Ford in reverse. Across the lawn, I glimpsed Mom. She ambled toward me with Jason trailing her and met me in the yard.

"You're not living here, are you?" Jason asked. "Isn't that your boyfriend, Cal?"

"He's not my boyfriend." I made a fist and rubbed my knuckles against his skull. His soft hair smelled like baby shampoo.

Jason smirked. "That's not what Dad said." He wriggled away from me.

Dad poisoned Jason's eleven-year-old brain. But why were they here? Did Bobby call Mom?

Mom stopped a few feet short of me and folded her arms. "We'd like you to come to dinner. Talk things over."

"Dad knows?"

She drew her lips into a strained line and fidgeted with her sunglasses. Bruised skin peeked out from under them. The cakey beige concealer drew attention to the new mark. "He noticed your room. I told you to spend the night, not empty your closet."

"Come home, Tracie. Or at least have supper with us," Jason said.

"I'll come if Cal can."

"Your dad won't like it."

"I'm not coming if Cal isn't invited."

"Okay, but you better warn him," Mom said.

What she meant was she expected Cal to mind his mouth. No snide remarks. No nosy questions. If Cal kept quiet and didn't pry, he could accompany me. It didn't seem fair to drag him into the family drama, but I didn't want to face Dad alone. Having Cal around made me safer.

"Okay," I said.

"Come at five thirty."

****

"Did you get rid of the creepy guy?" Debby asked, while stretched out on the sofa.

"He's not creepy." I took a seat in the recliner.

"Bobby said that. I never got a good look at him." She reached for a glass on the coffee table but couldn't lean over her pregnant belly.

I jumped up and handed her the drink. "Well, Cal is gassing up his truck. He's leaving in the morning."

"Good. I don't want to piss off Bobby again. We're having some problems." She took a sip.

"I know. He told me I'll have to leave after the baby comes. But you can change his mind, right?"

She shook the glass, ice clanking. "No, I can't. That's one of our problems. But whatever happens, you shouldn't live with your parents."

****

The guy who wore tattered jeans and sported longish hair escorted me to dinner. Black locks curled at his ears. I wasn't sure if Cal's looks bothered Mom more than his east-coast attitude. His jerky movements had her squirming in her chair at the dinner table more than once.

Jason and Cal scarfed down the meal, while the rest of us picked at our food as if Mom served live earthworms covered in tomato sauce.

Dad forked his lasagna and pinched off a bite. "Tracie, you can't impose on your friends."

"Debby wants me to stay with her," I said.

"And why is that? You cried on her shoulder, didn't you? You're spoiled. I didn't have anything when I was your age."

"I'm happier at her house," I said, avoiding Dad's stare and wishing I could say Grandpa didn't cover you in bruises.

"Debby has her own family. Whatever little fairy tale you two invented will come to a halt when she has her baby. She won't have time for you."

Cal wiped his mouth with a napkin. "I've been thinking about this too. Why don't you let Tracie move to Texas with me until she graduates? I live near her old high school."

Dad's eyes widened like a hoot owl. "Oh, that's why you're here. You think I'll let my daughter move in with you? She'll be a mother herself in a couple months—"

"No, Mr. Bigelow. No one wants to hop in bed."

Dad pointed at me. "You're moving home tomorrow. If you argue, I'll have a chat with Debby's husband. I'm sure he's tired of you."

"Mr. Bigelow, you're missing the point—"

Dad pushed his plate away and stood. "Tracie, you will move home tomorrow. Cal, you should head home tonight. Tracie will be busy with us." He left the table and vanished into the living room.

Mom followed him, abandoning her dinner.

Jason swallowed the last of his tea and set the glass down. "I'm done. Anyone up for video games?"

"In a little while," I said, knowing my twisting gut stopped me from having fun tonight. I gathered the dishes. "I'm not hungry."

Cal chewed his last bite of lasagna and carried his plate into the kitchen.

Mom returned and pulled me aside. "You need to say your goodbyes. Otherwise, you know what will happen. I'll finish clearing the table."

I found Cal in the hallway.

"Hey, I need to talk to you. Where's your room?" he asked.

"I'm not allowed to have boys in there. Dad will get mad."

Both Jason's video game and Dad's television blasted from the living room.

"Not even for a minute? It's getting dark outside."

Cal had a point. Everyone was occupied. After Dad's speech, they didn't think I'd break the rules.

We snuck into my room. With a soft click, I shut the door behind us. We took seats on the bed, since we had no chairs.

Cal ruffled his hair. "Are you moving back in here? Your dad is a maniac."

"You heard him. I don't have a choice. Debby will have her baby in a couple weeks, and I have nowhere to go."

"You can live with me. My place is small, but we could make it work."

I didn't know him well. What if we didn't get along after I went with him? Besides, Dad would call the law on us.

The door rattled, and my heart thumped when it flew open.

"You know boys aren't allowed in here," Dad said.

"Dad, we're just talking—"

"Shut your mouth, or I'll shut it for you." His posture stiffened.

We had to get out of here. Dad blocked the exit. Rather than challenging him, I stayed put. I could hear Cal breathing. He was no match for my father.

Dad glared at both of us. "Cal it's time to say goodbye." He stomped away.

I exhaled. It was safer with Cal here. Any other time, Dad would've stripped off his belt and whipped me. There was a five-minute window for Cal to leave before Dad threw him out and came after me next.

"He's crazy. Come with me." Cal sat on the bed's edge, one leg dangling, ready to stand.

"I can't."

I could only imagine the trouble I'd start if I left with this boy.

"You can. You're stronger than you think. What do you think he'll do when I leave?"

He sounded sincere, but there was always a limit to how far someone would risk their own wellbeing. What would happen if Dad called the police? When lights flashed and sirens screamed, Cal might not stand by me. When the cops snapped handcuffs on his wrists for aiding a sixteen-year-old delinquent, he'd regret ever meeting me. The risk he faced was too much to ask of someone only three years older.

Mom knocked on the door and popped her head into the room. Her lips pinched downward, and her frown lines between her eyebrows deepened. "Come here."

I was shaking but obeyed and met her in the hallway.

"Nothing will ever change. Get rid of him before your dad explodes." She padded away to the living room.

My heart pounded in my chest while Cal waited, and the clock was ticking. He had to leave immediately, and I'd have to deal with Dad.

Cal was ready to bolt when I returned.

"Okay, I'll go," I whispered, hoping he knew what he was getting himself into.

Together we walked to his truck, passing Mom and Dad on the sofa. Jason lay curled up in a ball on the carpet playing his game. Someone might as well have stabbed needles into my heart. There was no joy in leaving without telling Jason I loved him. I wished I could take him with us. But it was impossible.

Mom glanced up and acknowledged my nod which meant I'd be back. We hurried outside into the darkness. The kitchen light gave me the last glimpse of a house I might never see again. If I got into the parked truck, everything would change.

Cal wasted no time and hopped in.

Two angry people waited in the house to whip me. They'd just have to keep waiting.

My fingertips unlatched the door, and it only clicked a little when my shaky fingers pulled it shut.

The engine cranked.

Oh God, I'm really doing this.

"Go to Debby's. I need my stuff."

"She home?" Cal backed out, hit the gas, and zoomed toward her house.

"Who knows?" I couldn't call Debby from my parents' landline without tipping them off. "You have a cellphone?"

"Let's go."

Six blocks whizzed by.

Where is Deb's truck?

The porch lamp lit the way to the dark house.

I jiggled the doorknob, and it didn't turn. "It's locked, and she didn't give me a key."

"Let's go. Your dad will beat my ass if we aren't gone in five minutes."

"Go to the back door," I said.

We ran to it.

Thank God, it opened.

I flipped on a light.

Cal followed me to the bedroom where my clothes and makeup were strewn across the floor. My guitar was in the corner, leaned against the wall.

Headlights flashed the windowpane, and Cal tugged my arm. "There's no time."

"What about clothes?" A T-shirt and shorts wouldn't do. Going barefoot didn't cut it.

"Leave it. I'll buy you something later." His breaths grew ragged and heavy.

He was right. We'd better bolt before Dad missed me. Forget clean clothes.

I grabbed my Fender and notebook of music lessons.

We dashed to the truck. Every time a car drove by, we dodged the headlights. We had another hour to Texarkana and nine more total. When we made it to the state line, the game would change. Once we crossed, the law would call me a delinquent minor. It wasn't my fault. Dad was the boogie man and my aunt, mother, and a teacher ignored my pleas for help.

Ten hours of highway and the occasional small-town stoplight was a long time to think about who was the bigger asshole. Dad deserved an award. He was the king of belt-swinging outbursts.

Still, Mom gave Dad competition. Early memories sparked the times she sat me on a chair and positioned herself on another chair in front of me.

"I told you to stop banging the doll on the floor. You ruined my soap opera." Mom grabbed my chin, and her fingernails pinched my flesh. She stared me down. My four-year-old eyes watered until I dropped my gaze. Meanwhile my heart revved to full speed.

What kind of mother bullied her kid? The kind who shed the mold her own mother shoved her inside only to force me into the same punitive space. It didn't take long to shape me.

Over the years, we took turns being assholes. By age thirteen, I became an expert at forming my blanket over pillows and stuffed animals. Anyone checking would find a human-sized lump nestled under the comforter. If anyone knew I snuck out, they never told.

Once my shoes landed on soil, the wind called my name in the direction of booze and cigarettes. Warm Coors smelled like cat piss, and the bitter taste coated my throat. It was my friend's father's stash. We, the neighborhood rebels, met up and popped a few. All of us grimacing, then fake smiling as we swallowed.

As for the cancer sticks, they were butts collected from overflowing ashtrays. Lipstick stained the filter, and the crushed end held a few tobacco crumbles. We flicked a Bic, catching the end on fire. The heat scorched my tongue. I let the smoke linger in my mouth and wisp out without inhaling to trick the other kids. The one time I tried to suck it in left me hacking.

When everyone had enough talking, drinking, and

pretend smoking, we would slink home. I slipped behind the trees when the night owls drove by. The windowpane to my bedroom slid up easily. Teddy bears were still tucked in, keeping my secret.

I didn't have my teddy bear tonight, just Cal who stared at the yellow dashes on the street. White light streamed from his truck, piercing the darkness. The windows grew black, and in five minutes we'd cross the state line.

Maybe Dad didn't think I had the nerve to run away. Maybe he didn't predict I'd be an asshole. He probably forgot it was my turn.

Chapter 4

The grinding of eighteen-wheeler brakes woke me. I wiped my sleepy eyes. It was one thirty, and the bright lights served as a reminder. It wasn't a nightmare. I was with Cal as he pulled into a truck stop for fuel.

"You hungry?" he asked.

I stretched and adjusted my vision. "Nope, but I need to pee."

Who could eat with a belly full of jitterbugs? I had the same feeling the day my kitten died. For a month, I cried every morning when I woke up and my baby was gone. Something awful soured in my gut when the memory of his stiff body mashed on the side of the road came flooding back. What was done was done. I found him too late. Several cars had ground him into the asphalt until he was nothing more than a bloody smear with orange fur attached.

The cat was gone, scraped up and long buried under a maple tree. But the twisting in my stomach started again. Only this time Cal and I were on the run. By morning, Dad would realize I went to Texas. He would know when he pounded on Debby's door, if he hadn't gone there already. I wasn't safe. Dad would come for me.

Cal stepped out of the truck and raised his arms in a long, slow stretch. He strode toward the store. If he was nervous, he hid it well. At least as good as anyone. His confidence drew me to him when we first met.

I met him last October while Mom did errands at the bank. She had left me in the car and scurried into the building.

A motorcycle rumbled.

The young man straddled the Yamaha. He wore a leather jacket, boots, and weathered blue jeans. Jet black hair bloomed from under his helmet. The stranger smiled, revved the engine, and drove away only to circle the parking lot.

He didn't look like he belonged in Texas. Something about him screamed trouble, and that alone seemed like the cure for my boredom. I had to talk to him.

I lowered the car window. "Hey, nice bike," I hollered.

He pulled up next to me. "Just got it. Ever ride one?"

"Nope."

"Want to?"

"Yes, but I can't. Maybe later."

The short conversation led to a phone number exchange and plans to meet at the park. Mom didn't know I met a boy. It was best to keep him a secret. She had a way of nosing into my business which led to Dad asking questions. Heck, I just met the guy.

When it came time for the rendezvous, I called to Mom on my way out, "I'm going for a walk."

She was in her wing-back recliner watching television and didn't even blink or ask how long I'd be gone.

It wasn't far to the park. When I got there, dark clouds rolled in, and a distant thunderclap threatened rain. I didn't think Cal was going to show when a motorcycle in high gear plowed across the lawn.

He stopped short of running me over. "Ready? Maybe we can enjoy the beach a few minutes before the storm hits." He offered a helmet. "Put it on."

I hopped on, feeling like a renegade when he popped the gear into reverse. Tires dug a rut into the soft earth.

"Hang tight." He maneuvered over a curb, onto the street.

Arms around his waist, I leaned onto his leather jacket. Warm wind whipped my hair. Cal smelled like aftershave, something the schoolboys didn't wear.

When we zoomed down the road, my heart pounded. What if someone recognized me and told Mom? What if Dad saw? When the sun parted the clouds, light shone on my face. I no longer cared about the risk.

At the beach, the wind picked up, and the rain pelted us. The fall beachcombers gathered their seashells and dashed to their cars. Cal weaved around the vehicles and brought us to a hamburger joint.

We jumped off the Yamaha and hightailed it into the restaurant. There I stood, dripping wet. With the helmet off, hair was plastered against my head. We laughed at ourselves, both of us drenched.

Cal grabbed a napkin off the counter and patted my face dry. "Sorry, it's not a good day for a ride."

"It's fine."

Rain poured over the windows.

He smiled, water still clinging to his dark eyelashes.

"How old are you?" I asked.

"Almost nineteen." Cal removed the helmet and raked his fingers through dark, thick hair, flicking water onto the floor. Bushy eyebrows framed his brown eyes.

"I'm sixteen."

Mom would flip if she knew his age.

"Does your mother know you're with me?"

"No, she wouldn't like it. She hates motorcycles."

It wasn't entirely true. Mom had ridden one once.

A couple sat at the next table and bit into their sandwiches. The french fry aroma drifted to us. My mouth watered.

"I'm starving," Cal said. "Didn't eat lunch." He dug into a pocket and pulled out a wallet. Thumbed through the receipts inside and removed three dollars.

My own pocket had a five-dollar bill.

Cal added it to his own meager contribution and stepped up to the counter. He bought a hamburger, fries, and two soft drinks. We shared the burger. He wolfed his down like an animal, even licking his fingers clean, then started gobbling fries.

Plenty hungry, I stole a few fries. "Do you have a job?"

"I work construction," he said, chewing with a full mouth.

"For how long?"

"A couple months. Followed a friend here who said he made lots of money." His answer hinted of sarcasm.

"So the pay isn't what you expected?" With only two fries left, I snatched one.

"Nah." He ate the last fry.

The rain slowed to a drizzle, and we returned to the park. I didn't want to say goodbye. We only hung out a couple of hours, but I never felt freer than with him.

He kissed me on the forehead. "Better go before your mama misses you."

We had a couple of casual meetings and a few phone calls before Dad moved us to Arkansas. After that, we sent cards, emails, and spoke on occasion. He was loyal, the type of man who drove from Texas to check on a friend, even when her mother was crabby. He somehow understood something was wrong and wanted to help.

Happy teenage girls didn't leave their families on a whim. It wasn't my intention to screw up his life. A lie would've spared him, but the truth spilled out. And so here we were, at a filling station. If we could make it to his house, maybe he'd keep me safe. Part of me wanted to turn back. But I knew what was waiting for me. What was I doing here?

I took a deep breath and got a whiff of gasoline fumes. The pavement under me was cool on my bare feet. But it should be at one thirty in the morning.

Cal passed me carrying two Cokes and fried pies. "Hurry."

To my left, a police car pulled into the parking lot, and my stomach gurgled again. I wasn't the only one to notice.

Cal glanced at the state trooper and looked away.

He was probably thinking what I was thinking. It was time to go.

Chapter 5

Cal's mobile home looked like a chrome submarine missing its propeller. The door opened into a room probably eight feet wide and sixteen feet long. At one side, a cushioned bench doubled as a bed. A small kitchenette occupied the other side.

I set my guitar in a corner and pointed to a mystery door. "What's in there?"

"The bathroom." Cal pulled the latch and exposed a toilet inside a tall plastic box. There was no sink.

How gross. And not much privacy, either.

"Where do you wash your hands?"

"Oh, the kitchen." He bent his elbow toward it.

"You don't shower?"

"Don't insult me. The shower is above the commode." He pointed to a switch and the little sprinkler mounted to the ceiling.

I couldn't help from frowning. "So if I use it, the floor will be wet how long?"

"Until it dries." He stepped back and sat on the makeshift bed. "I'm beat."

A dump. He lived in a dump compared to my dad's house. But he warned me it was small. And to his credit, he shared what he had. Still, I wasn't thrilled about the arrangement.

Cal lay on the only bed, and I had slept part of the trip. Cal should rest since he drove the entire way. But

34

what would we do after today? His home wasn't much bigger than my bedroom. My aunt had an old camper like this, which she pulled to the lake. It wasn't supposed to be a permanent home.

Cal kicked off his shoes into the narrow aisle and closed his eyes. "It's big enough for two." He scooted to the wall and patted the bed.

It wasn't. Not unless he wanted to spoon—not a good idea. Every guy I ever cuddled with turned into a groper. They would press up against me until I felt something I shouldn't... This was already awkward.

What did I get myself into?

"I'm not tired." I retreated to a spot near the door and stayed quiet while he slept.

According to his alarm clock, three hours had passed, and the sun brought muggy heat. A dampness hung in the air. My skin was sticky and wet like sheets drying on a line in a light summer rain.

The *submarine* baked while air conditioner units hummed from five other mobile homes. There was one such machine mounted in the window, opposite of Cal. But its guts dangled from the broken plastic vent.

Of course, he'd live in the only trailer without air conditioning. For the life of me, I couldn't understand how he slept with sweat pouring off him. His hair stuck to his forehead. My T-shirt smelled like body odor and gas fumes.

I wasn't the only person awake this morning. Next door, a neighbor exited a blue-and-white mobile home and headed toward a car. He lit a cigarette and looked back at a young woman.

She stood in the doorway. Her mouth was moving, but I couldn't hear what she said. Tears streamed down her red, puffy face. He stomped toward a car, got inside, and drove away.

The woman appeared to be eighteen or nineteen years old. She held a tissue to her nose, and somewhere behind her a baby bawled loud and clear. She caught me watching her, straightened her blouse, and turned around. The door slammed.

Whatever went on at the neighbor's house was none of my business, but the man was a lot older than her. Maybe the girl was like me once. Only I didn't have a baby. Just a baby brother. Jason would go to school tomorrow. I should be in class too, but I dug myself a hole. Maybe I should call home. Tell them I made a mistake. But I didn't have a phone. Cal did, but his cellphone was probably locked.

Cal shifted on his bed. It was ten 'til ten. He yawned and slicked his hair back before squinting his brown eyes. "You're still here. I dreamed last night was a nightmare."

Seriously? He invited me here, not the other way around.

My spine stiffened, and my gaze went to his phone on the kitchen counter.

"Nope, it wasn't a dream. If you want me to go, I'll call somebody. I have friends, lots of them."

It wasn't true. Debby's baby was due in a few weeks, and her husband expected me to shove off once she delivered. Cal provided a way out—somewhere to go when Dad went apeshit. Dad would've punished me for letting a boy in my bedroom.

Cal yawned again. "You look like hell. Take a shower."

I exhaled with relief when he stopped with the

dream bullshit. "I know, but I have no clothes."

He pulled a drawer under his makeshift bed. Several clean folded T-shirts and shorts were inside. He tossed one of each to me. "Here. We'll shop later."

****

On Wednesday, the front door flew open.

"Bad news," Cal said.

The letter arrived in a small envelope. Oh God. It was Dad's handwriting scrawled across it. He must've found my address book or an old card from Cal. My stomach flipped over. We had a couple of quiet days, and I thought Dad accepted my choice.

"What does it say?" I asked.

Cal crumpled it into a ball. "It says you have two days to go home, or he's calling the cops. Says you're going to juvie 'til you're twenty-one."

"Let me see."

Hmm, Dad could've called. I wrote Cal's phone number next to his address. But Dad liked to intimidate me. It scared me more to get a letter than a call.

He handed the crinkled paper to me, and I unfolded it. "It's a lie. They can only keep me until I'm eighteen." I had researched the law weeks ago.

"Whatever." He grabbed the doorknob.

"Wait, where are you going?"

He couldn't leave already. He just got home, and sitting alone in *the sub* sucked. Who wanted to stay in a place with no air conditioner, no television, and no phone? Nothing to eat but dry cereal or canned tuna. Yuck. And my fingers throbbed from playing the guitar.

"Going for a beer." He shut the door and jogged to a white trailer. When he knocked, the door opened, and he disappeared inside.

****

The jitterbugs were back, and this time they kicked harder. The setting sun reminded me of Dad's ticking clock. What if the mail carrier delivered the letter yesterday and Cal found it today? Surely, he would have checked, but I had no recollection of him bringing in junk mail, bills, or anything else on Tuesday.

What if Cal's friend told him to bail? Who could blame him for having second thoughts? What if the police were already en route?

Since the eighth grade, I committed a friend's number to memory. Only I didn't have a phone.

Taking a risk, I headed next door. The man who lived there was still gone. Maybe the teenage girl would let me use her phone.

I knocked, and she answered.

"Hi, I'm Cal's friend, Tracie. Can I use your phone?"

Brenda let me in, provided I didn't wake the baby.

The call to my girlfriend yielded rings but no answer.

An operator put me in touch with Debby. "Tracie, where are you?"

"Texas."

"Your dad came over Sunday. He barged into my house looking for you and the creepy guy."

"What did you tell him?"

"I said I didn't know where you were. He called me a liar. He's a real jerk. Says he's going after you Friday if you don't come home."

"What should I do?"

"Get out of Texas… Oh, great. Bobby's home. Hey, can you call me later? There's corned beef hash in the skillet. Bobby gets cranky when I burn supper." She didn't wait for my reply and disconnected.

"Are you okay?" Brenda asked.

"Yeah, thank you for letting me borrow your phone."

In a crib, a baby bawled.

She turned to the infant. "Oh, he's probably hungry again."

"I better go." Leaving her, I headed to Cal's place.

If he knew I called someone, he'd have a fit. Dad was coming. The letter wasn't an idle threat. He would come on Friday. What were we going to do? I had to leave.

I packed my stuff. All the clothes Cal bought me, two pair of jeans, three tops, and underclothes fit into the paper sack I found in a drawer. I also found a bottle of Jim Beam in there. What was the harm in taking a few swigs? Cal was off drinking without me. Jim Beam was the only one around. And we almost became friends.

The liquor burned all the way down. Within ten minutes, the room spun, but the jitterbugs stopped kicking. A calmness swept over me after a few swallows. My throat went numb, making the heat simmer down to a pleasant warm.

No wonder people loved to drink. For a while, I had a brilliant plan. Hell, I'd move from Cal's trailer, rent my own. Someone at a fast-food joint would hire me part time. I'd enroll myself in school. I'd say I lived with Grandma, but she was home sick. Yeah, they'd let me back in class. My old friends at my old high school would jump for joy. Tracie was back.

At some point, I crossed the line from peaceful to hysteria. Probably at the halfway mark on the bottle because when it was empty, all my fears came spilling out.

Dad had to ditch work to come Friday. That cost him money. After he knocked me around a while, he'd make sure a grumpy judge threw me into a girls' home. Crabby old women with hairy moles ran those places.

Jim Beam wasn't a friend at all. There was a lot of banging and yelling going on in the trailer. It ended with crashing glass.

The door swung open, and Cal rushed in. "What the hell? Why are you destroying my home?"

I was lying down, and there was a hole in the window above me. Cool night air seeped in. "Look, someone cracked the windshield. You can't drive the sub anymore."

"Stop kicking. You, you broke it. The landlord will throw us out when he sees this." He picked up the empty bourbon bottle from the floor and shook his head.

Jim Beam did me a favor since there wasn't a bit of pain from the jagged glass stuck in my foot. "Debby said Dad is coming."

"Debby? You called her? When?"

"I went to the neighbor's house. Borrowed her phone?" I said, with difficulty since my words were slurring.

Man, oh man, I'm drunk.

"Oh no. You didn't. You can't tell anyone," Cal said.

"I didn't tell the neighbor. I just wanted to talk to Debby—"

"You think the neighbor girl can't hear? Don't you understand how serious this is?"

I fell back again onto the seat and let my eyes close.

This couldn't be real. A dream. This had to be a dream.

Hands grabbed my shoulders and shook me hard. "Sober up. We have to talk."

Chapter 6

I should've hurled instead of holding in a gut full of liquor. Burps and the taste of sour bourbon bubbled up into my mouth. I opened my eyes to a dark trailer. At some point, I must've passed out. The memory of Cal's words was hazy, like a dream with missing pieces.

The sub sucked. My back ached after sleeping on the built-in bench. I used the seat to keep the distance between us. No way I'd lay on the bed with Cal for the obvious reasons. Living here was awful. Not only that, Jim Beam left me a reminder of our time together. If my head was a rock, the hangover was a jackhammer.

Alcohol made nothing better. Especially when the fumes burned my nose. But that wasn't important while my world crumbled. After Cal left to have a beer, he trapped me here with my thoughts. When Dad caught up to us, he'd beat me, maybe throw a few punches at Cal, too. Jim Beam made me forget until morning. No one could help me. Not even Debby.

A yellow porch light filtered into our trailer. Balled up under his blanket, Cal snored. "Cal, wake up."

My throat dried up like day-old toast, and my stomach churned. Red numbers on his alarm clock were an unreadable red blur.

"Cal."

"What?"

"Can you get me a drink of water?"

He huffed. The floor creaked, and glasses clinked. "Sorry, the water is off."

"What do you mean?"

"The faucet is dry," he said.

I might as well have hot sand in my mouth. Even my tongue was parched.

"Please, get me some. Ask the neighbor."

"Tracie, it's too late to bother them."

My legs wobbled when I tried to stand, sending me back onto the bench with a thud. "I can't remember ever being this thirsty."

"Okay, okay." He didn't turn on a light but instead fumbled with a drawer and slipped outdoors. His flashlight guided him to Brenda's trailer. Faint knocks came before her door squeaked open.

The neighbors mumbled, and a couple of minutes later, Cal returned. "It's the best I could do." He handed me a tumbler. "They don't have water either. You're lucky they had something in the fridge."

I took the glass, and he returned to bed. The cherry drink did nothing to quench my thirst. It tasted like sugary cough syrup. After it went down, it came up along with big, curdled chunks, spilling onto my shirt and the floor.

Cal flipped on the light. "Gross, go outside." He hopped up and pushed me out the door. I stumbled and fell to the ground.

Nice of him to toss me out like a mangy cat coughing up hairballs.

The sour taste in my mouth made me puke more. Disgusting. I never had a strong stomach. Even in grade school, if I saw another kid barf, I'd upchuck too. It caused a domino effect. Before the janitor cleaned the mess, a couple more kids vomited, and I'd hurl a second time.

I lay on the ground and retched up my guts. "Ow!" I rolled away, trying to escape whatever stung me.

Cal peered down, shining his flashlight on the flattened ant hill. "Get up. Fire ants."

The insects swarmed my shirt. He jumped out and pulled me to my feet. We slapped at them in a fury, which woke me in a hurry.

"Sorry, Tracie." He pulled off my top and threw it on the ground. "Take off your shorts."

After a few wobbles, I freed myself of the clothes. My skin itched, and I scratched like crazy.

"Are you done puking?"

I brushed away more stinging insects and nodded.

"Get in the house. Do you remember what I said earlier?"

"The water is off?" It was awkward, standing there in my undies. I crossed my arms in front of myself. "You go first." I didn't want him to see me in my panties any longer than he had already.

"Can you turn off the light, please? And don't look at me."

He climbed into the trailer and hit the switch. "Don't you remember what I said?"

"About bothering the neighbors?" My eyes adjusted to the moonlight streaming through the window. I tiptoed over the vomit but still stepped in it. It squished between my toes.

"No, about my mom."

"Not a word, but I stepped in something nasty."

He flipped on the light.

Jim Beam had erased all traces of our conversation.

"Can I have a towel before I track the puke everywhere?" I was still in my underwear. "And stop looking at me."

He rummaged through the drawers and dropped his gaze when he passed a hand towel, a clean T-shirt, and a pair of shorts. "I called my mother. She told me not to bring you to her house. She said you should go home."

"Don't go telling people about me. I'm not a charity case."

The shirt he gave me had a black rhinoceros on it with a caption, *Save the rhino*. How fitting.

I flossed the towel between my toes, folding it over a clump of vomit, and repeated. "No one has to look after me. I'll get a job...rent a place. I'm a smart girl, you know."

"Yeah, you get drunk and kick out windows. The landlord will make me pay for the damage."

"I never drank much before. I'll pay you for the window. There are plenty of jobs out there."

"Yeah, maybe you can sit on the curb and play your guitar. I'll give you a tip jar, a box of cereal, and send you on your way."

I wadded up the towel and pulled a shirt over my head. "Nah, no need. It'll be daylight soon. My friends from my old neighborhood will feed me. I'll be fine." The shorts were too baggy, but a little pull on the drawstring cinched them at the waist.

"Well, if that's what you want. But you can't come back here." He opened a kitchen drawer, grabbed his wallet, and counted the bills. "Hmm, just enough."

He never offered a dollar. Instead, he shoved the billfold back into the drawer. "Better sleep, it's a long drive." He hit the lights, and darkness flooded the sub. His bed groaned when he lay down.

"What long drive? You can't force me to go home."

"Yeah, I know. I'm not making you do anything." The sound of a pillow fluffing followed. "My job with the construction company is over. They let me go."

"So what does that mean?"

"I'm moving to my mom's house, today," he said in a low calm voice.

"Oh." It hit me. Homeless…me…camping under bridges…dumpster diving…alone. I was alone. A strange man lay on a make-shift bed in a submarine-like trailer. I didn't know him, not really. He had no obligation to me. We weren't married. We weren't even related—not that family treated kin better than friends did.

Other than Jason, I didn't have a reason to go home. If I thought Mom and Dad would hug me and tell me they missed me, I'd walk back to Arkansas barefoot. It wasn't the kind of world I lived in.

A tear slid down my cheek, and I was thankful for the darkness. Cal was a silhouette. I probably looked the same way to him. He couldn't see my runny nose, or watery eyes, but my breathing grew heavier and louder.

Cal interrupted my thoughts. "I know you have other choices. You have friends, and Texas is a wonderful state, but you can go. Move with me."

"But your mom said no." The tremble in my voice betrayed me.

"It doesn't matter what she says."

"It does. What if she calls the law?"

"It'll be okay. If Mom tells, I'll get into trouble. Trust me, she won't."

I'd go anywhere but home. However, school would start again after summer break. I might lose credits for the spring semester. Cal wasn't my legal guardian, and I knew what happened to dropouts. They flipped burgers, cleaned houses, waited tables for their entire lives. Maybe Cal would convince his mom to help me get into school.

"Do you think I can graduate with my class?"

He shifted on his bed. "I doubt it. I didn't want to tell you, but I stopped by your old school Monday on my lunch break. They said you can't enroll since I'm not your guardian."

I wasn't thinking about graduation when I ran away. It wasn't fair. Teenage girls should be able to go to whichever high school they chose. Why should it matter who you lived with?

"Cal, do you think you'll find a job?"

"Sure, Mom will hook me up. Don't worry, it'll be great in Rhode Island." The mattress creaked liked he was as unsettled as I was.

My gut feeling said he had quit his job. Dad put a scare in him, and he wanted to move to a safer place. But his mom didn't want me hanging around. She knew about girls like me, nothing but trouble. Part of me wanted to right a wrong, go home, let Cal off the hook. But I couldn't.

"Rhode Island?" I asked.

"Yeah, what do you know about it?"

"It's the smallest state in the union." The tiny piece of land jetted out in the Atlantic Ocean. Water surrounded it according to maps in my geography class.

He chuckled. "Come lie next to me." He scooted to the wall, offering a spot.

He was nineteen, but his voice tensed in a vulnerable way, and I thought about Mom.

I wished I had a mother who cared as much as his did. One who wrapped her arms around me and pulled me close to her bosom. Mom never brushed my hair or kissed my forehead the way my friends' mothers did.

Cal wasn't a substitute for a mother figure, but I gave in and slipped onto the bed next to him. "I don't want, well, you know…"

He pulled the sheet over me. It was warm from his body heat. "Okay, I just need to get comfortable." He draped an arm over me, and something stiff pushed against my rear end.

"Cal, I'm not feeling well." I inched away. The last thing I needed was to prove Dad right. I didn't want to be a mother like Debby or the lady in the next trailer.

He rolled over, and I sighed with relief.

Within five minutes, the snores came. I closed my eyes and tried to block out Rhode Island.

Chapter 7

Wrong decisions messed up my life. A little voice in me said, 'Don't go with Cal. Don't go against his mother's wishes.' I didn't listen and dove neck-deep into trouble.

Concerns about showing up uninvited on his mother's doorstep bothered me. His mom would give me an accusatory look and say, 'So you've been sleeping with my son.'

I'd blush and shake my head, but mothers thought the worst about strange girls. Cal had quit his job. It paid his bills, and she'd have to support us. He planned to drive me there, despite their issues. He and his mother, Priscilla, didn't get along.

A conversation we had stuck in my head. 'She likes to build me up and break me down again,' he told me. 'She's a ballbuster, a man hater. Even took the dog to get cut because he humped her leg.'

People neutered dogs every day. When I said so, his lips twisted like he bit into a sour grape and he said, 'Buddy was horny. Nothing wrong with that, but Mom saw him riding my leg.'

Priscilla made a fuss. After all, it cost a fortune to dry-clean a Persian rug, the carpet he soiled. Cal said Buddy shot his wad right in front of her.

I wanted to tell him it was as much his fault as the dog's. But it was an argument I'd lose. Guys didn't like girls who sided with their mothers. Not that I cared much. He was only a boy I hung out with between boyfriends. Still, I didn't want to fight with him.

I had to stop these thoughts. Cal and I had a long day ahead. The clock said it was five forty-five. Soon, we'd be on the road, leaving this submarine-like trailer. So far, I managed to keep Cal off me. Dad's instincts were right, but I trusted Cal to do the right thing.

My tongue was dry and scratchy as a wool sock, and I went to the sink. When I turned the faucet handle, the pipes sputtered, and the water flowed. Thank the Lord for small favors. I ducked my head under it and gulped.

Cal yawned. "Oh, good. It's on again. I need a shower before we leave. How do you feel this morning?"

"Crappy." The thirty or so ant bites on my arms and stomach itched. Each scratch produced bigger bumps.

"Too bad. You'll just have to suck it up." His sarcastic remark warned me to watch out for myself. I was like gum stuck to his shoe. He probably wanted to dump me at Priscilla's house, and she'd get rid of me. Still, I didn't have any good options.

Outside, the black clouds hung low in the sky. A far-off rumble and silver flashes followed.

Cal rummaged through his drawers and pulled out clean clothes. The cubby near me stored paper sacks, and he grabbed one. "Let's get packed." He dropped it on the counter and disappeared into the bathroom.

My belongings were already in a paper bag on the floor, so I packed his while my head throbbed. It was my first hangover, and the baby screaming next door didn't help matters. Light shot between the drapes and wall, giving me a clear view. The woman and child cried, while a man yelled. She shirked away from him like she expected him to slap her. Instead, he ran to a car.

Whatever happened, I didn't want to get pregnant. The neighbor girl probably had nowhere to go. In a way, I could relate. That's why I had to keep Cal at a distance. Finding a new home alone was doable. Finding a home with a baby on my hip changed everything.

****

The truck's windshield wipers whipped side to side, unable to clear the gushing water. For an hour, Cal didn't say a word. I stuffed my bag along with Cal's shoes and clothes behind my seat. Pouring rain soaked the towels, a toolbox, and dishes sitting in the truck bed.

"Why are you taking me to your mom's house when she said not to?" I asked.

He kept his gaze on the road and the steering wheel steady. "My friend, Richie, said I'd go to jail, and you'd go to a detention center if we didn't leave."

It wasn't the answer I expected. I wanted Cal to say, 'You'll have a better life in Rhode Island. When Mom meets you, she'll change her mind. She'll invite you in, cook steak, and take care of you.' Instead, he worried about himself.

"The police can still track us. When Dad comes and can't find me, he'll call the cops. They'll talk to the neighbors."

He gave me a nervous glance. "No one knows where we're going. Richie thinks I'm driving you to Arkansas."

"When you don't come back, what will happen? You think he'll forget you? Just like that?"

Water fell in thick sheets and dimmed the headlights. Cal pulled onto the shoulder and waited for the brutal storm to pass.

"The neighbors mind their own business. No one

pries. They don't ask questions, and they don't talk."

The rain passed, and Cal pulled onto the road again.

"Cal, do you regret helping me?"

"No, I was homesick." He sighed. "Without you, Mom would call me a quitter."

"What do you mean?"

He kept the wheel steady though a driver near us weaved. "I hate Texas. It's so hot I could bake cookies on the asphalt, and I work outside in the sun. Mom knew I quit other jobs because of the conditions. She wasn't happy with me."

"Why? I mean, if it was a terrible job."

"She's a ballbuster. She thinks a real man is tough. When I was a little boy, she mocked me if I cried." He fell silent again.

"Cal, I think you're a real man."

He gave me a half-smile but said nothing more.

Why did parents delight in hurting their kids? And I thought I was the only one.

The pitter-patter started again, pinging his truck's hood, and the wipers ran full blast.

"Cal, do you think you'll find a job in Rhode Island?"

He stared ahead at the wet pavement. "Nope, something temporary maybe."

"What will we do for money?"

"Sponge off Mom."

I had a habit of making sour faces.

He snickered. "Don't feel too bad. She gets a ton in alimony."

Chapter 8

When Cal and I arrived in Rhode Island, the sun faded behind the multi-story homes. They looked like oversized grave markers in muted shades of blue, gray, and green.

"What drab houses," I said.

"Queenstown has codes. The city has to approve the color."

"Why?"

"It has to do with the founding fathers."

No wonder the early American settlers looked so miserable in old movies.

We pulled up to a gray house and cut the engine. It was a big place, larger than anywhere I had lived. Before I made it to the door, it opened, and a warm glow highlighted two figures, both feminine. One was taller than the other, and the shorter one stood in the other's shadow.

I took a deep breath and looked at Cal. His eyes lit up with hope. He was home with his family. I was the stranger. Everything changed again. It didn't seem real. It seemed more like a dream, and I couldn't wake up.

Cal must've seen the tension in my face. "Relax. She's a mom like any other. And my little sister, Bess, she's a sweetheart."

He grinned at them and got out. Priscilla displayed a reserved smile. The night air cooled my underarms, and

I tugged at my T-shirt. I felt grimy and windblown from Cal running the heater, and I realized how much chillier the evenings were here than in Texas.

Cal jogged to the door and embraced Priscilla in one swooping motion. "Ma, I missed you."

Their warm embrace shut me out, my feet shifting uncomfortably on this sidewalk far from home, far from my own family. When was the last time my mother gave me a hug? I couldn't recall, and envy swept over me. I didn't belong here.

Priscilla was taller than Cal and meatier, but not as chunky as my own relatives.

"Hey, kiddo, looking good." He hugged his sister next.

Bess was probably thirteen with soft curly hair stopping at her shoulders. Her wide eyes were curious. No malice in them.

I followed Cal to the house but waited at the threshold for an invitation. While he chatted with his sister, Priscilla fixed her gaze on me. Behind her blue eyes, I recognized guarded intrigue. She was sizing me up.

"Hello. You must be Tracie. Welcome." Her voice projected forced hospitality. It was the kind you offered to unexpected company.

"Thank you." A polite response was in order, no matter what I saw in those calculating eyes. I had to give her credit. She had manners even though Cal had put her in a compromising situation.

She gestured to me. "Come in, out of the cold. I made beef stew, one of my specialties."

The aroma of hearty beef and tomatoes filled the air. I was surprised she didn't make clam chowder, especially since Cal had told me he preferred it.

Beyond the door, steps led up and down. We went up, to a living room. No televisions or radios blared. It was quiet except for Priscilla's clicking shoes as she took us to the kitchen.

At the table, she had set out two placemats, napkins, and spoons for me and Cal.

"Ma is a gourmet cook, the best." He pulled out a chair and plopped down.

Cal gave her the right compliment because she spun around and flashed a genuine smile. "Sit, Tracie. You must be starving." She waltzed to the cabinet, retrieved the bowls, ladled a generous portion into them, and set them in front of us.

My stomach did a happy dance. The burger at lunch had digested. I didn't care if I ever ate another one. The greasy taste coated my mouth and lingered between meals. I was ready for a home-cooked meal. Every six hours Cal stopped at a fast-food chain.

He dug into the stew, biting into the cubed beef, carrots, and potatoes. I did my best to eat like a lady, sipping the broth from the spoon. Priscilla leaned against the counter, and her stare landed on me. She stayed there and kept the distance between us, never pulling up a chair. I tried not to shake. A potato fell off the spoon and splashed into the bowl.

God, I didn't need to splatter her table. I was already making a bad impression.

"Mrs. Russo, the stew is delicious." A chunk of carrot slipped off my spoon.

She must've realized the effect she had on me, and rather than torture me further, she turned and covered the stock pot. "I'm glad you like it. I have an early day tomorrow. You kids can stay in the basement. Cal, show her around and put the leftovers away when you're done."

Bess appeared and stood near the doorway.

"Bess, get ready for bed."

"But it's only eight," she said.

I was as curious about her as she was me, and I hoped Priscilla would let her hang around. Though she was probably three years younger than me, I was three years younger than Cal. Priscilla didn't send me to bed.

The neutral expression on Priscilla's face hardened, and the girl took a couple of steps backward before retreating.

Their mother seemed satisfied to regain control. "There are lots of pillows downstairs. Get up by seven and tidy up. We have sessions tomorrow."

"Sessions?" I asked.

"Mom is a doctor."

"I earned a PhD. I'm a private therapist," Priscilla said.

It was more like a reflex when my eyes triple blinked, but the surprised look must've pleased her because her face beamed.

"I'll see you kids in the morning," she said and excused herself.

Cal and I were alone again and banished to the basement. There had to be more bedrooms upstairs. The people I knew with basements filled them with old paint cans, ladders, cat litter pans, boxes of extra clothes the owner hoped to fit into again someday. They stored all the extra baggage. When it was down there below the earth, they forgot about their junk.

Basements were nothing more than underground

attics, but creepier. But then again, Priscilla held sessions there. It might mean it was more like a doctor's treatment room. Maybe it wasn't so bad except the *therapist* never considered maybe I didn't want to sleep in a room with her son.

"Tell me about her job," I said.

He snickered. "She runs the fat club."

"What?"

He got up and ladled more stew into his bowl, dribbling it onto the stove.

"Six or seven fatties come and lie on the floor to discuss their feelings." He returned to the chair, never bothering to wipe up the mess.

"It's not nice to make fun of them." I pushed my chair out and washed my bowl at the sink.

"Other than them shelling out a hundred dollars, it's ridiculous. They're like beached whales. And they pay Mom to give them advice."

I used a sponge to clean the spill on the stove. "What's wrong with that?"

"You see her gut? It's bigger than her breasts. She used to be hot."

My skin crawled. There was something disturbing about a guy who checked out his mother's body. After all, nineteen years ago he was a part of her. I never had dirty thoughts about my own parents. His expectations were odd.

"So what? People change."

"Only if you let yourself go. I like my flat stomach." He patted it before he took another bite.

Hearing his comments made me think of when we stopped in Mississippi. No wonder he gave me a hard time when I ordered a quarter pounder with cheese.

The kid at the counter punched in the request, and I thought it was a done deal until Cal interfered. 'Change that. Give her a small burger and small fries,' he said.

I didn't argue at the time, thinking he was worried about money but too proud to say it. So much for giving him the benefit of the doubt.

****

Priscilla's basement didn't have old buckets, spiders, or boxes of ill-fitting clothes. It smelled like strawberry air freshener. One wall had giant square pillows stacked neatly against it. Opposite to it stood a wood fireplace.

Cal grabbed two of the oversized cushions and placed them in front of the hearth. "I'm going upstairs a minute." He pointed to another room. "There's a bathroom over there if you want to shower."

Beyond the door, I found soap, shampoo, and bath towels. I peeled off my clothes and slipped behind the shower curtain. Warm water streamed over me, steaming away two days of sweat and body odor.

Cal didn't have money for motels when we drove here. It was a good thing. I accepted the grime to avoid laying in a bed with him. He made several vulgar comments about the servers who brought us breakfast at one small town. I changed the subject, hoping he'd stop. But he shared his opinions with me like somehow, I'd agree with him.

Afterward, I wanted to drive the truck while he slept. I didn't have a license, but he picked the long stretches of straight highway for me. It kept us moving toward Rhode Island.

Too bad his mother didn't offer me my own room. Thanks to her, I was stuck with him.

I finished my shower, dried off, and wrapped my hair and body in towels when music filtered through the wall. "Light My Fire" by The Doors played. Cal loved the old rock bands, but I didn't care for them. He often spoke of Jim Morrison and his untimely death. The obsession with a dead musician was creepy, especially when we were staying downstairs.

He tapped on the door. "Bess lent you pajamas for tonight."

It was thoughtful for him to ask his sister.

"Thank you." I cracked the door, grabbed the clothes, and shut him out.

"It gets cold down here. I made a fire," Cal said, while he waited for me.

"Good, I'm freezing." Once fully dressed, I traded places with him.

Burning wood scented the main room and chased away the chill. My damp hair dried much quicker near the flames than if pressed against a cool pillow.

Bess was sweet. Either she had plenty of pajamas, or she gave me her newest. The soft cotton nightclothes had *Hello Kitty* printed on them. Maybe when Cal saw me wearing them, he'd think of his sister, and it would crush any romantic thoughts.

So far, I avoided his groping hands with saying I'm sick. It worked perfectly ever since vomiting in his trailer. I wanted to tell him we were only friends. But whenever guys heard those words, the friendship ended. At least it did for me. This wasn't the right time.

Besides, Cal had lied to my dad. He planned to take advantage of me as soon as he felt safe. My own lies stopped him from dumping me in some strange town, leaving me homeless on the way here.

Tomorrow I could ask his mother for my own bedroom. Maybe her training in therapy could help me. I needed to talk to someone. Cal was a ticket out of Arkansas. How would Priscilla react when she realized I had no plans to go home? I'd consider returning to Arkansas if I found another place to live. Maybe the DNA test result would come in a few weeks.

The bathroom door squeaked, and he sauntered out. "Are you warm enough?"

"Yeah."

He wore a white T-shirt and briefs. It was the first time he didn't wear shorts to bed, and it bothered me. Back at his mobile home, he stayed dressed.

He fumbled with the stereo, and the Rolling Stones were up next. "Tracie, how do you feel?"

"Tired."

The fire threw flickers of red-and-yellow light into an otherwise dark room. It could've been romantic with someone else. After a relaxing shower, the calm swept over me until Cal plopped down next to me and tried to put his arm around me.

I squirmed away.

"Tracie, come closer." He rubbed my hand.

The Rolling Stones sang "Under My Thumb." It seemed fitting since he moved me into his mother's house. Without his influence, she might make me leave tomorrow.

"Cal, I'm tired." I tried to pull away, but he embraced me.

"Do you realize how beautiful you are?"

What a stupid line. Did he think I'd fall for it?

"Quit it. I'm exhausted and need to sleep."

His grip lightened, but he moved in for a kiss.

Considering my options, I broke free and ran for the stairs.

He jumped up.

Arms grabbed me before I reached the top.

"Stop it," I said, but gravity was on his side when he dragged me back to the pillows.

"C'mon, Tracie. I drove you halfway across the country."

"No, I don't want to mess around under your mother's roof."

I hoped by reminding him where we were, he'd stop. Even though Priscilla acted like we already did the nasty, maybe he'd feel weird about having sex in her home.

He held my wrist, and I couldn't pull loose.

Cal kept pawing me, and that damn song kept playing. I could scream for his mother, but she had those judgmental eyes that never left me while I ate her food. If she sent me away, I'd have nowhere to go. He knew that.

"Cal, I'm so tired." It was true. "The past week has been horrible. I'm not up for this. Not tonight."

He let go. "Okay."

"I want to sleep upstairs."

If I asked Priscilla, she might let me stay in another room.

"No, don't bother Mom. Stay here with me. I'm sorry I scared you," he said.

I ran halfway up the stairs before he caught me. "Mrs. Russo."

There was no pitter-patter of bare feet, no yawns, and no answer.

"Shhh, calm down. Don't wake her. Trust me." He pulled me downstairs, to his little den. "I'll sleep across the room. I promise you're safe."

He seemed sincere, and I relaxed once he kept his distance. Disappearing into the bathroom, he returned with a plastic jar but went back to his own pillow.

Glad he chose to stay away, I closed my eyes. Though persistent, he wasn't the type to rape a girl. We were friends, only friends.

A few minutes later, the smell of cocoa butter filled the room. Though I didn't look, I knew what he was doing. Every slippery stroke brought a moan or a groan. While trying to block it out, I recalled how Cal let Buddy hump his leg. He acted like dogs had a right to sexual gratification. His dog story should've served as a warning.

If I would've done it for him, I would've crossed the line from nice to naughty, like the prostitutes interviewed on a television show last winter. They had talked about the dirty deeds they did while working the streets.

One whore complained about oral sex, 'Those filthy men don't even bathe before they come looking for me. I got to get high so I don't gag.'

Some people liked it. My friend's older sister, Marnie, knew a lot about oral sex.

Out of curiosity, I asked her how hard to blow.

She laughed and said, 'No silly, you don't blow. You lick and suck him like a lollipop. It drives guys crazy.'

Marnie had plenty of experience, and two babies out of wedlock. She proved hand jobs led to blow jobs, and then you get the whole salami. My mother had said sex before marriage will lead to pregnancy. 'After a man gets a girl pregnant, he loses interest. He'll chase other girls and leave the last one to tote a baby on her hip.' I didn't want a baby.

I knew better than to let Cal convince me to touch him. Coming to Rhode Island was a mistake. What he did kept him off me. Some people said without intercourse, it wasn't sex—at least not for the girl. But once the girl agreed to do one thing, the guy usually pushed for more.

Afterward, Cal fell asleep, smelling like warm cocoa butter. He was satisfied. He left me alone one more night, but I had yet to suffer the consequences.

Chapter 9

Priscilla's heels clicked on the wood steps though she didn't come all the way downstairs. "Cal, get up. It's six o'clock. I need the therapy room."

"Okay, Ma." Cal stretched and rolled off his pillow.

Weak sunrays filtered through a filmy basement window, and Cal turned on a lamp.

I squinted into the bright glare and buried my face into my pillow.

What happened last night? Oh, he pleasured himself while I listened a few feet away. Today, he seemed fine with it, like we had played a game of Monopoly. But of course he did. He was a guy.

I snuck another peek at him. He moved his bedding against the wall like his mother wanted.

Did she know what happened? She didn't bother to come when I called. Maybe she didn't hear me, but what if she did and chose not to answer? Two against one. Them against me.

I couldn't look at him without thinking about the greasy jar of cocoa butter and how he used it. The faint scent still lingered in the air, and the queasiness of uncertainty settled in my gut.

"Tracie, get up. The fat club is coming. We have to go." He dashed to the bathroom.

I scooted off my pillow and tidied the room.

After dressing, I found Priscilla upstairs in the

kitchen, drinking coffee. She looked like a therapist in her smart gray skirt and her mint green blouse. Her hair was swept into a chiffon bun, not a strand out of place.

"Good morning," I said.

Her lips strained into a forced smile. "Morning… There's something you should know. Number one, I consider you an adult. I expect the same from you as any other adult. If you act like one, you'll be treated as such."

She didn't mince words. I never thought she'd be so direct.

"I'm sixteen—"

"Not anymore, you're not. You're in a relationship with my son. If anyone asks, you're eighteen. Don't tell anyone your real age. I don't want trouble."

Man, oh man, she must've heard Cal moaning last night. Priscilla had a gleam in her eye like she assumed we were intimate. Maybe she could smell the cocoa butter on my clothes. She probably walked in on him with other girls.

"Yes, ma'am," I said to keep the peace and because I was at a loss for words.

She never asked me how I felt. The tightness in her face rippled to the rest of her body, making her appear stiff and unyielding. Not what I expected from a therapist. I never met one before, but I always imagined they were like school counselors—someone who listened. Not her. She'd never let me lay on a pillow and unburden myself, though I needed to.

Priscilla continued with her rant. "Number two, you'll both get jobs. I've already talked to my dear friend, Trisha. She owns The Lobster Palace, and she needs help."

Cal appeared in the doorway. "Ma, can I use your

credit card? We need things."

Priscilla's piercing blue eyes left me and landed on Cal. The tension in her face doubled.

"Tracie, go put on your shoes. I'm taking you to breakfast," Cal said.

I stepped away, happy to escape.

Let Cal take the heat.

In the living room, I met Bess. Questions danced in her eyes.

"Thank you for lending me the pajamas," I said.

At first, Priscilla's low snippy voice kept their conversation private.

Cal's voice grew louder. "Ma, my girlfriend needs a jacket. Don't worry. We'll pay you back, and we won't ask for another dime."

"You better. Don't take advantage of my good nature. I used my favors for you. And I expect you to work hard for Trisha. Do you understand the entire town will watch you bus tables?"

"I know, you are the great Priscilla Russo, therapist to Queenstown."

"People judge. Remember that," she said.

Bess smiled, despite the firestorm blazing in the kitchen. "How long have you dated my brother?"

"He's not my boyfriend. Just a friend."

It was the first time Cal called me a girlfriend. I had to escape Cal before he did something worse. He misunderstood. We never kissed or held hands. The leap from friend to girlfriend started with the move from Texas. Somehow, he trapped me under his thumb, like in the song he played. It was a giant thumb with more pressure than I ever imagined.

****

Friday night, the patrons arrived by dozens at The Lobster Palace. Cal pointed out doctors, lawyers, professors, and other professionals. He said only rich people ate the king crab, Maine lobster tails, and giant prawn. They paid a la carte. Not like at the diners in Arkansas where an entrée came with biscuits and two sides.

White linen tablecloths dressed the tables. In the center, a flower bouquet added class. Fancy. With everyone in dinner jackets and elegant gowns, it looked more like a party than a restaurant.

Trisha, the owner, circled the room, welcoming her guests. She smiled all the time. But who wouldn't when a meal cost a fortune? The money poured in as fast as they could eat their food.

She assigned me to the kitchen. For hours, my hands soaked in hot, soapy water, while I scoured pots and pans. When I wasn't washing dishes, I scraped the oily salmon skin from the plates into the garbage.

Why did so many people like to eat creatures with gills and slippery tails? Gross. It didn't take long before the trash smelled fishy. I had no desire to eat fish, crab, or lobster. It didn't help matters when Mac, the cook, pulled a live lobster from a bucket and set it belly up on his butcher block.

He wielded a knife, which resembled a medieval dagger. "Goodbye, Mr. Lobster." With a swift jab, Mac stabbed the poor thing, and the metal ripped through the crunchy shell.

Its tail curled, and it died.

The animal might've suffered less than if dropped into boiling water. But I cringed just the same. Mac enjoyed his work too much, eager to oblige another order. All those rich bastards had to have their seafood. Only hours ago, the animals swam happily in the ocean.

The supper rush ended at eight thirty, the same time the yelling began. Cal spouted four-letter words. Crashing glass had the staff running toward the commotion.

When I got to the dining room, Cal clenched his fists and swung at the head busser. Blood poured from both their noses.

She ducked. Then her wicked right hook caught him under the chin.

He fell.

She jumped on him and pounded his face. It took two guys to pry her off him.

Stupid. Priscilla will bust his balls. He'll lose his job before he earned a paycheck.

The customers stopped eating.

A breathless Trish rounded the corner. "What's going on?"

Cal wiped his battered nose, smearing blood across his face. "Crazy woman attacked me for no reason."

"He's a thief. He stole the tip," the head busser said.

They were surrounded by the staff, and the servers grimaced at the accusation.

Trisha had her hands on her hips. "Turn your pockets inside out."

"I keep some money on me. It's all mine," Cal said.

"Mr. Greeley left a fifty-dollar bill on the table. I know Cal has it," the head busser said.

"Let us see," Trisha said.

Cal dusted off his slacks and turned away.

With all eyes upon her, Trisha nodded, and two male servers seized him while another dug into his pockets.

Sure enough, it yielded the loot.

Oh, how could he? The others would judge me by association.

"Hey, give me back my fifty." Cal lunged at the server who held the bill, but didn't get far with two guys restraining him.

"I saw him take it," the head busser said.

Trisha frowned at Cal. "You're done. Go. I'm going to tell your mother."

He left without saying a word. I continued working until the manager dismissed me, but found myself on the outs with everyone. No one smiled or talked to me. Other than pointing out my next task, everyone ignored me.

When the shift ended, everyone gathered their things. One server rammed her hand into her purse and pulled out a key ring.

"Do you know where Cal lives?" I asked with as much nerve as I could muster.

"Yes."

"I'm staying with his family. Can you give me a ride?"

She looked at her watch. "I can't, but it's only two miles." The woman gave me directions instead.

I stood in the parking lot, in the dark. Everyone jumped into their cars and drove away, while I walked to my new home, alone.

Chapter 10

When I reached Pricilla's house, yellow light washed over the Cadillac in the driveway. Cal's truck was missing. After the awkwardness at The Lobster Palace, it was better he was gone than to recant what happened. He would try to convince me he didn't steal the tip though we both knew otherwise.

Inside Priscilla's dining room, flameless candles radiated a warm amber glow. Fatty scraps from a steak dinner and the hollow skins of baked potatoes remained on two plates.

A man laughed from Priscilla's room. His low voice wasn't familiar. It was past my bedtime, and I never asked Priscilla for a bedroom. It wasn't the right time, not when she entertained a male visitor. She called me an adult, so I hunted for a spare room.

Cal never gave me the grand tour, but the main hallway had several closed doors. I opened one. A Hello Kitty nightlight shined bright enough to see Bess tucked under her covers. She didn't stir.

The next door solved the problem. Behind it, I found a bed fit for a princess, adorned with a gold and plum blanket and a dozen frilly pillows. The dresser drawers were empty, ready for clothes. A digital clock on one nightstand blinked *10:00*.

Without delay, I returned to the basement for my clothes, guitar, a toothbrush, pajamas, and the makeup bag Cal bought me with Priscilla's money. He generously gave me a new hairbrush, mascara, eyeshadow, and lip balm. A couple of tops, nightgowns, underclothes, and a light jacket were courtesy of his mother as well. The money we earned tonight at the restaurant didn't come close to paying for it.

The bathroom in the hall had a container of decorative barrettes, like others Bess wore in her hair. I moved my cosmetics into a drawer and took a shower. Afterward, I dressed for bed but needed to score points with Priscilla.

She'd be pleased to find the dinner table cleared, dishes washed, dried, and put away. No one wanted to deal with greasy pans the next morning. Besides, I spent hours in a kitchen at work. A few more plates wouldn't kill me.

I expected fallout when Cal discovered me locked inside a separate bedroom. Priscilla's support would come in handy, and if the cost of loyalty came in the form of maid service, so what.

****

Someone knocked and rattled the doorknob. "Tracie, are you in there?"

I opened my eyes. Was I dreaming, or did Cal call me? It took a few seconds for the red numbers from the guestroom clock to blur into *2:30 a.m.*

"Tracie." Cal waited outside the door.

Jiminy Christmas, he came home. Of course, he couldn't go to sleep downstairs. That wasn't the Cal I knew. He always found a way to complicate everything.

I pulled down the soft covers, hopped out of bed, and whispered to him through the wall. "Yeah, I'm here. Go away."

"Let me in," he said, while jiggling the locked knob as if it would magically release.

"No, I need privacy." I turned around and hobbled in the dark, arms outstretched to reach the mattress.

"You can't keep me out. It's my mother's house."

A click and footsteps meant someone joined us.

"Cal you're being too noisy," Priscilla said.

"Ma, Tracie is using the guest room and won't let me in."

Oh, my. He resorted to tattling on me the way he might with his sister. No matter what Priscilla said, I'd never open the door and allow him in—even if she asked me to.

My breathing quickened during the painful silence, partly from anticipation and anger while waiting for her response. He didn't own me, even if we stayed at his mother's house.

"Go to the basement and leave her alone."

"But, Ma, she's my girlfriend. Why are you taking her side?"

"Go. Don't disturb me again, or you can sleep in your truck." The steps were louder when she walked away.

Ha. She found him disturbing. She would know him best after raising him. But I lay there most of the night wondering if her answer would've been different if the gentleman didn't stay over. It made sense that she sent Cal away. No one wanted to fight with their kid when they had a lover warming their bed.

****

The next morning, when Priscilla and her boyfriend stirred, I waited for them to exit their bedroom before leaving the safety of mine. They mumbled in low voices in the hallway. Their footsteps were quick like the man was in a rush.

Outside, an engine turned over. Below my window, Priscilla stood on the porch waving and blowing kisses as the Cadillac sped away. She swayed back and forth in her kitten-heeled slippers.

Before the gentleman disappeared around the corner, another car pulled into the driveway. A teenage boy hopped out, carrying a backpack and a cocker spaniel. Priscilla greeted him on the sidewalk. He hugged her, and they made their way inside the house.

My door squeaked when it opened. I edged toward the living room, stopping short of them. The kid came into view. He and Priscilla were sitting on the sofa.

Toenails clicked on the hardwood floor. Buddy, the infamous humping dog, ran toward me. I ducked and stayed quiet.

Someone whistled.

As fast as he came, the dog bounded into the living room.

Curious, I resumed spying.

The boy, who looked sixteen, picked up the cocker spaniel and set him on his lap.

"Are you hungry?" Priscilla asked the boy.

"I'm starving. The step-monster never cooks." He scratched the pup's ears. "Can I move back in after the school year?"

"Maybe, I'll talk to your dad. The kitchen is a disaster, but I'll whip you up pancakes." She glided in the fancy shoes, pink feathers stirring as she breezed that direction. She took the shortest path and didn't notice me watching.

With Priscilla in the kitchen, I inched closer to the

living room.

He looked up and smiled.

"Hi, did you spend the night with Bess?" he asked. "I'm Logan, her older brother."

I shook my head and didn't know how to explain myself. Good first impressions were harder to make when I couldn't stop staring at his big brown eyes and shiny dark hair.

The creaky stairs interrupted my thoughts.

Cal reared his head over the banister. "Hey, bro, I forgot you were coming. You met my girlfriend?"

My face heated like I had a sunburn. "I'm not your girlfriend. Stop calling me that." It wasn't the best time to announce it, but it slipped out.

Cal's jaw tightened. "Since when?"

"Since never."

The brother leaned back on the sofa, still holding the dog. He had a smirk on his face as if he found my denial amusing. Most guys would accept the rejection, but not Cal. He kept pressing me.

"Come downstairs. We need to talk." Cal stomped toward me, but I ducked into the dining room.

"She said you have the wrong idea. Why don't you leave it alone?" Logan said.

"Mind your own business."

In the kitchen, Priscilla stood at the counter mixing pancake batter. A skillet heated on the stove. She ladled batter into the pan, and it sizzled.

With the breakfast table near her, I planted my butt in a chair, feeling safer.

Cal followed me into the room. "C'mon, Tracie."

"No, I'm not going downstairs with you." If I could help it, I'd never let him corner me again.

Priscilla looked up from the steaming flapjack. "What's wrong?"

"She won't listen to me. I did everything for her, and now she acts like she's not my girl."

"Cal, you don't own her. She's in a relationship with you."

He clenched his fists, and it made me glad she was the authority figure.

I had to fess up and tell the truth regardless of his reaction.

"Cal never was my boyfriend, just a friend. We never dated." It wasn't clear to me if she heard me calling her that night from the basement. Either way I had to admit how I felt, and maybe she'd understand.

He tugged at his ear. "Why'd you let me drive you here? And what about everything I did for you?"

"You talked me into going to Texas, then brought me here. No offense, Mrs. Russo. You have a lovely house."

"For someone who's not my girlfriend, you sure wrote me a lot. Spent a lot of time with me on the phone. Until last night, you didn't have any objections to staying with me in the basement."

My face warmed up, and I didn't want to say what he did in his little den, a few feet from me. Priscilla probably knew about his cocoa butter.

She kept flipping and stacking golden pancakes onto plates. She poured the batter, and it sputtered when it hit the hot pan. "Cal, quit referring to her as yours. Consider her feelings."

"Stop with the therapy session. Don't tell me how to run my life when your boyfriend's married. When will Dick leave his wife? Huh?"

Priscilla frowned but said nothing.

"Tracie, let's talk somewhere else." His bony fingers clamped down on my arm.

"Ow, stop it." I pulled away, but we were in a tug-of-war though I never left my seat.

Priscilla smacked him with a spatula, and he let go. "Don't put your hands on her. I'll throw you out, if you do it again." She waved the spatula at him before setting a plate on the table. "Logan, honey, your breakfast is ready."

Cal glared at me, and I looked away to see Logan and Buddy standing in the doorway.

Logan scooted a chair back and joined me at the table. "Thanks, Ma."

"You're all ganging up on me. I don't need this shit." Cal dug his keys from his pocket and stormed out.

With him gone, half the tension lifted. Half lingered since Logan knew our business. It was awkward, and yet I was drawn to him. I didn't know why, but I was usually right about these things.

"Good morning." Bess entered the kitchen and kissed her mother on the cheek before hugging Logan.

Priscilla placed a bottle of pancake syrup on the table and poured more batter into the skillet. While it bubbled, she stacked two more hotcakes on a plate and placed the dish in front of me.

"Thank you," I said.

"Sure, it's one of my specialties. And thank you for cleaning the kitchen last night."

She did notice, and it was nice of her to appreciate me. I had done enough for her to come to my rescue when her awful son cornered me.

Logan didn't pick up his fork and stuff his face. He

waited for his mother to serve everyone first. Cal would've scarfed down the food, licked his fingers, and begged for more. Already, he was Cal's opposite at the breakfast table.

Bess caught me staring at Logan, and I diverted my attention to the stove as Priscilla flipped another steaming pancake. His good manners, handsome face, and long black eyelashes hooked me. He must've resembled his father. His mother didn't wear makeup this morning, and her lashes were brown and stubby, a lot like mine.

"What should we do today?" Logan asked Bess.

Bess shrugged.

Whatever they decided, I hoped they invited me.

Chapter 11

On Saturday afternoon, Priscilla dropped Logan, Bess, and me off at Jump City. From the outside, it was a gray bubble, a massive jellyfish. Inside, trampolines circled a giant pool of blue and yellow sponges—a kid's fantasy come true.

Logan held the door for us. "It opened three weeks ago."

Beyond the reception counter, a teenage girl launched herself from a mat and back-flipped into the pit of colorful squares. I had heard of these places, but we had none where I used to live.

Logan pulled the cash from his wallet and strolled toward the cashier.

The attendant smiled at Logan and Bess. But she frowned at me and flipped her hair over her shoulder. "Hi, Logan. How many, two?" she said in a pitchy voice.

"Three." He handed her the money.

The girl snatched the crumpled bills, fumbling a few. They landed on the floor beside the counter. She was quick to jump out into view, bending over in tight shorts that rode up her long legs. In slow motion, she reached for one of the bills.

This was a kids' hangout, not a bar. I could've slapped her butt cheek into the parking lot.

I wasn't the only one disturbed by the show. Bess coughed, and Logan diverted his gaze to the remaining money scattered on the floor. He picked up the bills. When he passed them, she slid her fingers across his hand and gave him a devilish grin.

"How long you staying?" she asked.

Her intent on stretching out the transaction and the chitchat grated on my nerves.

An overhead sign listed the price options, and Logan pondered at it though he already knew when Priscilla would return. "Two hours."

The girl straightened the bills one at a time, rubbing out the wrinkles.

Logan yawned. "Shea, hurry up and give me my change, already."

It was a relief once it was a done deal. She had a thing for him, but he wasn't into her even though she gave him a look at her butt.

Bess pointed at a trampoline. "There's one we can use."

We headed toward the fun, leaving Shea at the counter.

Logan put the extra cash in his wallet and followed.

"Thanks, I'll pay you back when I get paid," I said.

He patted his billfold. "Don't worry. It's on Dad. He's in New York with the step-monster. He wants me to spend his money. It eases his conscience when he dumps me on Mom." The comment rolled off his tongue as if he had a bitter taste in his mouth.

I guess I wasn't the only one who felt ignored. He suffered, too.

Bess ticked off the outings on her fingers. "Hmm, Dad's fifth trip this year. He buys his stepdaughters earrings from Tiffany's, but he never thinks of me."

It seemed trivial compared to my problems, which I

wasn't ready to share. They didn't know my dad made an average living. Mom didn't have expensive jewelry.

"Who cares about earrings? You can't jump on them." Logan ran toward the vacant trampoline and hopped on. He bounced several times before diving into the pool of sponges.

Like a graceful cat, Bess leaped onto the springy tarp. "Tracie, c'mon. It's big enough for both of us."

She waited while I climbed over the spring pad onto the rubber mat. We synchronized our moves. Those training weeks at cheerleading camp came in handy when we did the pikes and the herkies. People on the floor stopped and watched as Bess called out the next stunt. She had a knack for choreography—toe-touches, tucks, and power jumps.

Shea stood on the floor, arms crossed, glaring at me.

Logan waited his turn since kids occupied the other stations. "Yeah, everyone knows you're good. Dive into the pit, already."

Bess sprang off and did a flip, and I did a couple more jumps to irritate Shea before following Bess's lead. We were angels landing on marshmallow clouds.

When other people fell into the sponges, they shook us, the way it felt when someone got off a springy bed. Bess didn't stay in the pit long. She popped up and headed back for another turn, repeating the performance. I sank deep into the sea of yellow and blue squares. If only I could kick Shea out of here and live at Jump City, I'd forget I was a runaway.

Logan bounded off the mat and plummeted toward me, landing on the next sponge.

His hair was damp and his breathing heavy. "Sorry, that was close."

For a few seconds, he lay next to me, and the urge to roll toward him crossed my mind. I wanted to fall into his arms and hug him. We were so close I could feel his body heat, and he smelled nice, like spring leaves kissed by rain. It could've been his cologne.

I didn't dare move nearer to him. He'd only been polite and never signaled he was attracted to me. So instead of throwing myself at him like Shea did, I took his hand when he offered to pull me to my feet. It was warm and firm, and I probably held it too long, but he didn't seem to mind.

We ran back to the trampoline and took more turns. After an hour, we needed a break. The sweat poured off me the way it did when I ran high school track. My mouth dried up like I sucked on cotton balls. A concession stand sold icy soft drinks and giant cinnamon pretzels. Logan bought snacks, while Bess hunted for a free table. We sat around it and ate.

Bess noted the time. "Mom will come soon."

"Where did she go?" Logan asked.

"I think she met Dick, but I don't know where."

I had forgotten about Cal's news. Their mother chased a married man.

Spending time with Bess and Logan at Jump City made me ooze with guilt too. I was having a good time. After I ran away, Dad probably kept Jason locked in the house like a caged parakeet. Jason and I used to ride go-carts, roller-skate, play laser tag at places like this. He would love it here.

"Tracie, are you okay?" Logan's question ripped me from my thoughts.

"Yes." I sipped the fizzy orange drink he bought me.

"You don't look okay."

"I miss my little brother." I bit into a pretzel. Sugary cinnamon melted in my mouth.

"How old is he?" Bess asked.

"Eleven… He loves trampolines."

"How old are you?" Logan asked.

"Sixteen."

"I'm seventeen. Bess is fourteen."

Bess wiped her hands on a napkin, removing the sugar grains. "What happened to you? Why did Cal bring you here?"

"My dad used to beat me."

Their eyes widened while I told them about the abuse. By the time I finished, Bess's eyes watered. I didn't know if I should've shared my problems, but talking about it made me feel better.

****

We were watching a movie in the living room when banging came from the kitchen.

Bess got up and checked on Priscilla. Within a minute, she returned.

"Is she okay?" Logan asked.

"I don't think so. It's about Dick. She's making lasagna for dinner, but she dropped a can of tomato sauce. It splattered all over the floor, and she won't let me clean it up."

A bad love affair could derail anyone, even a woman as educated as Priscilla.

"We should go downstairs when she's upset," Bess said.

In the kitchen, pans rattled. Their mom didn't seem violent other than popping Cal with a spatula. Considering the finger imprints he left on my arm, he deserved more. But maybe she wanted her privacy, and this was her way of telling us.

Before we could go, part of a conversation filtered through the walls.

"No, Dick… When? When did you plan to leave her for good? You promised."

There was no need to listen further. Cal did this. He knew which switch to throw to spoil his mom's day when they argued earlier. What he said must've gnawed on her all afternoon.

Grown women wanted a full-time man, and from what I heard, Dick didn't want to trash his marriage. He gave Priscilla just enough attention by staying the night to build her hopes only to crush them.

Bess turned and headed for the stairs. "Let's go."

"I'll be down in a minute. Just want to see Mom." Logan tiptoed toward the war zone.

"I have to use the bathroom," I said, leaving Bess to descend the basement steps alone, though I knew about the toilet downstairs. I was more interested in watching Logan deal with his mother than going with Bess.

I spied from the dining room. The kitchen had its own ears plastered within its walls. The family gathered here to talk, eat, laugh, cry, and even yell. If the walls had a mouth, they could tell me their secrets, but since they didn't, the arched entryway provided a view.

Logan wrapped his arms around his mother while she sobbed. "It's okay, Ma. Let it out."

Priscilla needed her own therapist, someone to help her cope. Logan did his best to comfort her. What a guy. He stood barefoot in a puddle of tomato sauce, holding her while she cried.

****

From a basement cabinet, Bess retrieved a bean-bag

toss game. "I saw your guitar in the guest room. Did you take lessons?"

"I did for six months. I know a few songs," I said.

"Go get it."

Since we were downstairs, Priscilla wouldn't mind me strumming a few tunes, so I went to get it. I returned with one of the things that reminded me of home and noodled a few chords.

"It sounds good," Bess said. "Do you remember your songs?"

"Stand By Me" came to mind, and I played and sang. Bess knew the lyrics and joined in. Music always seemed to make my troubles disappear.

Bess set up the frame of tic-tac-toe and gathered the square sacks as we belted out the tune.

Once finished, I set the Fender aside. "Jason always liked to sing."

She threw a beanie to me. "Want to play?"

"Jason loves this, too," I said.

Logan emerged from the stairwell. "You want to call your little brother?" He offered his cellphone.

Just the thought made my heart patter into a snappy rhythm that rat-a-tatted in my ears.

"Yes, but what if someone finds out?" The landline we had at home didn't have caller ID. Dad was too cheap to pay for the luxury. But since leaving, he might've bought it in case I called.

Logan unlocked the phone and handed it to me. "If the conversation goes bad, hang up."

With a nervous finger, I tapped the numbers.

After three rings, Jason answered. "Hello."

"Jason, it's me, Tracie." The words came out croaky.

"Where are you? Dad is going crazy, and everyone's looking for you."

Mom yelled in the background. "Who is it?"

"Don't tell," I said.

"It's Tracie—"

"Jason, no one can know."

"Hang up, hang up." Logan snatched the phone and shut it down.

Logan had the final say. It was his phone, but I wanted to talk to my brother. It was too long since I'd heard his little-boy voice.

The disconnect affected me in a way I didn't expect. It brought back memories of what Jason and I shared. We went to the movies, rode bikes, and ate birthday cake. We used to split the last stick of Juicy Fruit gum.

I missed folding his T-shirts that came warm from the dryer, scented with fabric softener. Oh God, he'd grow up, and his face would change. He'd shave and trade his bicycle for a car. After a while, he'd forget about me. What have I done?

Chapter 12

After another sleepless night, the solution popped into my head. Mom had to defend me against Dad. She had to let me come home and make him leave. Maybe by now, she missed her only daughter. Good moms kicked the bastards out when they raised a clenched fist or had a belt-swinging fit. I had to convince her to make him leave if I wanted to go home. However, I wasn't sure if our time apart worked to my favor.

The floors creaked as if to say everyone woke up. Priscilla's routine didn't vary. She spent the early hour with her nose in the newspaper, sipping coffee. When her children woke, she cooked pancakes or omelets.

After dressing, I joined her in the kitchen. "Mind if I browse the classifieds for a new job?" I poured a cup of brew to make her believe we had something in common, though I didn't care for the bitter taste.

She glanced over her reading glasses, perched on her nose. "What happened to the job at The Lobster Palace?"

Trisha must've forgotten to call. Or she gave Cal an empty threat.

"Your friend didn't tell you?"

"Tell me what?" She passed the newspaper.

"She fired Cal and told me my job was temporary. She'll call you, if she needs me again."

Trisha did me a favor. The Lobster Palace reminded me of the jolly cook who rammed the knife through the lobster's belly. I cringed, thinking about the horrible crunching sound the blade made as it ripped through the shell. Never again. Civilized people didn't work where the chef murdered dinner, then served it with melted butter.

Priscilla lifted her cup and took a sip. She paused before setting it down. "Let me guess... Cal broke the dishes while bussing tables."

"He should tell you himself."

"He should, but he's not here."

She didn't cuss, yell, or throw her beverage against the wall when I spilled the details. The little sigh that escaped her was no louder than her dress rustling as she stepped past me to put her cup in the dishwasher. If I didn't know better, I might've mistaken it for boredom. My mother would've flipped if the boss fired me for stealing. Instead, she stood, opened the refrigerator, and gathered eggs, ham, and cheese for omelets. She cooked meals to cope with stress the same way my friend's alcoholic father reached for another beer.

"Can I ask you for a favor? Can I call home for my social security number? My mom keeps it tucked in her dresser. Someone will ask me for it. You know, work applications."

It was true. A potential employer needed the number, but I committed it to memory. Priscilla didn't suspect, but since I had to work, the excuse validated the need to borrow her phone.

"What did you do when Trisha asked?"

"I left that part blank."

She removed six eggs from the carton and placed them in a bowl. "Of course, you can make a quick call."

She never asked me if I was homesick. Or how I felt.

Were we thinking the same thing? If the lines of communication opened, she'd no longer have to keep me. Cal had left me here, whether she liked it or not.

Priscilla gave me her cellphone, and I took it to my room. The walls sheltered me, kept me in a safe cocoon away from open ears. The less they heard the better.

Mom answered on the second ring.

"Hey, it's me." A weighty silence followed.

Mom cleared her throat. "Don't tell me you're pregnant already."

She always said the most judgmental things, assuming the worst.

"Give me credit. I'm not an idiot." It came out as harsh as her accusation.

This wasn't going well. The gloom in her voice reminded me about her uncaring nature. She was like a sea turtle who swam to shore, laid eggs, and left the hatchlings defenseless. When the birds swooped in and pecked off their heads and legs, their mother had long returned to the ocean. The turtle never worried about her young after she laid eggs.

"Only a dummy runs away. What's wrong? Don't like living with Cal?"

"What if I didn't?" I said. "Would it matter?"

"Yes, your dad said you can't live here anymore… It's not up to me."

She passed the blame, but her chilly response froze me to the core. She was a cold-blooded reptile. If she wanted me home, she'd fight for me. Good mothers put their children first. But if she didn't care, why should I let on how sad I was?

"Well, I'm fine. Got a great job, making my own money."

"Good, glad to hear it. I have to go—"

"Wait, can I talk to Jason?"

"No."

My heart sank into my stomach. "Why not?"

She drew in a ragged breath. "Your dad says you're a terrible influence on him."

"Let me say hello, please."

"No." She disconnected and left me hanging on the line.

She might as well have stabbed me in the heart. Her words stung. She never asked me any questions: *are you okay, do you need money, why don't you come home*? I couldn't believe how easily she dismissed me. She probably fretted more about losing a grocery coupon than a daughter. I was expendable.

****

"Monday, Monday." Gloomy songs reflected my job-hunting mood. It got worse when the fast-food manager took a potshot at me.

Who knew a fast-food joint could be so picky? It didn't take an American president to lift a basket of fries from the hot grease or build a burger. The dinging bells and flashing lights cued the employees to flip the patties, eggs, and pancakes. The tasks were foolproof — at least for a fool with a high school diploma. After filling out the two-page application, I knew I was screwed.

The manager glanced over it. "Why aren't you in school?" The nip in his voice frosted my lips shut.

It was late spring when students still attended.

He judged me. No one else asked for the job. People weren't lining up to wear the drab uniform. No one wanted to feel vegetable oil misting their skin and slicking their hair. Why should he care if I didn't go to school?

"We don't hire dropouts here." He looked me in the eye and said it like a snooty maître d' I had seen in a movie.

"I'm not a dropout." Losing a semester didn't mean I'd never go back. Besides, I had extra credits from the year before. If I missed another semester, I'd fail to graduate, but time was on my side.

"Girls your age are in school." He wasn't changing his mind or his tone.

This was too familiar, too punitive. Shaming me, really? He didn't know me. But I knew this all too well, and I wasn't going to take this garbage. This guy had a corncob up his butt.

I snatched the paper from his hand and crumpled it. "Working here sucks. Even for you, doesn't it?"

His mouth flew open, but he said nothing before I zipped away.

Outside, a string of businesses lined Coast Road—donut shops, pizzerias, delis, and grocery stores. Help-wanted signs hung crooked in windows and on doors that led me to believe someone might hire me.

I stopped at several places. The managers gave me the same bad news, for different reasons. 'No, we need to see a social security card. You don't own a car? Where is your driver's license? I'm sorry, we're looking for someone with experience.'

Someone would hire me, and then a few paychecks later I'd buy a bus ticket to Arkansas before the fall semester started. The clock ticked—a reminder to leave before Priscilla booted me out of her house. Though she didn't hint at it, the day would come.

Chapter 13

When the marijuana burned, it screamed, "Joint here, joint here." And there were lots of screams the day Cal returned. The cannabis scent drifted through Priscilla's house like incense smoldering in a New Age store. No one could mistake it for sandalwood or lavender.

My nose followed the distinct odor to the basement. Downstairs, Cal and a girl giggled in the therapy room. They must've slipped in while I cleaned Priscilla's shower. She said to scrub it good, and the blast of rinse water must've covered the voices and footsteps.

Bess had gone to school by seven thirty, and at midmorning, Priscilla left me in charge of the housework while she went shopping. "I made a list for you." She handed me the paper. "You have to clean. My maid quit, and the house can't clean itself."

Rather than whine and have her accuse me of free-loading, I accepted the chores and checked off each room as I finished. The upstairs sparkled. No doubt Priscilla would smile when she saw how I scrubbed away the grime and freshened her home again.

She'd let me stay here longer, but room and board didn't buy a ticket to Arkansas. Rhode Island wasn't the paradise Cal promised. I'd have to call and beg Aunt Martha for a place to stay and enroll in school. No one was around to ask permission to use the landline telephone.

I took a mini-break from the housework and glanced at the help-wanted section in the newspaper. The employers required experience, and one listing caught my eye. Housekeeper. Priscilla might even give me a work reference. Since the job paid four dollars more an hour than minimum wage, I should call.

I tackled everything on Priscilla's list except the basement. It was next. But not when the stereo blasted "Light My Fire" by The Doors. Experience taught me that when Cal's music played, he was horny, and the moans downstairs proved it.

No doubt Cal and the girl ripped each other's clothes off and were screwing. Their sweaty bodies likely slapped together and peeled apart with each lustful thrust, not something I cared to see. Thank goodness he never convinced me to get naked.

The front door squeaked, and Priscilla waltzed in carrying three full grocery bags. "Tracie, take one, please... whew! I know that scent. That's not allowed in my house."

Before she lectured me further, the music stopped.

Priscilla peered down at me. "Ah, Cal is here. I thought you were playing his CDs and..." Her eyes shifted, in a calculating way, the way they did when she shuffled her thoughts.

I relieved her of a bag and continued to the kitchen with her in tow. In her own time, she'd confront Cal. Once we unpacked the goods, I placed them in the pantry but didn't complete the job before her son and the girl greeted us.

"Hey, Ms. Russo." The young woman stood as tall as Cal, and she was thin except for her pregnant stomach.

Her stretchy white blouse outlined the outie belly-button front and center. It was as big as a walnut.

Priscilla's jaw dropped. "Kimmie, it's been a while," she said, in a stutter. Her gaze left the girl and settled on Cal who smirked, most likely from his mother's slack mouth.

In those first few seconds, I couldn't have described the girl's hair, eye color, or complexion. The obvious question dominated over any other observation. Did the baby belong to Cal? If not, at least he couldn't get her any more pregnant—a little bonus for him.

The whole idea of what he did pissed me off the way it did when my old boyfriend dumped me for the new girl at school. I didn't know why. It just did. At the moment, I rooted for Priscilla. She'd lay into him.

Cal reached for a bag of Doritos on the kitchen counter. "Yum. We have the munchies."

Priscilla frowned. "I bet I know why. No pot in this house, got it?"

"Ma, it's just a harmless herb. Besides, Dad said you smoked more than a campfire when he met you."

"We're talking about you. And you." She pointed at Kimmie. "You'll give the fetus a birth defect."

"The baby isn't his, so don't be all up in my business." She grabbed the bag from Cal, ripped it open, and crammed a fistful of chips in her mouth.

Priscilla snatched the Doritos and folded the top over. "Don't disrespect me in my home… Don't you get it? You're ruining your lives." Her voice screeched an octave higher.

Cal pulled a joint from his pocket and lit it. "Ma, you're overreacting. Take a toke and relax. You'll feel better."

"I'll feel better when you hold a job, take responsibility. I didn't raise you to steal or smoke weed."

He inhaled, passed it to Kimmie, then turned to me and blew smoke in my face. "Why did you tell her I got fired? To get even with me?"

"No, it wasn't like that. I swear."

"Put it out." Priscilla wagged her finger at Kimmie. "No drugs in my house, ever. Got it?"

Kimmie passed the joint to Cal. He took another pull before he spat in his hand and snuffed out the flame. "No problem. I came by to pack my clothes. We have a place, an apartment."

This complicated my situation. Cal should've come home alone and apologized to both me and Priscilla. Since he brought me here, he should help me. I wanted to return to Arkansas. I needed to find somewhere to live other my parents' house. His new living arrangements messed up my plans. He shacked up with a pregnant girl, really?

The lines on Priscilla's face softened into that of a worried mother. "What apartment? Where?"

"It's a communal house. Russ, Maggie, Ralph, and other people live there. Our spot's in the attic. Everyone has a part-time job so we can write music, play guitars, enjoy our lives."

Priscilla's jaw dropped again. Cal and Kimmie left her speechless, going back to the basement.

I headed to my room and stretched out on the bed. The jitterbugs were back, kicking and punching inside my stomach. Had I known Cal would bring me here, then leave me on my own, I'd never have gone with him. While he screwed Kimmie, I'd have to scratch up enough money to leave.

****

The job in the newspaper held promise. After the brief job interview, I became the third person in a housekeeper team. A married couple, "Gary and Shelly," needed a girl to help them. They paid cash. It solved my work documentation problem. They never asked to see a social security card or anything else.

Priscilla didn't live in a big house compared to the ones we visited. Gary and Shelly cleaned mansions, and they drove me to one the next morning. The entryway was the size of half my parents' home. Stepping inside dwarfed me to the size of an ant. Somehow, I knew I'd work as hard as one too. Backbreaking labor ahead.

Gary divvied up the tasks. "Tracie, you'll dust, including baseboards and blinds, make beds, pick up the kids' toys, and dirty clothes. Toy boxes are in their bedrooms, and hampers are in the bathrooms."

Shelly cleaned closets, kitchens, and vacuumed while Gary scrubbed the bathrooms.

I wasted no time getting on with the unpleasant business. Holy cow! There was a mountain of puzzle pieces, Lego bricks, and filthy socks under the kids' beds. It kept me busy.

Not only that, Gary inspected my work afterward and scowled. "When you make a bed, you smooth the wrinkles. Pull the blanket tight and tuck it under the mattress."

It didn't matter. Not to the five little piggies who slept in them, each in their own queen-sized bed. Still, I needed this job, so avoiding an argument was best.

"Sorry, I'll redo them." I yanked the cover tight and tucked it under like he said.

"There's no time. We're late for our next job." Gary

wiped his sweaty forehead. "Do it again, and I'll dock your pay. We have a reputation to uphold."

Was he kidding? Jerk. No wonder he had an ad in the paper.

I didn't challenge him as we exited the room. "After the next house, are we done?"

"No, two more after lunch. You have to speed up. You're too slow."

I bit my lip to keep the words in my mouth. If he heard them, he'd fire me.

****

Gary put me through hell the next couple of weeks. I gritted my teeth with every hateful comment. My jaw ached, and each of his insults gave me evil thoughts. So much that if I died, I'd probably land in Hell, inside a filthy house. The devil would expect me to untwist the dirty bed sheets and pick up stained underwear. His dust bunnies would hiss and hop away while I swatted at them with a Swiffer duster.

Miserable.

Gary made the housekeeping job a living hell. He stood behind me and barked orders. "Move faster." If he had a pitchfork, he'd poke me with it. He was vying for Satan's job.

When Gary dropped me off at Priscilla's house after work, I praised God for giving me the strength to tolerate my boss for another day. Lately, his demands mounted to making me clean bathrooms in addition to my original duties.

The next day I had regrets about working for him when he told me he added more tasks.

"Clean the second level." He passed me a sponge which substituted for a mop. "You'll have to scrub the bathroom floors by hand."

I understood what he meant when I saw it. A bulimic teenager's bedroom connected to the first bathroom. She had puked everywhere. Brown streaks dried on the side of the toilet bowl. When I scrubbed the caked-on vomit with a wet sponge, it revived the sour smell—a logical reason Gary assigned me this job.

Disgusting. The girl should have the decency to clean up after herself. This was beyond the call of duty.

The bathroom in her parents' room was just as nasty. Her mother shed like a dog too—long brown hair all over the sink and countertop. The urine smell hit me like it did in a public bathroom. The man who lived here had a poor aim, and the yellow splatters on the white tile proved it. After scouring everything for thirty minutes, I rinsed the sponge and caught Gary peering at the floor.

"Tracie, you missed a spot." He pointed to a wad of hair behind the commode. "We have a reputation to protect."

I had finished washing my hands. "Do you mind getting it?"

"If I do it for you, you'll never learn." The devil's smile emerged, and the fire flashed in his eyes. He prodded me for the last time. It was my fault. I failed to defend myself, and my grandma always said *you get what you settle for*—a lesson I relearned today.

"You have a reputation to uphold. Get it yourself," I said.

He crossed his arms and blocked my exit. "I told you to do it."

"Go to hell." I raised my head high and stepped forward until we met nose to nose. We stood too close. I breathed in his hot air as he blew it out.

"Move, asshole." I held my voice steady though inside my nerves rattled, and the jitterbugs kicked.

Chapter 14

Gary stepped aside when I challenged him in the master bathroom. He was a bully. Bullies picked on weak people. But the fire raging in the pit of my stomach made me as strong as a dragon. When we were nose to nose, he knew he'd pushed me too far.

Enough already. I didn't move to Rhode Island to take abuse. I got too much flack at home. Dad was an expert at torturing me.

I ran downstairs to the bay window. Shelly carried a pail of dirty rags to the car. She never hassled me like her husband did, so I caught her in the driveway.

"Can you take me home? I quit."

She opened the trunk and placed her load inside with her back still to me. "It's Gary, isn't it? He's picky because people expect a spotless house. If the clients aren't happy, they'll fire us."

"I can't deal with him any longer," I said, hoping she'd understand.

She spun around, while the morning sun streamed into my eyes.

A pang of discomfort swept across her face, and she slammed the trunk. "We have three more houses to clean by five. Can't you help us finish, then quit?"

Over my shoulder, Gary stood near the house. His glare burned a hole in my back. "No, he's mean."

"Don't quit. I'll talk to him."

They were opposites. When they worked, Shelly hummed while Gary grunted and checked his watch every few minutes. He stayed tense and grumpy, unless he flashed a malicious grin. I'd stay, if he'd stop harassing me. Maybe she'd scold him and tell him to leave me alone. I needed this job.

She jogged his direction, while I hovered near the car. Their voices were low and controlled. When they returned, Gary stayed quiet.

"You can't take it personal. The clients have high standards," Shelly said.

"I understand, but it's not *what* I'm told. It's *how* he tells me. I'm not stupid."

Gary jiggled his car keys. "No, you're not, but we have to train you." He slid inside the vehicle, and Shelly and I jumped in, too.

Perfection. That's what Gary demanded. He never considered rich people lived like pigs. They saved up the filth and sprinkled it behind toilets and under furniture. If they had to clean up after themselves, they'd never pee on the floor or throw wads of hair behind the toilet.

Gary started the car and drove ahead, passing a street I recognized.

"Hey, you missed the turn to take me home," I said.

"We're late for the next job. You have choices." He stared at me from the rearview mirror. "You can help and get paid or sit in the car. I'll take you home at the end of the work day."

We were on a stretch of road dotted with small delis, and he drove farther into unknown territory.

Why didn't Shelly stop this nonsense? Instead, she sat silent, leaving me to deal with him. He probably bullied her when no one was around, and she was glad she wasn't the target.

"Pull over and let me out," I said, my hand on the door latch daring to jump into the street.

Gary snickered and veered into a small parking lot in front of a quaint gift shop. "Okay, have it your way. Walk."

Were we still in Queenstown? As the car slowed, my heart beat faster. It was hard to tell where one city ended and another started. The storefronts were identical with their muted shades of gray, blue, and the occasional mustard yellow paint.

Shelly twisted in her seat. "Are you sure you want to quit? Do you have anyone to call?"

No, and no.

A quick glance at Gary's sneer in his rearview mirror helped me decide. "Yeah, I'm done." If I didn't go, he'd never quit hassling me for missing a hair or speck of dust. I already felt like an idiot most of the time and didn't need his criticism.

"What do you want? To flip burgers for a living?" Gary taunted me with his malicious smile, one last painful jab.

"Whatever I do, I won't be scrubbing dried puke off bathroom floors." With a slam of the door, I was outside but gasped for air like I locked the oxygen in his car.

They sped away without looking back, a red streak vanishing over a hill.

Alone, without a soul to help me, I stood penniless in the near empty parking lot. What have I done? Damn. I forgot to ask for my pay. How would I find another job? What would I do for money?

A block away, the street sign blurred into a jumble of words. No one was around except an elderly lady who gimped out of the gift shop, lugging bags toward her sedan.

I stepped between her and the car. "Excuse me, where are we? What city?"

She dodged me like I planned to mug her. "Queenstown."

"Where's Main Street?"

She pointed. "A few blocks south."

****

When I arrived at Priscilla's house, I got two surprises. Priscilla had gone out and locked her door. I didn't have a key, but it opened when I jiggled the knob, a nice surprise.

"Logan, hey, what are you doing here?"

He mirrored my smile and let me in. "Dad and the step-monster are on a cruise to Puerto Rico. I'm staying a week. Mom said you went to work."

"I did. I'm done for the day." There was no reason to rehash unpleasantries. With Logan here, Gary became a patch of fog that lifted after the sun rose. This gorgeous guy was the burst of light that made terrible memories vanish in a flash.

"Mom didn't say how long she'd be gone, but she packed a picnic basket. She's meeting Dick at a park." He shut the door and sat on the sofa.

Of course, they'd go to a motel. They'd screw the day away while Logan and I had the house to ourselves or at least until Bess came home. We had at least four hours.

Whoot, whoot!

I joined him on the couch, and I told him all the news of Cal and Kimmie.

"Oh, that's why Mom was edgy. She never said

Kimmie was pregnant. She said they were smoking weed. The way she reacted you would've thought they did heroin."

I never took anything stronger than an aspirin. Cannabis seemed to crop up everywhere. But not in my parents' house.

"How often does Cal smoke?" I surrendered to the leather cushion and rested my tired body.

"When I lived here, he smoked all the time. Have you ever tried it?"

"Nope. Maybe someday, if I wouldn't get caught." The smell of body odor wafted from me. It wasn't something I wanted to share. "Excuse me. I need a shower. It was a long morning." I left him alone, gathered fresh clothes, and headed to the bathroom.

Once the Dove soap replaced the stench of sweat, I dressed again. I found Logan in the kitchen eating a sandwich.

He looked up at me. "There's more in the fridge if you're hungry. Mom made them. She even cuts off the crusts."

I had missed breakfast, and these were yummy. Priscilla baked her own sourdough bread. And she layered the sandwiches with smoked ham, lettuce, tomatoes, and provolone cheese.

"Thanks." I filled a glass with water. "Where does your dad work?"

"He owns a dozen clothing stores."

I set my drink on the table and joined him. "Does he know about me?"

"No. Not that I know... Don't worry, Dad's too busy with the step-monster and her kids to care."

"Do you go to school, or did you graduate early?"

"I do go, but not with Dad away. My teachers gave me my homework to do here."

We finished lunch and tidied up the kitchen.

"Tracie, there's something in the basement I want to show you."

These Russo boys sure spent a lot of time in the den downstairs—a man cave for entertaining girls. I couldn't deny my attraction to him and the rare opportunity we had to be together.

Logan led me there and took two overstuffed pillows from the stack, the ones Priscilla's clients used. With eight pillows, we had a sporting chance of picking clean ones unless someone had done the nasty on them all.

Logan placed a pillow next to me. "Relax, I'll be right back."

I examined the checkered cloth for stains before I sat and waited. Well, anticipated. What was he looking for? I hoped it wasn't what I thought it was. I shouldn't be down here alone with this guy. He tempted me. Part of me wanted to be tempted, but part of me thought about Kimmie's pregnant belly.

Logan reappeared and popped a CD in the player. He didn't play old tunes, preferring millennial pop songs. He had something hidden in his palm, and he showed it to me.

It would be my first time. We would share something special, but not what I had predicted.

"We won't get caught," he said and flicked the lighter. The fire jumped onto the joint as he sucked the other end.

"Is it Cal's?" I asked, listening for noises upstairs.

Cal could barge in on us any minute.

"No, it's my own stash." He passed the joint to me.

"This sounds stupid, but when I tried to inhale a cigarette, it nearly killed me. You'll have to teach me how to do it without coughing up a lung."

He gave me a quick lesson, and after the second pull, we were giggling. We were lying side by side, sharing the joint, my mouth where his mouth touched it. The paper end was hot and moist.

Thoughts came to me in spurts and then disappeared just as quick. I tried to talk, but my sentences spilled out unfinished. All memories drifted away. At some point, the joint was gone. Getting stoned, then realizing we smoked it all was like getting drunk and eating apple pie, later asking, 'who the heck ate my dessert?'

We sank into the pillows. He wrapped his arms around me, and I rolled toward his firm, warm chest. Everything else disappeared—the walls, the ceiling, and the floor beneath us. My head floated on the cushion like the cannabis dissolved my brain. His parted lips brushed mine, his breath sweet. Just as my lips pressed into his, a squeak from upstairs interrupted our kiss.

Chapter 15

The mantel clock over the basement fireplace said *3:30*. Time slipped away while Logan and I smoked dope. It was easy to lounge on the pillows and forget other people lived here. Light footsteps treaded the floor above us. It sounded more like flats than Priscilla's clicking heels.

"Logan, where are you?" Bess's worried voice called to her brother.

Logan stretched and yawned on the giant cushion next to me. "Downstairs."

Thank God, it wasn't Priscilla. Otherwise, I'd find my stoned butt on the curb, homeless.

A minute later, Bess came running with the air freshener, turning the basement into a faux orange orchard. "Mom will have a fit if you're smoking weed in her therapy room."

"Are you going to tell?" I rubbed my eyes, and she came into focus, frustration crossing her face.

Bess gave the air one more quick shot of freshener. "Yeah, that's why I'm covering it up."

I sat up. My head drooped forward like a bowling ball wired to a stick. "Sorry, I'm stoned. How long does it last?"

Logan tossed his pillow onto the stack against the wall. "It's different for everyone. Just sleep it off."

The longer I stared at him, the more my eyelids

sagged until they shuttered down. Besides making me hungry enough to eat a cow, smoking pot only intensified my fear. What now? Priscilla wouldn't tolerate me quitting my job.

****

My buzz was long gone when I had my next encounter with Priscilla. Someone should've hung a sign above the kitchen door that said, "War Zone." My feet ached from the job search as if I marched across Rhode Island barefooted. I wasn't prepared for an unexpected battle. Neither was she.

Priscilla stood at the stove, swaying side to side in her high heels, frying up a blob of egg foo yung. A goblet of Chardonnay sat on the countertop. My mouth watered. Not from the wine, but from the aroma of Chinese sausage and fried onions. Especially when she plated the golden omelet and ladled hot gravy over the top.

"How was work?" Priscilla asked.

I faked a smile, the kind I gave whenever I spun a hasty lie. "Okay."

"Do you like working for Gary and Shelly?" She never asked before. The sarcastic ring in her question alerted me she might've heard the news, but then again, I wasn't certain.

"No. It's temporary."

"Funny you say that… Shelly dropped by and told me all about it."

My mouth went dry like she powdered it with flour. What exactly did she want me to say?

"Well?" She slammed the spatula on the pan the way people smacked flies, picked up her drink, and gulped the wine.

"Uh—"

"Uh isn't an answer."

This woman already heard Shelly's version of the story. She had the wrong idea in her mind.

"It didn't work out. Gary was a bully." I didn't want to rehash the whole ugly story, but her words shamed me. It was the alcohol making her go on a rant.

"Shelly said you were horrible. They kept their end of the bargain and paid you, while you glossed over the work. Gary had to go behind you and do your job."

The heat flushed through me. What did she know about housework? Up to a few weeks ago, her maid scrubbed the toilets and swept the floors free of loose hair. And Priscilla only worked a few hours in the mornings. Her ex-husband supported her. Though I wanted to tell her so, I took a deep breath and forced the words into a deep place where I stored things I couldn't say.

"Did she bring my pay?" I asked, not even knowing how much I had earned.

"Yes, in cash. But I'm keeping all of it. And you still owe me sixty dollars, so you better find another job," she said.

Really? Nice.

An uncomfortable silence fell between us until the front door squeaked.

"Ma, where are you?" Cal called to her. "I need Grandma's rings."

Priscilla turned off the stove and stumbled toward his voice. "What rings?"

He stoked my interest. Heirlooms?

I followed, keeping a safe distance, in case things got nasty.

"The engagement and wedding rings. You know, the

ones you said I could have when I get married." He met his mother in the living room, and he wasn't alone. Kimmie stood next to him, and they held hands. Their interlaced fingers rested on her enormous pregnant belly.

"You're not getting married. Not to her," Priscilla said. "You're too young."

"We are too. Already applied for a marriage license." He kissed Kimmie. "Our wedding is next Saturday."

I stifled a giggle when Priscilla frowned like she swallowed vinegar. He reminded her that teenagers did worse things than quit jobs. At least I wasn't dumb enough to get pregnant or marry Cal. Their stupidity shifted Priscilla's focus off me and onto them— something to celebrate.

Cal glanced up and delivered a blow to me. "Another thing, we're moving in. The house we're renting is going up for sale. Tracie's room will do since the baby will come in a few weeks."

What?

I moved closer to them. "Why can't you stay in the basement? I'm already settled in the guest room."

From the corner of my eye, Kimmie scowled at me.

"Because your squatting days are over. You should move out—you don't belong here," Kimmie said.

My gaze drifted from Cal to Priscilla. Cal didn't object to his girlfriend's remark, but Priscilla's expression said she was in control. She didn't like Kimmie, and it worked to my favor.

"It's my house, and I make the rules. Because there's a baby on the way and because I don't want my clients smelling cannabis, you two will take the guest room. Tracie can stay in the basement or the living room when Logan sleeps over."

Relief washed over me. She banished me to the basement, not to the streets. It was a decent thing to do, only I knew there was more to this. She wanted her son close, not in a stranger's house. It made perfect sense. She used me to irritate Kimmie.

Kimmie's eyes went wide, and her face turned deep red. "Cal, I can't live here with your ex-girlfriend. Make her leave."

"No, I can't."

He must've noticed the worry in my eyes. I was an outsider. Just like Kimmie. He must've felt responsible for me. Only a monster would kick a girl out after bringing her here, and he knew it. Whatever the reason, it worked to my advantage.

Kimmie stared at a plastic vase on an accent table before picking it up and throwing it at him. "Why not? Get rid of her. You said you loved me, not her."

Cal dodged the vase, and it bounced off the wall. "I'm not making her leave."

"You will or else." Kimmie huffed and stomped out the room.

"Wait," Cal called to her, but she sped up and ran outside. The door slammed behind them.

For now, I won the battle. I'd have to be careful. One slip, and I'd lose the next round. Still, I couldn't help from thinking Priscilla had plans for me.

I went to the kitchen.

Priscilla followed and put the plate of egg foo yung on the table. "Eat if you're hungry. I'm making another for myself."

I took her up on her offer. She cooked better than my mother, grandmother, aunt, or anyone else in my family. Within a couple of minutes, she had her own dinner and sat across from me.

Still rattled from the drama, I picked up my fork and tried not to gobble or spill my food. "Thank you for letting me stay. I promise to help you more and get a job."

Priscilla chewed and set her fork down between bites. "There's something you can do for me, and for Cal though he doesn't understand what it'll mean for his future."

"Sure, anything." I was so happy she didn't kick me out that I promised in haste.

"If he marries Kimmie, the relationship will last a month, tops. He'll end up divorced. I can't let it happen. You can stop him."

I paused mid-chew and swallowed a chunk of egg foo yung. The cabbage in it scratched my throat on the way down. What she said next didn't surprise me, but getting involved was risky.

"Cal cares about you. This thing with Kimmie...it's just a phase. More of a conquest, only she's already been conquered as you can see."

She wanted me to bend the line between them into a triangle—a love triangle. She knew Cal's head whipped in whatever direction he saw a girl. A wink or smile would send him running from fling to fling. I didn't care for that sort of thing. I never tried to steal anyone's boyfriend and didn't appreciate Priscilla using me as her pawn. It was too bad I had to play to stay in the game.

I set my fork down and said it like I read the lines in last years' drama class. "Sure, I can help. It makes me sick to see them together."

Little did she know I'd never do it.
"I'm glad you understand."

Chapter 16

The sun glittered between the buildings, highlighting Sprinkles Donut Shop. On Friday, I strolled past the 'help wanted' sign on the window. Cranky customers swarmed the counter. They needed help.

Young women in pink uniforms ran between tables. They carried hot coffee, glazed donuts, blueberry muffins, and brownies, while an older woman mopped up a spill.

I had no ID or a social security card, but what they didn't know wouldn't hurt me. Honesty didn't pay in this town. If I wanted to land a job and leave Priscilla's nut house, I'd have to change my strategy. Then I spotted her.

Her name tag said *Tammy*, and something about her clicked. She wasn't in charge, but when she smiled at me, the flutter in my stomach stopped.

I drew in a deep breath of fresh-brewed coffee and approached her. "Hi, I want to apply for a job. I have experience."

It was a lie, but she didn't know. Besides, anyone could box donuts, pour drinks, and run a cash register. Couldn't they?

"Sure, how much experience?" Tammy asked.

"Two years at Martha's Donut Shop, in Arkansas. Used to help my aunt on weekends 'til she sold the place."

The light in her eyes brightened. "Wait here." She darted through a doorway and returned with the forms.

This time I took Priscilla's advice and claimed to be eighteen.

After I signed on the dotted line, Tammy snapped up the paper and read over it. "Oh, you're married?"

My confident nod convinced her but didn't stop the question. "What brought you to Rhode Island?"

"My husband wanted to move near his mother." Claiming Cal as my husband was a nice touch to help me blend in. Otherwise, they might not hire an Arkansas girl.

The manager had a telephone to her ear, and if Tammy kept asking questions, she'd catch me in a fib, so I told her everything she wanted to hear. 'I can work any shift you want. I'll fill in if someone calls in sick. I worked every station at my aunt's business.' By the time the boss hung up the phone, Tammy was jumping to tell her the news.

Even through the morning chatter, Tammy's voice squeaked above it all when she told the manager. "She has experience. You should hire her."

The manager, with a name tag *Gloria* beckoned and led me to a corner table. I sat stiff and waited for her to fire off questions, and this time the answers had to fool her. If they didn't, she'd never give me work.

Gloria stared at my tummy. "You look young to be married. You have a baby at home?"

I didn't think they were allowed to get that personal.

"No, and don't plan on having kids," I said. "I can work any shift."

The worry lines on her face relaxed, and soon I had a handful of payroll paperwork.

"Wendy, our human resource lady, has Fridays off.

Fill those out and give them to her next week. How's your last name pronounced?"

"It's Russo, like *you sew* but with an R." It was better to use Cal's last name instead of my own.

"Come back at eight. You'll work with Dee."

****

Since I didn't have to report to Sprinkles until the evening, I walked home carrying my pink uniform. When I arrived, Cal and Logan were watching a movie and eating chips.

Logan looked up when I entered the living room. "You found a job?"

"Yes, success at last. But my feet are killing me." I showed him the smooth soles of my cheap shoes. "I'm wearing a hole in them."

I plopped down on the sofa next to Cal, and it was as if a bell rang when Kimmie stormed into the room.

She glared at Cal who was more interested in the movie than her. When he didn't notice her, she cut her eyes toward me. "I moved your shit downstairs."

"You mean you dumped it on the floor," Logan said.

"What?" I knew what she meant, but the nerve of her. She threw my panties, bras, and other belongings in Logan's room.

"Tracie has to move to the basement, anyway. What's the difference?"

"Mom would've given her a chance to collect her stuff herself. You don't have the right to bother her things," Logan said. He turned to me. "Don't worry, I put your clothes in the bathroom."

"Hey, are you going to watch movies all day?" Kimmie said to Cal.

He kept his eyes fixed on the screen. His mouth fell

open as the actress bent forward, her ample breasts in full view. It only took a second before Kimmie popped him on the head.

Cal scooted closer to me, avoiding her while she swatted at him. "Quit it. My show isn't over yet." He sat on the remote control, while she tried to pry it free. But he was stronger.

"Stop." Kimmie yanked the wall plug.

"What?" he asked. "What's your problem?"

"Every time I turn around, you're staring at another woman. Always some half-naked chick." Her face flushed a bright shade of red. "And why do I have to catch you snuggling with your ex on the couch? Huh?"

He was never my boyfriend, and we weren't holding hands. We weren't leaning against each other, either.

"Nothing is going on between me and Tracie. You're too jealous."

Kimmie picked up a book from the coffee table and smacked him over the head.

He chased her to the bedroom.

A door slammed, and Kimmie screamed.

Logan stood and took a few steps that direction before he stopped. He must've decided it was none of his business and went to the kitchen instead.

A sandwich sounded good, so I followed him.

He filled a glass with water. "Sorry she was rude to you."

Cal had a huge problem that was bigger than ogling women. If Kimmie kept acting jealous, Priscilla wouldn't need me to break them up.

"Hormones," I said.

"What?"

"I heard pregnant women go temporarily insane

116

before they have a baby."

He took a sip of water, then dumped the rest in the sink. "She was crazy before she got pregnant."

The screams grew louder, and the bedroom door slammed again.

"Kimmie, wait!" Cal called to her, but she ran outside.

He didn't chase her. Instead, he went back to his movie, but I knew we wouldn't get rid of Kimmie. She'd return in a few hours, and I was still on her hit list. The less I hung around, the better. To get to work by my shift, I'd have to leave an hour early. It was a long walk to the donut shop.

"Hey, Logan. Do you or Cal have a bicycle?"

He pulled a jar of peanut butter from the pantry. "Yeah, it has a flat tire. Why?"

"So I can ride to work."

"We can look at it, but I don't think we have a pump. I can drive you in Cal's truck." He smeared the peanut butter on two slices of bread. "Want one?"

"Yeah, I'm starving."

He made two sandwiches and gave one to me. "I appreciate the lift, but maybe we can fix the bike anyway, for next time. Sprinkles scheduled me to work the night shift. I get off at midnight when the baker comes in."

It would be dark. Not safe for a girl. Any set of wheels would help keep me at an arm's length from creepy men lurking in the alleys, the laundromat, or gas stations.

"You can't be walking or riding around at a late hour. I'll come get you tonight. Maybe next time Cal will. Especially if I gas up his tank. It's running on fumes."

I gave him an agreeable smile but knew Kimmie would have a fit. Maybe I'd be able to go back to Arkansas before Logan went home. He said his father was on vacation for two weeks.

Logan always had money in his pocket. He was bitter toward his dad for marrying again, but at least his dad supplied him with cash. And he didn't mind sharing the wealth. A gentle suggestion might help me get something I needed.

I took a deep breath, hoping it would. "You think you'll still be up that late? You should give me your cellphone number though I'm not sure if Sprinkles will let me use their phone. They have rules, you know."

He stuffed the last of his snack into his mouth and chewed. He took his time like he was thinking. "You should have your own phone. One without a contract."

"Well, if I ever earn enough, I could buy one. Your mom kept my last paycheck, and I still owe her. I don't have any money."

He pulled out his wallet and offered a wad of bills. "Here, take it. There's always more."

The possibilities were in his palm. He might be giving me enough for a bus ticket. If not, he could take me shopping tomorrow. It was a lot of cash. He'd expect something in return.

"You sure?" I tried not to count the twenties he waved in front of me.

Part of me didn't want it. But the greedier part did. Money gave me choices and hope. I longed for Arkansas even if I didn't know where I'd stay.

He passed the money. "Take it, Tracie."

"Thanks. You know it will take me a month to repay

you while working at a donut shop." I kept rubbing my fingers over the stiff bills. The money smelled new and stuck together.

"Consider it a gift, since Mom kept your pay."

"Logan, I don't want to carry cash around at work. Any idea where I can hide it?"

He touched me lightly on the arm. "Downstairs."

Of course, he stashed his weed there, and no one ever found it. He led me to an unfinished part of the basement. It had a cement floor, and studs held a place for walls if someone were to hang sheetrock. In a corner, he showed me the plastic pipe — a hollow safe for valuables.

After we stuffed the green roll deep inside, he placed his hands on my shoulders and turned me to face him. His brown eyes looked through me. He'd expect something for the cash. A kiss was all I could afford.

Chapter 17

East coast people were hangrier than southerners. If I spread a little sugar on a piece of cardboard, they'd mistake it for a graham cracker. I learned the lesson while working the night shift at Sprinkles Donut Shop.

It was eight o'clock when two women, one middle-aged and the other in her mid-twenties, sauntered into our store. They lugged oversized handbags on hunched shoulders and plopped down on the barstools.

The older one held up a palm when I came running with a menu. "We want blueberry muffins and medium diet Cokes."

Okay. It seemed like an easy order. First, I retrieved the drinks. The muffins were in the kitchen on a cooling tray. I placed them on small plates and set them down at the counter in front of the ladies.

The younger woman frowned. "Where's the butter?"

"I don't know," I said.

The older of the two pointed a red fingernail at a miniature refrigerator next to the drink station.

"Oh, sorry. I'm new and I never eat butter with muffins. Actually, I never ate a muffin here."

She glowered at me like I insulted her. Her eyes drifted to my tiny waist. It was as if my words translated to, 'I'm thinner than you because I don't like muffins. You have lots of experience gobbling them. I can tell.'

Dee stood back, behind the register taking in the scene. She must've thought I was an idiot. I hoped not. I already felt like a buffoon without one more person judging me. So I hurried to get the ladies pats of butter.

One of them already finished her Coke and sucked on the straw, making the annoying slurping sound. I set the cold yellow squares on each plate.

The older woman gave me a sarcastic smile. "Warm it up."

"Huh?"

"In the microwave. You can't expect me to eat a cold muffin." She pinched the pat of butter between her long, manicured nails and set it beside her glass.

The other lady pushed her dish toward me.

"How long do I nuke them?"

She rolled her eyes. "Try fifteen seconds."

It wasn't easy to serve them. I turned my back, and they stabbed me with insults.

"The girls here get dumber every day," the younger one said.

"She's the worst. Good looks get you hired, but I'll bet you a donut she'll get fired by next week."

Meanies. I wasn't trying to screw up on purpose. Not only that, I had to refill their drinks, retrieve more napkins, and feed them a second muffin.

The women never once thanked me. They wiped their mouths and left lipstick-stained napkins wadded up next to their dirty plates.

I sprayed down their places and cleaned the crumbs.

Dee strolled toward me. "Jealous, they're just jealous. We're younger and prettier."

I cleared my throat and croaked out my own judgment. "No, they're hangry. You know, a cross between hungry and angry, but more hungry. You'd think they wouldn't wait 'til they're starving to come in here."

"I know, but they do. You'll get used to it," Dee said.

Back in Arkansas, no one ever treated me awful while working at a restaurant. But then again, I threw birthday parties for children. The kids came in all smiles, ready to play games and dig into cake. At the end, I'd say, 'Let's have a contest. Who can throw away the most trash?' The children giggled and laughed while their tiny hands gathered up all the plates and napkins. I'd only have to wipe down the tables and sweep the floor.

The second lesson at Sprinkles came as a surprise too. Regular customers expected me to move at rocket speed. But only two of us worked the night shift. For the next hour, no one came through the glass doors. The tables and bar remained empty.

The job seemed like a snoozer when a stream of factory workers jostled in, elbowing each other in a frenzy to buy java before heading to work. Dee and I rushed behind the counter and poured the coffee.

A gray-haired man flashed his five-dollar bill and shuffled his feet. "Make mine tall, with four pumps."

"Four what?" I asked.

"Creamer, now hurry, girl."

I turned to the steel canister behind me and pushed the lever. It didn't move far enough. It resisted like when I pumped too much air into a bicycle tire.

His nostrils flared when a little blob of cream dropped into his coffee. "Put some muscle into it. Girl, you're making me late."

I leaned over the canister, using my weight to press

harder. Once it delivered enough, I passed the cup to him.

His voice grew louder with every comment. "No, put the top on it. Don't you know anything, kid?"

It wasn't as easy as I thought. Fumbling the flimsy lid, I pushed it against the cup. But the edges caved with the pressure. The whole drink toppled over. Hot brown liquid spilled onto the glass display case of fancy donuts and brownies. Coffee puddled onto the floor.

Oh, this wasn't going well.

Customers grumbled. And the crowd took turns sighing and groaning. I dropped a stack of napkins onto the spill. While it soaked, I poured him a new coffee.

Dee was great. She picked up the slack. The line in front of me split, and most of them gave her orders. I served three people to her dozen. The customers ran out the door within ten minutes.

Dee huffed when the last one left. "Whew, that was rough."

"Sorry, the old man made me nervous." I tugged at my pink uniform, straightening a wrinkle.

She smoothed back a wisp of hair that had fallen from her ponytail. "It's okay. I'm used to it. This place is a revolving door."

Besides the griping, the customers left black scuff marks on the white floor. Great. I'd have to get on my hands and knees to scrub it clean.

"So they'll be back?" I asked. "How often?"

"Not 'til tomorrow. Revolving door means people quit. Customers crab at you. Most new hires don't have the patience to deal with it."

"How long you been here?" I asked.

Dee took a deep breath. "Too long. Six months. I've

trained at least twenty girls."

"Do you hate the job?"

"No, not really. It gets easier the longer you stay. Unless someone quits and there's a gap between then and when the manager hires someone new."

I hated the job so far. But Dee was pleasant enough. I didn't intend to make her work nights alone until Sprinkles hired another person. She could've let me piss off more factory workers or let me mess up more orders. Instead, she bailed me out.

"With some practice, I'll get better," I said.

The door swung open, and Tammy, the girl who convinced the manager to hire me, staggered in. "Hey, ladies, slow night?" She slurred her words.

"You missed the night crew," Dee said. "Tracie's doing great."

It was nice of her to cover for me. But she put me in debt to her twice.

Tammy kept going to the soft drinks and carried something, a miniature bottle. She turned her back to us but twisted off a top and laid it on the counter. She dumped the contents into a cup and filled the rest with Coke.

Tammy turned around and took a swig. Dark bangs fell into her eyes. She had bedhead, the way hair looked after sleeping on it when damp. "Gloria asked me to check in on you. What's your name?"

"Tracie," I said.

Something was wrong with her. Drunk. Tammy stank like bad breath and booze.

"Well, Tracie, did you make any tips tonight?"

"No. I didn't know we get tipped."

Tammy spun around, knocking the bottle on the

floor. It bounced and rolled under the counter. She staggered to the other side of the bar and retrieved a cracked coffee cup. The coins inside clanked as she dumped them onto the countertop. A quarter rolled off the edge and hit the floor with a ping.

We moved toward Tammy. Dee picked up the mini liquor bottle and tossed it into the trash can. The same kind my friend's father collected.

"Dang, only three bucks here. Cheap-ass customers." Tammy palmed the change and dropped it into her pocket. "Since you're not claiming it, I must've earned it on the day shift." She took the money and left as fast as she came.

"Did you get a whiff of that?" I asked.

"No, what?"

"Alcohol. Those fumes...vodka." It was the same smell my friend's dad used to have on his breath when I visited. The odor lingered like bad perfume. "She'll get fired if Gloria finds out." I stared out the window while Tammy's car weaved out of the parking lot.

"I didn't detect anything... She likes to tinker with cars. Helps her dad in a garage. You confused alcohol with some other chemical," Dee said.

It was vodka, but I let it go. I owed Tammy at least one favor for helping me land the job.

The tip cup concerned me more. Nothing for me.

I walked to it and placed it in its spot. "Have you made any tips?"

"Not much, a quarter here and there. Customers leave their loose change sometimes."

Donuts and coffee were cheap compared to meals. But any money helped me get to Arkansas sooner.

"If you get a tip, stick it in your pocket. Management

says we share the money, but take what you earned," Dee said.

There was a crumb on the counter. It gave me an excuse to spray the disinfectant and wipe with a paper towel. Afterward, I discarded the dirty towel in the trash, on top of the bottle Dee threw away.

I was right. She drank vodka.

Something odd was going on between Dee and Tammy. I didn't need to involve myself. But by keeping Tammy's secret, I'd soon learn another lesson.

Chapter 18

It was midnight when Logan pulled up in Cal's truck at Sprinkles Donut Shop. Dee wrung out the mop and worked it, smearing Lysol-infused water across the floor. She had to close the place. With nothing else to do other than stand under fluorescent lights, I clocked out and ran straight for the door when Logan came for me.

The stars sparkled in the clear night sky. For a mid-size town, the city skimped on streetlights, making it peaceful like the small towns in Arkansas. I hopped into Cal's truck and settled into the cold bucket seat while getting a whiff of roast beef and onion rings. Two drinks were in the cup holders.

"How's the job?" Logan asked. "I didn't know if you're hungry, but I am, so I bought sandwiches." He threw the gear into reverse and then forward, rolling out of the parking lot onto a street covered with more shadows than light.

"The job's okay." It sucked lemons, but guys didn't want to hear complaints. "Thanks for the dinner, I'm starved. I don't care for the sweets we sell." My stomach did a happy dance. What he bought was better than the donuts dripping with sugar glaze or bursting with Bavarian cream. It was hard not to dig into the crumpled bag sitting on the console between us.

He turned left, the opposite direction I wanted to go. "I know what you mean. If you're not too tired, I want to take you somewhere."

I glanced down at my pink uniform and sneaked a quick sniff. My underarms didn't stink though they were clammy since my deodorant rubbed off hours ago. "I'm not dressed for going out."

He continued driving, passing parked cars on the street. "Don't worry, it's not that kind of place. It's better."

We were alone. Worry set in. What would Cal say about us taking his truck? What would Priscilla think if she knew her younger son bought me a late dinner, gave me money, and took me somewhere after midnight?

Though I had concerns, the idea of spending time with him gave me a buzz. We could touch each other without interruptions, judging eyes, or open ears. Lately, I fantasized about him. After our kiss, the memory of pressing my lips against his came to me at least fifty times. Tonight, I'd try not to fret about what other people thought.

We drove a good distance before Logan turned onto a road along the seashore. He flipped on the high beams. White streams of light cut through the dark, while we rolled along the pavement. To our right and below, a restless sea sloshed against the steep bluffs. Up ahead, the lighthouse flashed a veil of red onto the water every few seconds. The building was far away, and I couldn't see an access road.

When Logan reached the end of the street, he cut the engine. "It's ancient, built in the 1800s."

The mysterious stone cylinder sat on the hilltop and seemed to grow out of the ground.

"It's beautiful." I had only seen them in pictures, and this one towered above us as it guarded the bay.

"I thought we should have a view while we picnic." Logan unpacked the bag, handing me a sandwich and onion rings before taking a meal for himself.

This was far better than going to a fancy restaurant or eating one of Priscilla's specialties, though I loved her lasagna, sandwiches, and stew.

"It's perfect." I unwrapped my sandwich and bit into the sesame bun, getting a mouthful of roast beef and tangy barbecue sauce.

Outside the windows, a howling wind raised the waves that beat against the rocks. For a while, we feasted on the sandwiches, onion rings and slurped icy soft drinks. We didn't talk. He gazed at the lighthouse that flashed red onto the sea for boats gone adrift. A foghorn blew in a high pitch, guiding mariners safely inland.

"People believe the lighthouse is haunted," he said.

I swallowed another bite of the onion ring. "A ghost?"

He gave me a slow nod, and his brown eyes grew serious.

Logan wiped his mouth with a napkin. "When the fog rolls in, she slinks around in a white nightgown. We might see her."

With the late hour, the heavy air drifted over the land, clouding the trees. Something pale moved in the shadows. Something big.

Logan's phone rang, and I jumped.

He glanced at it. "I have to take this."

Two stray dogs ran into the street. One mounted the other.

So much for phantoms.

The door clicked. Logan slipped out and walked away from the truck. While he mumbled into his phone,

I strained to hear his end of the conversation. Something told me trouble hung on the other end, Priscilla, or Cal.

People were probably looking for him.

Logan finished talking and returned to the truck.

"Is everything okay?" I folded the foil around my half-eaten sandwich and stuffed it into the bag.

"Yeah."

"Is someone looking for us?"

"No, it's nothing." He sipped his drink with an annoyed expression.

If he didn't volunteer to tell me, I wouldn't nag. Why spoil the night?

"Isn't this place great?" he asked and scooted closer to me.

The console separated our seats, but he leaned over. When his warm fingers interlocked with mine, his thumb traced my palm in little circles. A warm tingle shot through my body.

My heart raced. Since he kissed me in the basement, I couldn't get the taste of him off my mind. We were alone, far from his mother.

He lifted my chin. "You're gorgeous...and easy to talk to."

Without waiting for a reply, his lips touched mine. They were hot and moist. Mine locked onto them. He pulled me closer, and his eager hands slid over my back.

I made out in trucks before. After Friday night football games, my boyfriends drove me to a dirt road. If I liked the guy enough, I might let them cup my breasts through my blouse, but my bare skin was off-limits.

Logan breathed harder and crawled over the console. He moved my seat back, giving us more space. Our heat steamed the windows until the haze surrounded us. It separated us from the rest of the world.

I lost my head when he ran his hands under my shirt.

He unfastened my bra, and my breasts spilled out. "Tracie, I never wanted anyone like I want you." Hot and stiff as a tree limb, he pushed against me.

His heat caught me on fire, and the fire spread between my legs when he started grinding, though I still wore pants. While he rubbed against me, he nibbled on my neck.

His raspy zipper groaned on its way down, alerting me he was ready to do the deed. It didn't matter where. We could've been lying on a cactus bed, and I wouldn't have cared.

All modesty flew out the window. I tossed my top behind the seat and wiggled out of my uniform.

Once I stripped down to my panties, another car roared from behind. Headlights brightened the cab.

Oh no.

Whoever it was stopped.

The hum of a motor was too close. My clothes.

In a frenzy, we grabbled in the dark, bumping heads while clawing at the seats. My foot was in a pants leg. I yanked it up and stuck my other leg in its opening.

We weren't fast enough.

Fingers tapped the window. A flashlight invaded our privacy.

Logan jumped into his seat and lowered the window enough to see the man in uniform. "Hi, Officer."

The police officer peered through the gap, shining his light. It highlighted my backward fitting shirt and Logan's bare chest. I crossed my arms over my britches which gaped at the zipper.

"It's past curfew. I need to see your driver's license,

proof of insurance, and registration," the man said.

Logan opened the glove box and handed the guy a wad of papers. While he fished his license from his wallet, the officer panned his light over each piece.

"Step out of the car."

"Both of us?" I asked, wondering how I could rezip without drawing more attention to my nakedness.

"Not you, miss," he said. "Him." The officer stepped back, allowing space for Logan's door to swing open. Logan wiggled into his shirt and hopped out. They moved toward the police car. The muttering wasn't loud enough to decipher.

I finished dressing.

My heart pounded in my chest. What was going on? I swiped the damp, foggy glass which cleared the view.

The cop held a clipboard.

Next to him, Logan crossed his arms.

A ticket?

Logan's phone sat on the dash. It vibrated, and a name splashed across the screen, *Stephanie*. He never mentioned her. Who was she? His stepmother or stepsister? Only someone close to him called after midnight. Was it the same person he spoke to earlier? I could answer. But she'd ask questions. We had enough to deal with tonight. After five buzzes, the phone stopped ringing.

The motor was off, and the night air cooled the truck cab. I shivered.

More mumbling.

Logan's voice was low and controlled. He stayed calm, while the officer scribbled on a form. Did Cal fail to buy insurance or register his truck? It wouldn't surprise me.

Logan raked a hand through his thick hair and accepted the ticket. At least, the officer didn't question me.

The phone rang again. Stephanie. She didn't give up.

The door clicked, and Logan climbed in. He glanced at the flashing screen and flipped the phone facedown. "It's okay. Got a citation, but it's Cal's problem." He started the engine and spun the truck around.

The officer sat in his car, eyeing us as we rumbled away. The phone buzzed repeatedly, but Logan never looked at it.

We headed to Priscilla's house, and I asked, "Who's Stephanie?"

"Nobody," he said in a clipped voice.

I couldn't dismiss the girl. She kept calling, and it was after one a.m. If she were his stepmother or sister, he would've said so. He never denied having a girlfriend, and I never asked. I should have.

When we were halfway home, sitting at a stoplight, the phone buzzed again. He picked it up and hit the power button.

"Who is Stephanie?"

"Don't worry about it," he said.

He kept a secret, though I had shared my life story with him. And I let him grind on me. He had seen me topless, too. In a heated moment, he almost stripped me naked and took my virginity.

If not for the cop, Logan would've had me. He would've humped me like the dogs mating in the road. If he had a girlfriend, I meant nothing to him. He probably didn't care if he got me pregnant. I was glad it didn't happen. Who wanted to have sex with a guy who wouldn't tell me why another girl called him at one a.m.? So why did I feel sick over this?

My stomach turned over like Logan forced me to swallow a stone. Stones were cold, hard, and I had an awful taste in my mouth.

Chapter 19

It was still dark when cold hands clamped down on my ankle and yanked my dream away. "Wake up."

I stretched the length of the sofa, and my feet hit an armrest. Before Priscilla disturbed me, I dreamed of stepping on soft, cool grass. "What? Is something wrong?"

"Yes, there is, and you know it." Her raspy whisper alarmed me. People didn't talk before dawn unless something bothered them. All the possibilities swirled in my mind. Logan's money, smoking cannabis, and the police officer catching me undressed at the lighthouse. Which one? Or did I forget something? It was too damn early for this.

"Cal says he's getting married this weekend. You were supposed to stop him, but you're focused on Logan. Going to the lighthouse with him after midnight, really?"

Oh no. She found out. My heartbeat finished waking me.

She patted me on the arm. "Don't look so shocked. You know teenage boys talk. I'm putting you on notice. Logan is off-limits. Get your head on straight and work on Cal. Remember our agreement?"

I had plenty of words for her, but anything I said would make it worse. I dug myself a hole when I moved here. I made it easy for Priscilla to use me when she didn't want to dirty her hands. But if she kept at it, I'd make her miserable. For now, I'd do whatever she said.

"Well?" she asked.

"Yes," I said, aware that she might throw me out if I didn't agree to her terms. With nowhere to live, I had no choice. My other options amounted to hanging around the twenty-four-hour laundromat. A co-worker might let me crash on their lumpy couch a week or two.

She switched on the lamp and gave me a satisfied smile. "Good. I'm glad we've got that settled. I have something else for you." She passed a piece of folded paper. Her generous list of chores included dusting, vacuuming, mopping, laundry, bathrooms. And the list went on and on.

"This will take all day. Is anyone helping me?"

"No. Bess goes to school. Kimmie can't be exposed to chemicals since she's pregnant," Priscilla said.

"She can vacuum and dust," I said.

"No, she's too close to having the baby."

"Can't the guys help?"

"No. They don't do a good job. You can handle it. Besides, you still owe me sixty dollars. Think of it as paying me back." She didn't wait for another objection and padded away.

Priscilla meant payback. She punished me for showing Logan my breasts and failing to break Cal's engagement to Kimmie. She let me know I screwed up.

I shouldn't have to clean the house alone when five other people made messes. They all showered, used the toilets, dirtied dishes, and filled the hampers with stinky clothes. Kimmie wasn't related to them, and she didn't get a chore list.

After dressing and eating a boiled egg, I tackled the rooms. I stood on a chair, on tiptoes to reach the top of

Priscilla's antique hutch when Logan showed his face.

"Good morning," he said.

"What's good about it?" I wiped my damp cloth across the oak furniture, and the dust transformed to mud. It must've been months since anyone touched it.

"Well, the sun is shining. I thought we could take a walk. I'd like to take you to the park and show you the swan in the little creek."

"I could, except your mom thinks I have too much free time. You know, time to go to lighthouses and take off my clothes. So she gave me chores." I hopped down and rinsed the cloth in a bucket, turning the water gray and dingy.

"I'm sorry. She overheard me talking to Cal."

"Oh, I know. I'd hope you didn't share that with her directly. If you did, your family is more messed up than I thought. It's bad enough you told Cal."

He looked down at the floor. "Sorry Mom's giving you a hard time."

His apology didn't repair the damage. I couldn't rewind the clock and change last night any more than the night I ran away with Cal. The brothers were comparing experiences, exchanging stories about me. It made me feel cheap and dirty like the streetwalkers in Dallas, the ones wearing see-through dresses without panties so the men could see the merchandise before buying.

"I said I'm sorry. Cal had to know about the ticket. I didn't know Mom was listening."

I moved on to the dining table and swiped it clean. "Well, she did. And she's not happy."

"Can I help?" When I didn't answer, he went to the linen closet and returned with another towel. He dusted the table legs. "When we finish, will you go to the park

137

with me?"

"Why not ask Stephanie?" I said, trying not to sound too bitter, but the words came out stiff and angry.

He rinsed the cloth in the bucket and squeezed it until damp. "Oh her, she's my ex-girlfriend. She calls, bawling and screaming. She's too needy. That's why we broke up."

"Why didn't you just say so when I asked?" I picked up a broom in the corner and swept the floor.

He fidgeted with the wet rag, while looking down. "It's embarrassing. I didn't want to admit I had a stalker. I kept hoping she'd go away, find another guy." Logan sounded sincere, but he had a big mouth, telling his brother about us.

Still, I had misjudged his relationship with Stephanie. Lots of people attracted creepers. It was part of dating. At least Logan recognized she was a problem and ended it…if he told the truth. He probably did since I never caught him in a lie. And he was a rock star with big brown eyes, dark wavy hair, and the confidence to take the stage. I bet girls chased him, swooning, throwing themselves at him. Just because they did, didn't mean he gave them a second look.

"I'm sorry I got mad about Stephanie. But I'm still pissed you told Cal what happened between us."

"Tracie, he wanted to know what we were doing at the lighthouse. I told him we were eating sandwiches until the cop came. That's all."

If that was it, his mother guessed the rest. She knew I'd fall for Logan, her handsome son. What else would we be doing at the lighthouse after midnight? Priscilla was smart and had twenty-five years of life experience on me.

I stopped sweeping. "Logan, I'm sorry. I don't know what's wrong with me. Of course, you wouldn't tell Cal what we did. I guess I'm paranoid."

He stepped closer and set my broom aside. "It's okay. You've been through a lot." He hugged me, and his warmth chased away my doubts. He did care. I was safe in his arms, right where I wanted to be. Priscilla didn't have to know, not today. She'd forget about me and Logan soon. I'd make sure she had bigger problems.

****

A certain level of craziness tended to invade my dreams. Butterflies baring fangs, dead babies floating in bathtubs, birds with a taste for human flesh worked their way into my nightmares.

I shaded my eyes from a merciless sun, squinting at the crows sailing toward me.

Caw, caw. Hundreds of black birds aimed needle-sharp beaks at me.

Knock, knock, knock... "Dick, I know you're here." An unfamiliar female voice called beyond the front door.

My eyes, half-mast slits, opened to the dark living room.

Dick... Dick, oh Priscilla's married boyfriend.

She pounded louder, while I turned on my side and covered my head with the throw pillow. Sleeping on the couch put me closest to the visitor. But it wasn't my place to answer the door, not with five other people living here. Dick's Cadillac was as visible as an elephant in the driveway, his misfortune.

The sound of sticky bare feet slapping the wood floor came to a stop. "Why don't you get the door?" Kimmie asked. "I can't sleep with that noise."

The banging came faster and more determined.

I wanted to let the woman in. Let the lady go nuts flipping on lights, opening bedroom doors, waking everyone until she found Dick and Priscilla lying in the same bed. Priscilla was sleeping in one of her tacky nighties she made me wash and fold. I hoped it was the bright-red one with the butt-flossing thong. Since her lecture, revenge entered my mind. And best of all I could get Kimmie to serve it without appearing guilty.

"Kimmie, I can't answer her. She's pissed. She'll rip his head off."

The floor creaked when Kimmie moved closer. "Who?"

The woman kept pounding the door, but she'd leave if someone didn't answer her soon.

I sat up and wiped the sleep from my eyes, which gave me a shadowy view of Kimmie's rounded shape. "His girlfriend."

"What the hell are you talking about?"

I whispered the answer. "She's asking for Cal."

"I thought I heard her ask for Dick," Kimmie said.

"No, she said, Cal you dick."

Kimmie got quiet a minute as if deciding what to do.

The woman stopped beating the door. "I know he's here. Why don't you answer?"

Kimmie growled like a hungry alley cat guarding its dinner and stomped toward the woman's voice.

"No, Kimmie, don't. She'll tear you up," I said.

"I'm not afraid of her." She flipped on the lights, both outside and inside, and revealed the middle-aged woman.

My vision adjusted in time to bear witness to the lady's slack mouth and bulging eyes lingering over Kimmie's swollen belly beneath a transparent

140

nightgown.

"Oh, my. You're pregnant?"

Kimmie gave her a victorious smile, took a step back, and placed her hands on her hips. The woman frowned at the display of super-sized stomach, even more when Kimmie thrust her hips forward.

"Where is he?" The stranger pushed her way past Kimmie and ran into a partially lit hall.

"Hey, I didn't invite you in," Kimmie said. "Cal, Cal, get up. You have some explaining to do."

"Dick, you sick bastard. She's practically a child." The woman went from door to door, banging.

Kimmie seized my arm. "She said Dick."

"Yes," I said, breaking free and heading into the hall.

"Hey, you said she was after Cal."

"I did not. I told you she was looking for Dick. You totally misunderstood me," I said.

A door squeaked, and Dick stood in boxers at Priscilla's doorway. "Michelle, what are you doing here?"

"Oh, Dick, you're in big trouble. Had to go to an out-of-state conference, did you? Well, I had this feeling you didn't, and you know what? I called. Called your office. Your assistant said there was no conference." She threw her arms up. "You like this better than Vegas? You promised me, and all this time you've been sleeping with a child. You, you pedophile!"

Priscilla's bedside lamp lit the room. "Who's a child?" She sat up and reached for a robe draped over a chair next to the bed.

"The teenager who answered the door." The woman pointed at Priscilla who stood up in her red-and-black nighty with a thong wedged somewhere in her butt crack. "And you're sleeping with her mother too? What the hell is wrong with you?"

Priscilla slipped on the robe and tied the belt. "Dick, who is this woman?"

"No, you have the wrong idea. I haven't been sleeping with the kid," Dick said.

"Either way, it's over, and this time, I'm telling your *wife*." The woman spun around and pushed her way past me, Kimmie, and Cal.

Chapter 20

Trouble started with a capital *K*, followed by *i-m-m-i-e*. Kimmie was on a mission to torment me ever since I set her up. When Priscilla's house of cards fell, I never predicted a complete victory. With Dick's wife and girlfriend folding, Priscilla had him all to herself.

Having another person living here didn't irritate me as much as Kimmie's accusations. She knew I fooled her into letting Michelle into the house. I refused to tell the truth. My lies started a war.

Of course, Kimmie never admitted to pouring bleach on my uniform while my clothes were in the washer, downstairs. When I went to move my stuff to the dryer, it had huge white splotches. The bleach fumes stung my eyes. I knew it was Kimmie who did it. She scowled at me more than usual when I wore my Sprinkles uniform.

Kimmie left her dirty clothes in the laundry room. It was hers since no one else wore tops big enough to cover a beach-ball-sized belly. I could've returned the favor and drizzled Clorox on her belongings. But she deserved better. Since she liked to roll naked on the carpet with Cal, she didn't need her blouse. She didn't need panties, or the armpit-stained bras, pants, or her maternity dress, either.

Kimmie's clothes went into the fireplace. After a healthy squirt of lighter fluid and a strike of a match, the flames jumped on. What was cotton shriveled to thin, black curls.

I stirred the ashes with the poker, and the evidence blended into a swirl of gray. I had no choice but to wear the blotchy uniform to work. With a little luck, someone might've left the storage closet unlocked at the donut shop. A secret exchange was in order before starting my shift.

My life here soured, and I didn't like these petty games. Kimmie brought out the worst in me. I needed to go. But where to?

I tapped Debby's number into my new cellphone. No answer. The money Logan gave me covered the cost, but not enough for a bus ticket, too. When I called Mom, a recording said the number was disconnected.

My stomach twisted. What the heck was going on? Did my family move away? Even worse, Logan, my confidant, left the house.

Logan said he had errands to run and left with Priscilla. They didn't go into detail, and I had other things on my mind, like finding my mother. Why did my parents disable the phone? I always felt grounded before, knowing there was a home base in Arkansas. My family foundation fell into a dark void. No mother, no father, no brother. I was out here, in a strange state, living with crazy people.

I put on my worn-out shoes and headed upstairs. Cal sat alone on the sofa, watching television.

"Hey, the tie-dye fashion looks good on you," he said.

I glanced down at the white splotches. "You think? My uniform got into a fight with the bleach and lost. It happened when I wasn't watching."

"Oh." His listless reply said he suspected who did it, but he didn't admit what I already knew. "Do you want a ride to work?"

"Sure. It's a long walk."

It was four thirty. I still had ninety minutes.

"Where's Kimmie?" I asked.

"Her mother picked her up. She had a medical appointment, you know, the baby."

Relief swept over me. The last thing I needed was for Kimmie to burst in here and accuse me of stealing her clothes.

"Where's your sister?"

"School, but she has dance class later. Do you have time to talk?" Cal asked.

"Sure." I plopped down on the couch, sinking into the pillows.

Cal fidgeted like he worried. Not the kind of worry when you missed the school bus or if you got caught sneaking in after curfew. It was more like when you got an F on a test in a class you were already failing. Only his serious expression meant it was worse than I predicted.

"What's wrong?" I asked.

A commercial blared, and he turned down the volume. "I don't know how to deal with Kimmie. We're supposed to get married this Saturday. I'm having second thoughts."

"Don't marry her if you don't want to."

"But she has her heart set on it. And I did agree when she brought it up." He twisted his garnet class ring on his finger.

"So you didn't actually propose to her? Is that what you're saying?"

Kimmie was the type of girl who told her boyfriend when to wed and where to honeymoon. She'd decide how many kids they'd have, and even their names.

"You see it's like this… Kimmie's a great girl. The guy who knocked her up didn't want a baby, and I offered to help. After all, we did grow up together, same school, church, neighborhood."

"I get it. You felt sorry for her."

Cal liked to play the hero. If he didn't, I wouldn't be in Rhode Island hundreds of miles away from my family.

He scooted closer to me. "I care about her. I do. But she has a temper. Always mad, always picking on me."

"I know. And when you agreed to marry her, you didn't think you'd spend your life with a jealous woman."

Cal was a guy who enjoyed looking at women of all shapes and sizes. He ogled girls with big breasts and lean legs. And the prettier they were, the longer he stared. Kimmie made it clear several times she didn't appreciate his gawking. They were a match made in hell.

"So what do you plan to do?" I asked.

"I don't know. I already gave her Grandma's engagement ring."

It was like he asked my permission to welch on a promise. The baby would come, and it needed a father. Cal could provide a last name, but he didn't have a job or any way to support a family.

I turned to him, more directly now. "Cal, you can't marry her. Just be her friend, help her through the pregnancy." I rubbed his arm as reassurance, not as a sign of affection.

A door slammed outside. "Thanks, love you too." It was Kimmie's voice, and a car rumbled away.

Cal pulled me closer, hugging me. "It has to be Kimmie's decision, understand?"

I tried to wiggle loose when the front door opened, and Kimmie walked in on us.

"Cal, get your hands off the slut." Something crashed against the floor. "I can't even trust you for a couple hours."

Bony fingers clamped down on my throat. Freeing myself was like pulling up a tree root, only the root strangled me.

"Kimmie, stop it. You're hurting her." Cal hopped up and pushed her back.

Kimmie jumped on me, and I choked.

He ran around the sofa and wedged his arms between us. Wrapped them around her, while I squirmed.

"I didn't do anything," I managed to croak, though I knew it wouldn't convince her.

He pried her hands loose and slung her off me.

With a thud, she hit the floor.

"The engagement is off. We can't get married if you're messing with other girls." Kimmie yanked off the ring and threw it at him. It pelted him in the chest before pinging across the floor.

Legs splayed, she somehow righted her pregnant body and pushed herself to her feet. She spat in my face on the way to her bedroom.

I wiped away the spittle and considered pouncing on her, but she outweighed me by at least fifty pounds. Besides, I was still gasping for air. "Cal, you're a jerk. I can't believe five minutes ago, I felt sorry for you."

Cal picked up the gold ring and slipped it onto his pinky finger. "Problem solved." He headed to the bathroom and shut the door.

What happened would please Priscilla, but what concerned me more was Logan's reaction to Kimmie's accusations. I didn't want him to think I threw myself at Cal. Maybe Kimmie would call her mom and leave before giving Logan an earful.

A ringing phone interrupted my worries. No one answered. Kimmie was probably packing, and Cal didn't come out of the bathroom. It didn't seem like a big deal when I went to the kitchen and picked up the landline receiver.

"Hello, is Logan there?" Her perky voice came through clear.

"No, he's out. Can I take a message?" I asked, wanting to know this girl's name more than relaying her news.

"Sure, tell him Stephanie called. Tell him I'll be ready at eight."

Logan always had his cellphone with him. I was sure Stephanie called his number first. Still, her surprise sucked the breath out of me.

"Are you still there?" Stephanie asked.

"Yes…I'll tell him."

"Thanks." She disconnected before I could ask questions.

The worries set in. What did Stephanie mean? A date? Did Logan lie to me, or was the girl delusional? Was she a stalker who knew where he'd be at eight?

The television droned on without anyone watching. I turned it off before sitting on the sofa. For a few minutes, it was quiet, except for the chatter in my head.

The toilet flushed. Cal came out of the bathroom the same time the front door opened. Priscilla waltzed in with Logan in tow. He carried a fancy tuxedo under the clear plastic wrapper.

The hallway door slammed, and Kimmie turned the corner with a paper sack full of clothes. She set them on the floor and stomped past everyone, heading downstairs.

Oh no. She's going to tell everyone.

Priscilla glanced at the bag crammed with Kimmie's belongings, then at me. "What's going on?"

"I've had enough," Kimmie said, on her way downstairs.

Puzzled, I couldn't stop staring at Logan's tuxedo. Was he meeting Stephanie in these clothes tonight? It was prom season. Maybe Stephanie knew he was going.

Priscilla zeroed in on the white splotches on my top. "What happened to your uniform?"

"Someone bleached it. It's ruined."

"Where are my clothes?" Kimmie screamed downstairs, feet pounding as she hit the steps. "My stuff is missing. I left my dirties by the washer, and now they're gone." She glared at me. "You did something to them, didn't you, Tracie?"

I shrugged as if I had no idea her garments were cinders in the fireplace. "Maybe you only *thought* you left your clothes there."

Logan admired his new suit and didn't concern himself with the screaming. After all, this was our new normal.

"Yeah, like I *thought* I saw you and Cal stuck together like magnets. I hallucinated."

Logan stopped and turned. One corner of Priscilla's lip lifted into a crooked smile.

"We weren't messing around," I said, more concerned about what Logan thought than trying to please his mother.

Who would Logan believe? Kimmie told everyone I was a liar. She was right. I tricked her the night she let Michelle into the house. We were at war. Kimmie was a grenade, and Cal had lit her fuse.

Just when I thought things couldn't get worse, Cal took another shot at Kimmie. "So what? While you were at the doctor, we had sex on the sofa. I enjoyed her much more than you."

Logan's eyes widened, and his neck snapped backward.

The room grew silent.

"He's lying. Nothing happened," I said.

Kimmie was speechless, and Priscilla's crooked smile widened.

Logan had heard enough. He disappeared to the safety of the basement.

After our night at the lighthouse, he must've believed Cal's story.

Fat tears rolled down Kimmie's face. Cal stabbed us both with a knife of lies, twisting it good and hard, making it burn, bleeding us dry. With precision, he cut out Kimmie's heart and sliced off my relationship with Logan.

"I swear, it never happened," I said.

"Shut up." Kimmie picked up her bag and balanced it on her humongous belly. "You and Cal deserve each other. I'm outta here."

Chapter 21

I slinked into work with my palms covering the white splotches on my uniform. I needed eight more hands to hide the stains in the front. When I got there, Dee had called in sick. It was Tammy who greeted me.

She smiled as she looked me up and down. "Bleach?"

"Yes, ma'am, I'm sorry. My friend's girlfriend—"

"Don't worry. It happens all the time." She led me to the dim hall behind the storefront. "Wait here."

Tammy slipped through a nearby door. As she rummaged around, the sound of drawers rolled on rails, then there was the clinking of metal. She returned with a silver key which slid into the lock on the supply closet. With a click, the door sprang open.

"We keep extra uniforms for a reason. But don't blab. The bookkeeper's supposed to charge it against your paycheck." She offered a small top and pants she pulled from their hangers. "We'll throw your old ones into the dumpster after dark."

I took the new uniform that reeked of faux lavender. "How much do they cost?" I was going to borrow them, not steal. Her tone hit a nerve and made me suspicious of her favors.

She fiddled with the wire hanger. "More than they're worth."

This was the second time she helped me. Maybe she

did it because I didn't rat her out to the manager when she showed up stinking like alcohol. She must've wanted to make sure she was safe. What better way than to encourage me to steal?

"I don't mind paying for them. Don't want to get anyone in trouble."

"Listen, no one will notice. Don't overthink it. Take the damn uniform and be grateful someone has your back." As she moved closer, fumes blew into my face.

Drinking before work or on the job was wrong. I tried not to dwell on it, while I peeled off the spotted clothes and dressed in the new ones. I had a gut feeling something awful was going to happen tonight. Tammy had a purpose for me.

A gaggle of customers clamored through the door. Once they bustled in, we hurried behind the counter.

"I need a dozen glazed." The woman fumbled with a twenty-dollar bill, while I whipped out the container. I transformed the flat box into a three-dimensional rectangle. Before I could fill it, Tammy's register cha-chinged twice.

No matter how fast I moved, even dropping a couple of pastries on the floor while rushing, Tammy beat me. No one said it was a contest, but I had to earn my place. My clumsy fingers kept hitting the wrong buttons on the register. The machines looked like the ones in flea markets back home.

"Oops, sorry, ma'am…Tammy." The drawer jammed, and no amount of jiggling it helped.

Tammy finished stuffing a jelly donut, oozing with raspberry cream, into a bag and slapped the change into the man's hand.

"I'm stuck," I said.

"No problem." Tammy sidestepped toward me and punched a button. The drawer popped open, displaying a zero on the monitor. "Let's see." She grabbed six one-dollar bills and a quarter, folded the paper money over and passed it to the lady who was huffing like she had run a 5K race.

The woman snatched the box, turned, and headed for the door.

"Have a nice night," Tammy said.

The grouch was the final customer, and I sucked in a deep breath to cool my frustrations.

The math was flawed. Even a high school dropout knew if a dozen donuts cost eight dollars plus tax, and the woman gave me a twenty, we owed her closer to eleven dollars. In a tense moment, Tammy rushed and opened the drawer without ringing up the merchandise. Instead of fixing the mistake, she scribbled on a piece of scratch paper.

"What are you doing?" I asked.

"We, my friend, are keeping tabs." She finished her note and tucked the pen behind her ear.

"That's a good idea since I'll probably screw up another order before the night ends." I licked my dry lips. "I don't know how you check them out so quickly."

Tammy picked up the paper and smirked. "There's a trick to it."

Old-fashioned registers were hard to operate. Intimidating was the best way to describe them. No one trained on machines like these. Not anymore. Heck, everyone scanned the goods or had foolproof keypads. We should have pictures of glazed donuts, jelly donuts, bear claws, eclairs, and coffee instead of numbers to punch.

"You want to learn how it's done?" she asked. "Don't look so scared. It's easy."

Maybe for her, but I'd better listen anyhow.

"Most of our customers carry cash. The owner doesn't like credit cards though he'll take a local check."

"Why?" I asked.

"Keeping credit card records and paying the bank fees takes a bite out of his wallet. It's a cash business. No one returns or exchanges a donut. You buy a donut, eat, and you're done."

"How is it easier? If we had a credit card machine, I'd swipe it, they'd sign, and it's over."

"Watch." She hit the same button she did before, and the cash drawer sprang open.

"So…that's what you did when I got stuck." I knew what to do if in a jam, but it didn't help me learn the task.

"It's all you have to do…well, almost. Add up what you think the purchase costs and give the customer half their change. If they give you a big bill, it's not noticeable."

How sad, yet terrifying. My stomach flipped over at the thought of cheating customers. Tammy never counted the change back to the people. She slapped it in their palm and sent them packing.

When I stood in line at a store, the stranger behind me always stood too close, almost on top of me. Hot breath steamed my neck. Nasty. I paid and stepped aside, never counting the money I had stuffed into my jean pocket. Did the cashier cheat me?

"Tammy, what happens if they realize you gave them the wrong amount?"

She crossed her arms. "It only happens maybe once a month. Tell them you made a mistake and give them the money. It's simple. They already think women who work in donut shops are idiots."

She spoke the truth. My first day on the job, the two muffin eaters had a good time taking jabs at me. Still, I would've never shortchanged them.

"I guess if someone notices, you'd want to remember them. Never try it twice on the same person," I said.

It was better to make her think I was on board with this, while I figured out how to avoid scamming customers.

"You got it. See how simple it is? When our shift ends, we split the pot."

It could be easy, but restaurants had cameras. People went to jail for stealing from their employer. They called it embezzling. Only Sprinkles didn't have many customers. How much money could Tammy hope to make? A few dollars here, a few quarters there. It wasn't worth the risk of going to prison.

"Here they come." Tammy pointed to the onslaught of factory workers, rolling into the parking lot. "Now's your turn to make money. I've been doing all the work."

The door flew open, and customers flooded the lobby. With only seconds to spare, I ran behind the counter. Tammy zipped the opposite direction.

"Wait, where're going?" I asked.

"Restroom. You can handle it." She jogged away.

A man flashed his five-dollar bill.

I gave him a nervous smile. I knew him. "Coffee, four pumps?"

"You bet." His lips peeled back in a grin, exposing yellow teeth.

My heart beat in my chest like someone knocked at

155

the door when I pretended to be gone, only they knew I was home. I couldn't cheat him. Instead, I fixed his coffee and did my best to do the math in my head.

He smiled when I passed the cup and his change. "You're getting the hang of it, kid."

After a grueling twenty minutes, everyone had their drinks, and the lobby cleared.

Tammy sauntered to the register and smiled at the zeros on the tabulator tape. "Good, you did fine."

Perspiration rolled down my neck, and my hairline was damp with sweat. She'd notice later. There had to be a minimum the store collected at night. I made no effort to add to the amount.

She presented the paper and pen. "How much?"

"I don't know. Got nervous, lost count. I'm still learning the system. You know, making the coffee the way they like it."

She tapped the pen on the countertop. "What I don't understand is you have experience. Don't tell me your aunt, the one you worked for, didn't line her pockets. You're not stupid."

It took a minute to collect my thoughts, shuffle them in a way that sounded logical. "If she did, I didn't know about it. But it's different here. The customers rush me. They run in, scream their orders, and leave. In Arkansas, they sit around the tables and talk for hours, nibbling on donuts and sipping coffee."

She chuckled. "Thank God the customers don't stay here all night. The more flustered they are the better."

She seemed satisfied with my answer.

For a long while, we were alone. Then three men, who looked to be in their early twenties, blew through the door. Two of them sat on the bar stools, while the one with a full beard met Tammy at the counter.

Tammy pulled her head out of the donut case she was cleaning. "What can I get you?"

"Three Cokes."

It was well past eleven thirty, and I swept the floor. My broom dislodged dried crumbs wedged under the tables as the frayed bristles scraped across the tile. Every so often, the straw broke under the pressure and joined the pile of dirt and sugary sprinkles.

While she made their drinks, the other two men burned holes in my back.

"I could watch you work all night." He had a ball cap crammed tight on his head with boyish curls poking out. The chauvinistic smirk on his face was contagious. His friend sported the same unsavory expression, and it raised my goose pimples.

"That'll be seven fifty," Tammy said to their friend.

He gulped his drink. After he drank half of it, he stopped. "Nah, it's on the house."

Tammy held out her palm. "Pay up, buddy."

The other two men hopped off the stools. One swatted my backside on the way to the counter.

"Keep your hands to yourself," I said.

He turned. "Or what? You and your co-worker here gonna kick us out?"

"No, but the cops will," I said, eyeing the wall phone.

The shmuck with the ball cap jumped over the counter and blocked me, positioning himself in front of the telephone.

Tammy pointed to the ceiling and walls. "We have hidden cameras. Your ugly mug is on them. You'll get arrested for harassment, theft, and whatever else we can think of."

The doubt crossed my mind. Within twenty minutes, before the baker arrived, they could rape us, rob the place, and head on their merry way. But they didn't work here, so they didn't know about our security.

Inside I trembled, but I spat the words out rock solid. "She's right."

The one who spanked me in passing came toward me, dug his fingers into my arm. I yanked back, but no matter how hard I pulled, his grip pinched me to the bone. "Gimme the tape."

His dirty fingernails dug into my skin. He towered over me and twisted my arm.

"You think the owner is stupid? The tape isn't on the premises. Bells blasting as we speak. Cops are coming for you," Tammy said.

The men gave each other worried looks. Their eyes questioned whether we triggered a silent alarm.

With confidence I grinned and nodded. "Get off me." My inner strength kicked in, and the knee jerk reaction hit him in the groin.

He let go as if I turned into a live wire of electricity. "Ow." Hands cradled his private parts. He'd have no normal function there tonight.

The first guy slammed a ten-dollar bill on the counter. "Here, keep the rest." He and the guy who blocked the phone grabbed their drinks.

They made a hasty retreat with the butt spanker in third place, limping out the door.

I headed to the phone, ready to make good on the harassment and assault charges. My arm had red marks on it.

"What're you doing?" Tammy asked.

The white beams flashed through the window as they peeled away.

"Reporting them."

"No, don't."

"Why? So they can murder us next time?" I held up my injured arm. "It still hurts."

"You'll live." Tammy opened the cash drawer and pulled out the money and counted.

I dreaded this moment. She'd figure out I didn't cheat the customers.

"It's usually twice this much," she said, waving the cash.

I swallowed hard. "I suck at math." She didn't need to know I aced calculus, trigonometry, and algebra. Every customer received enough change, though I might've come up short on the sales tax.

Tammy replaced the money that belonged in the cash drawer and made neat piles with the extra on the counter. "You need to practice. Since you didn't get much, I'll keep this." She stuffed the loot into her pocket.

Her decision gave me an internal sigh of relief. If she kept it all, no one could accuse me of robbing customers. Any respect I had for Tammy sank like a brick in a mud pit. She'd never rise above the scum in which she settled, not after cheating hardworking folks. Those people slaved at night to pay their bills. My God, they had children at home. Little boys who ate cereal, pizza, and sandwiches, like my younger brother did.

She patted her pocket. "You need to get the hang of it. Understand?"

I understood. She didn't want to call the police. They'd snoop and bust her scam wide open.

Headlights flashed through the windows and saved

me from Tammy's lecture.

"I've got to go," I said.

I didn't know which was worse, listening Tammy's speech or talking to Cal.

Chapter 22

Cal never showed. In the shadows, I slinked toward Priscilla's house. My frequent calls to her sons went unanswered. No one drove me home. No one cared.

Cold wind blew my hair in ten directions, and without a jacket, the chill set in. I stopped every few minutes and called Logan and Cal. After five rings, Priscilla's phone landline delivered a generic message. Logan's phone went straight to voicemail.

As I passed a fenced yard, a dog yipped. It alerted everyone I didn't belong here. The boys had forgotten me. What was I to them? Nothing...nothing at all. I might as well chisel *nothing* into a stone and carry it in my pocket as a reminder.

Beyond the windows of each looming house, people slept. They dreamed, while each tiring step carried me closer to Priscilla's sofa. I had little in common with the strangers in their beds except somewhere, I had a family. My brother was tucked under the covers, not roaming the streets like a stray animal.

Two miles later, I arrived at Priscilla's driveway. The white Cadillac, Dick's car, glimmered in the moonlight. Cal's truck was gone. I had no house key, and someone locked the door. At least the wind stopped howling, and Bess heard my knocks.

"Tracie?" Bess said, in a sleepy voice. "Sorry, I forgot you were at work and locked you out."

I stepped inside, glad to thaw my frosty nose. "Thanks for getting up. Where are the boys?"

"I don't know where Cal is, but Logan went to the prom. He should be home soon."

"Prom?" I said, but suspected all along.

"Yeah, with Stephanie, his girlfriend." Bess covered her mouth and yawned. Her news shattered my heart into a million pieces.

"His girlfriend?" I asked, to make sure I understood.

"His sometimes girlfriend. They break up and make up." Bess padded back to her room.

Logan and Stephanie...together tonight. Until now, Logan made living here tolerable. I looked forward to seeing his smiling face, kissing his soft lips. Until now....

Logan met Stephanie after I started my evening shift at Sprinkles. When Cal and Kimmie pulled me into their drama, I forgot to say Stephanie called. It didn't seem necessary. He labeled her a stalker, and no one wanted to know their stalker called again.

Stephanie's chirpy voice popped into my head. No wonder she sounded chipper, like the happiest girl in Rhode Island. Tonight, she wore a formal gown, and Logan stayed by her side. He wore the fancy tux Priscilla bought or rented.

A black limousine threw light onto the wall clock. *1:20*, it said. The car idled on the street, and two people emerged. A gap through the blinds gave a view of Logan and the girl. They embraced, and he kissed her. It wasn't a peck on the lips. Logan had his tongue in her mouth.

Damn...why didn't Priscilla tell me? She said Logan was off-limits, but she never mentioned Stephanie. Stephanie must not be the reason. Priscilla's boyfriend was married, but it didn't stop her from dragging him to bed.

I had to end my relationship with Logan. No decent girl ever kissed someone's boyfriend. I ignored the warning signs the night Logan drove me to the lighthouse. And he lied about Stephanie the next day. I trusted him and convinced myself she stalked him.

The lovely girl with long wavy hair released Logan's hand and lifted her dress. Like a gentleman, Logan opened her door. She slid into the luxury vehicle, gathering her glittery red gown onto her lap. With a gentle click, Logan shut her door. Her window lowered. He leaned inside for another kiss. But it wasn't the final one. They blew kisses to each other as the car sped away. Logan remained still, a statue gazing at the empty street long after she left.

Prom. Everyone went but me. I wore this crappy uniform while my crush took another girl. He spent the night dancing with her. I couldn't face him.

Anger and jealousy seethed in me the same way when my boyfriend, Jake, took Tia Perkins to a concert. He bought the tickets for us. At the last minute, he canceled. He blamed it on a migraine headache. The following Monday, Tia's friends huddled and whispered in the school hallway. They knew Jake dumped me before I did.

Logan turned and strode toward the door. He approached the house with confidence. What guy wouldn't? Stephanie was a princess. No fairy tale for me. My foolish choices landed me in a New England nightmare.

I darted into the dark kitchen and waited for him to disappear downstairs. If only I could vanish.

Minutes passed before the doorknob jiggled. What was taking so long? Every second he lingered outside was another stab to my heart. I didn't want him to see me windblown after the long walk home. Besides, what would I say to him? My will to keep the tears in my eyes hinged on staying calm. I didn't want to cry tonight.

Suction from the door seal broke the quiet. A soft clack followed. Instead of leaving, hollow footsteps drew nearer on the oak floor.

Tap, tap, tap, then they stopped in the hallway.

I tiptoed to the dining room.

Tap, tap, tap, they came closer.

I crouched behind a chair and held my breath.

He flipped the light switch.

A glare filled the kitchen.

Logan drank a glass of water.

The walk home dried my mouth, and I longed for relief.

He disappeared somewhere between the stairwell and the basement. I went to the kitchen and quenched my thirst.

Oh no. I didn't go downstairs to get my clothes. If I waited until he undressed, I could pretend I came home and prevent an embarrassing encounter. I'd rather let Logan go on thinking I didn't know about his date. He didn't need to know how it upset me.

After twenty minutes, I reopened the door and closed it with a thud. If he teetered on the edge of sleep, he'd recall the noise. He'd figure it was me.

With quiet steps, I descended the stairs, guided by his nightlight.

On the floor, Logan rested on giant therapy pillows. His cologne perfumed the room.

I tiptoed past him, gathered my clothing, and headed back.

"Hey," Logan mumbled in the low light.

I stopped. "Hey."

He sat up, dressed in a T-shirt and boxer shorts. "Come talk to me."

"No, I'm tired."

"Too tired for me? Come here, I missed you earlier."

Seriously? He must've mistaken me for an idiot, a slut, or both. A half-hour ago he kissed Stephanie. With her gone, he'd settle for me? Did he believe I messed around with his brother? He probably did and wanted a piece of the action. If he thought I threw myself at every boy, he had the wrong idea.

"I walked home after work. Tried to call you for a ride," I said.

"Sorry. Something's wrong with my phone. It doesn't always ring."

Oh, please…

His cellphone flashed and vibrated, but I raised my hand and yawned. No need to look. It was Stephanie. He swept it under his pillow, stowing it away. Stowing her away. She was home unaware I had his undivided attention. She missed him. We both missed his kisses when he was gone. But he'd never touch me again.

Logan leaned back on his pillow. The nightlight outlined lean muscles beneath his T-shirt. For a split second, I wanted to reach out and run my hand over the ripples. Stephanie wasn't married to him. They weren't even engaged. Despite what he did, he looked delicious. What the heck was wrong with me?

I remembered my older friend, Tabitha, had said, 'Deep down every woman is a slut.'

'No, some women are virgins until they're married. Grandma was. Not everyone's a slut,' I said, sure I was right.

Tabitha giggled. 'Yeah, they are. Everyone loves sex. They just pretend they don't.'

Logan adjusted the pillow. "I'm sorry you had to walk home. It's too bad my phone broke." The pillow muffled the buzzing cellphone.

Tabitha was right. A part of me wanted to rip off his clothes. But he wanted a fool.

"Yeah, they always break, and they cost too much." I left him alone, looking as sly as a snake. Cold-blooded creatures always struck when you least expected it. I needed to climb out of the snake pit.

Chapter 23

Pink light chased away a somber moon into the clouds. A new sky promised a better day.

Debby. I had to call her. She'd help me find my parents, and we'd work out our differences. If not, I'd find another place to live.

After a quick shower, I dressed and went to the kitchen. In the refrigerator, I picked through the leftovers. Pizza. Not a typical breakfast, but a slice wrapped in paper towels kept the dishes clean. Rattling the plates would rouse Priscilla and the others. I didn't care to see them, so I took my jacket, phone, and slipped outside.

A few streets over, the park provided privacy. Crisp air held the fragrance of spring flowers growing in patches of yellow and violet. Trees sheltered a bench. Beyond it, a swan swam in a babbling brook. Anyone standing on the road might notice me, but my lime-colored jacket blended into the greenery. To a keen eye, I was just another person enjoying the birds.

I strolled to the wooden bench. The last time I sat here, Logan was with me. He made a game of brushing his lips across mine. The third time he did it, he let me kiss him. Before we left, he had his tongue in my mouth. We both wanted more, but not in public. After seeing him with Stephanie, I was glad nothing serious happened.

My finger quivered as I tapped Debby's number into the phone. It was an hour earlier in Arkansas, which meant I'd probably wake her.

Debby answered after the fourth ring. "What? It's seven o'clock."

My heart beat as fast as a hummingbird's wings. "It's me, Tracie. Thank God, you're home."

"Got home yesterday. It's a boy." The joy of motherhood had deflated along with the pregnant belly.

"Congratulations."

Debby cleared her throat. "His name is Robert, but we call him Junior."

"Bobby's happy, I bet."

The ultrasound technician told Debby she'd have a daughter. Since then, she collected frilly dresses and bows. Unless she repainted the nursery, her little boy stayed in a pink room. His blankets were covered with daisies and kittens. Bobby scoffed at the rosy room. He told her he didn't want a girl, and they'd try again as soon as Debby healed.

"Yeah, he's happy all right. He has planned the kid's whole life. Fishing, hunting, football, baseball…all the things I hate."

Since I left Arkansas, Debby went nuts. Her hormones were *out-of-whack* as my aunt Martha used to say. It was hard not to judge her, but then again, I wasn't married to Bobby. If only people were one gender and could reproduce at will, then everyone would lay eggs whenever they wanted a baby. A single-gender world could solve a lot of problems.

"At least it's over. He got the son he wanted," I said. Though I didn't believe it was a woman's duty to produce a boy. The health teacher said a man's sperm determined the child's gender. Someone should remind the husbands of the fact when an unwanted girl was born. Mom told me Dad griped when he realized I was female. He praised God when Jason was born.

Debby's grogginess changed to sniffling. "Are you kidding? Bobby's planning on having more boys. He wants the kid to have a brother. It's not right. I was supposed to have a sweet girl. The boys will be like Bobby." She broke down into sobs.

Why didn't I keep my big mouth shut?

"Don't cry. Tell him you don't want another child. Don't get pregnant." I didn't know much about marriage other than witnessing my parents' dysfunction. But if Bobby loved her, he'd consider her feelings.

"I'm not having another kid with him. He gets the baby, and I'm getting a divorce."

Mothers weren't supposed to abandon their children. Hearing her troubles made me glad I didn't have sex with Cal or Logan. I could end up like her or Kimmie. No matter how awful my life seemed, it could get worse.

"I'm sorry," I said.

If she ever stopped rambling, I could ask for help.

"I haven't told Bobby. I'll be twenty years old next month. And divorced before I'm twenty-one." Her bawling upset Junior, and his screams joined hers.

I needed to ask her. It felt wrong to burden Debby when her marriage fell apart, but she was my best shot at getting help. "There's a reason I'm calling. Mom's number is disconnected, and I'm afraid she has moved."

"Hold on." The receiver clanked in my ear.

"Junior, shut up."

The baby bawled, and yelling at him didn't help.

Poor kid.

"I'm sorry. He won't stop crying."

Junior screamed louder like someone pinched him.

"Have you seen my mom?" I asked, competing for her ear.

"Who?"

"My mom, brother, dad. Have you seen them?"

"Shut up, Junior... I saw your dad after you left. He came over—"

"You told me that last time I called. Have you seen him since?"

"I can't hear you. Speak up."

For goodness' sake...why didn't she stuff a binky in his mouth?

"Have you seen my family since then?" I asked, trying to stay calm.

"I saw your brother, Jason." She cleared her throat. "He rode his bike past here, a week, no, maybe two weeks ago."

My parents could move within a week. They could easily pack and load trucks within a few days.

"Can you go by their house and check? See if they're still living there?" I asked.

"I could if Bobby let me out. He left me here this morning, stranded without my truck. Like I said, I left the hospital yesterday. Suffered in labor a whole day. Should've had a C-section only Bobby didn't let me. He wanted me to have a natural delivery. We can't *afford* a C-section. And if the doctor cut me open, he'd have to tend Junior while I healed. The moon would catch fire before he'd change a diaper."

"Please, go over to Mom's house and check what's going on. Walk if you have to," I said.

"You're as inconsiderate as my husband. I don't feel good, and I can't walk far. Not like this. Besides, I'd have to take the baby with me."

Friends helped each other. If she wanted to, she'd explain my problem to Bobby. She overreacted. He'd understand. After all, I didn't have anyone, not even Logan. Since I ran away, my life fell apart. How could she be this selfish?

"I'm sorry I came across as insensitive. But I'm stuck in Rhode Island and can't get to Arkansas. I don't even know if I have a home anymore. I'm so scared."

People milled around the park. My throat hurt from yelling into the receiver, and a woman walking her dog stared at me. A man in dark sunglasses stood at the creek bank and tossed bread into the water. Two swans ate it before the pieces sank into the muddy stream.

The birds survived better than me.

"Okay, I can check next week, when I'm better." She hollered over the screaming baby.

"Can you loan me some money, so I can buy a bus ticket? I promise to pay you back. Let me stay with you until I can settle things with Mom and Dad. I'll help you with the baby, cook, and clean your house. I'll do anything."

"I don't have any money. If I did, I'd hire another attorney. He said pregnant women didn't get divorces. He wouldn't file the papers. It's a sexist world."

She didn't have to tell me. I already knew. Every guy disappointed me, even my own father. Debby had a decent mother. One who'd help us both if Debby would think straight.

A door slammed on her end. "Get off the phone," Bobby said. "Junior's screaming his head off. I can hear him from the yard. You're a bad mother."

I'd leave too if Bobby jabbed me with insults. He deserved to raise Junior alone. Though guys like him never did the dirty work of raising kids. They simply replaced their wives before the divorce announcement made the newspaper.

"I did my part. I had the baby."

The man feeding swans strolled toward me and frowned. Though I held the phone away from my ear, we both heard Debby screaming.

"Can I call later?" I asked.

"Get off the phone."

The line went dead.

Chapter 24

For every door that slammed in my face, another opened wide enough to squeeze inside. Sometimes I sucked in my gut to slip through. I needed a second job, and it was my lucky day when Rae hired me.

The checkered pastel walls in shades of yellow, pink, and blue warmed Flavors Ice Cream Shop. The place reminded me of a baby's blanket, cozy and inviting. And who didn't like ice cream? Chocolate was the best. It melted into a smooth slurry, coating the mouth with all the creamy goodness.

Rae handed over a white cotton uniform. "Can you start pronto?"

"Absolutely." I accepted the folded tops and pants which resembled medical scrubs.

For once, I got what I wanted. She gave me a clinical-looking outfit. I'd make her proud, digging the frozen treat from buckets and piling it high on cones. I'd do such a great job the customers would ask for me by name.

"Good. Wear white sneakers, something with tread on them tomorrow. We don't want you slipping on a spill."

I nodded. My gray shoes were slick on the bottom. With all the walking, the soles had worn to the thickness of a dime. Sprinkles paid me on Fridays, two days from now. If Priscilla felt generous, she might lend me a few dollars. The thrift store on Main Street carried used shoes. I didn't want to buy second-hand clothes, but they were cheap.

Flavors sold twenty-five types of ice cream. Favorites included birthday cake, coconut cream pie, french vanilla, strawberry cream, and chocolate chip. The manager allowed employees to eat as much as they wanted. It was a bonus. And to ensure I'd stay, Rae offered me more money than at Sprinkles.

"You'll train with Jill. I have to go." Rae picked up her keys, and with a jangle she was gone.

Jill, a thin, young woman with long brown hair wisped into a ponytail, smiled like she could light up the state. "Rae manages two other stores."

"I'm glad I caught her today. Good timing, I guess."

"Two people quit. We had to work their shifts. The Easter bunny could've applied, and I bet she would've hired him."

Pff, what was she getting at? Or was she making small talk? Maybe she was one of those people who always said the wrong thing when they met people for the first time. Whatever. I needed friends, not enemies.

The tinkling bells alerted us we had customers. Two ladies with three toddlers strolled in. In a jiffy, Jill scooped blue balls of birthday cake ice cream into paper cups for the children. The women each settled for french vanilla on sugar cones. I moseyed to the edge of the bar while Jill handled the transaction.

One lady dug into her purse. "I'll pay this time." She plucked out a twenty-dollar bill and passed it to Jill. Jill tapped the keys on the register. She set the money aside.

Looking at the overhead sign, I tallied the prices.

When Jill counted back the change, it was correct.

She placed the twenty into the drawer. "Have a great day and come back soon." The smile plastered across her face never waned. And it wasn't fake. Her cheekbones lifted, and the corners of her eyes crinkled. It was different from Tammy's smile at Sprinkles. Tammy's lips moved upward when she greeted customers while her eyes flickered over their pocketbooks.

After a quick tour of the building, Jill plopped down in a chair and beckoned me. "What's your story?"

"What do you mean?" No one ever asked me outright. It was none of her business. The less she knew about me the better. I couldn't tell her I ran away from home.

"Everyone has a story."

"Then tell me yours," I said to get the attention off me. This strategy worked well at parties when someone forced me to talk.

"I grew up in New York. But moved here to be with my boyfriend, Eddie. He's into real estate."

"A real estate agent?" I asked.

"No, but he rents out the rooms in his house."

Oh, good to know. Maybe he has a vacant room. But then again, I'd have to pay him. That would cut into my savings. I better suck it up at Priscilla's though it didn't hurt to ask…just in case.

Before I could ask, a car parked out front. Someone approached. We jumped up and moved behind the counter. The bells jingled when Tammy popped through the door.

"Hey, Tracie… Jill, you're still here?"

Oops. I didn't plan to tell anyone at Sprinkles I took a second job.

Jill's lips tightened into a sickle. Her gaze landed on

Tammy like a suspicious guard dog.

"I want two scoops. Butter pecan and chocolate mint on a waffle cone." Tammy unfolded a five-dollar bill and slammed it on the counter.

Jill scraped the bottom of the butter pecan bin and packed it onto the hollow cone. Once she had the second flavor on top, she handed it to Tammy.

Tammy scowled at the ice cream. "You call that a serving? It's the size of a golf ball."

"If you want more than two scoops, a five won't cover it," Jill said.

"Never mind. Gimme my change." Tammy held up a palm and turned to me. "You are coming to work tonight, aren't you?"

"Yeah."

"Good, don't tell Gloria you're working here. She hates moonlighting." Tammy zipped out the door, to her car. Instead of driving away, she sat and gabbed on her phone, while she ate.

Was she tattling on me? Didn't I have a right to do whatever I wanted on my own time?

"How well do you know Tammy?" I asked.

"Too well. She worked here a year ago. Rae fired her."

"Oh," I said, not wanting to divulge my knowledge of Tammy's drinking and cheating customers. Thanks to Tammy, Rae would put me under a microscope. And since I worked here with Jill, Tammy could use it against me. She'd run her mouth to Gloria the first time I refused to swindle a customer. If Rae gave me enough hours, I'd quit Sprinkles.

Jill swished the metal scoop in a bucket of water. "Where else do you work?"

"Sprinkles Donut Shop." I didn't want to say it, but in a town this size, she'd find out, anyway.

"For how long?"

"A few weeks." The lie sounded better than admitting I started a week ago. "Tammy works days. I work nights."

Jill wiped the scoopers dry and stood them on their handles in a bucket. "But she's on the night shift with you tonight?"

She weaved her way inward like she solved a puzzle. Only she didn't have to. She put this image together before. It was a picture of Tammy with one hand on a liquor bottle and the other in someone's wallet.

"Someone must've called in sick or quit. I have no control over the schedule. I'd quit Sprinkles if Rae let me work here full time."

Jill's smile returned. "So what do you think about Tammy?"

"I barely know her... Tell me about you and Eddie."

Between serving the orange sherbet and cherry jubilee, Jill rambled about her life. She spoke about her childhood, high school years, and her boyfriend. Her father was an Alabama preacher who married a New York chef. Her mother owned a French bistro.

Jill fell in love with Eddie, a guy who never went to church. When her father found out, he accused Jill of dating a heathen. She stayed with him anyway and moved to Rhode Island. She hadn't seen her parents in a year.

"Are you going to marry Eddie?" I asked.

"He hasn't asked, but I will if he does. He said he'll pay my tuition for nursing school. If he said that, I'm sure he plans to keep me."

By the afternoon, the air seemed lighter and the sun brighter. Tammy's haze over me evaporated. Since Jill left her childhood home, she'd understand my problems.

"Does Eddie have any vacant rooms for rent?"

Before she could answer, the bells tinkled. The customers streamed to the counter, eager to select their favorite ice cream. They peered through the glass at the bins, taking their time. A lady picked the coconut cream pie flavor. The steel spoon sliced through the velvety treat which I slopped into the empty cone like filling in a pie shell. Packing it into a frozen tower made the customer smile.

While everyone ate, we tidied the counter. I waited for the people to leave before asking Jill again. Was it too soon to ask? We only met today. She didn't know me. How much did her boyfriend charge for rent? It was tempting to think I might have a chance to move out of Priscilla's house. But every dollar I spent kept me from saving for a bus ticket.

What if Jill and her boyfriend lived in a shack with peeling paint, dirty carpet, slow drains, mice, or even worse, roaches? Priscilla kept a clean house. In the time there, I never saw an ant, spider, or even a cobweb. I'd sure hate to pour a bowl of cereal and have a dozen roaches scurry over my cornflakes. But Jill evaded the subject, and I didn't push her.

After the last patron left, I sprayed a table and wiped away the drips of melted pistachio. Moving on, I cleaned the chairs. The clock said *4:00*. I had to walk home and change for the night job. If no one gave me a ride, I'd have to walk to Sprinkles this evening.

"When am I working again?" I asked.

Jill replaced the empty butter pecan container with a

full one. "You'll work the ten-to-four shift the rest of the week. We're closed on Sundays."

Six hours minus a lunch break. Not bad.

Chapter 25

Since my second job required white shoes, I went shopping. Celia's Attic on Main Street had a pair of sneakers in my size for ten dollars. With no scuff marks and clean insoles, they were perfect. But there was a problem. I only had three bucks in my pocket. While I inspected them, heels clicked behind me.

"Finding what you need?" The lady's black cape fluttered behind her and skimmed the floor. Her thick eyeliner and indigo lipstick contrasted against skin as pale as a lizard's belly.

A real live witch? Or was she Gothic? Her clothes looked like a Halloween costume.

"Yes, I guess so." I tried not to stare at her and glanced at the price tag. "Do you ever have sales?"

"No. The merchandise is already discounted." She held up a pair of black leather wedges, like the ones she wore. "These are better. Versatile, and only five bucks."

Of course, she thought so. The color matched her lacy dress and patterned stockings. She loved black enough to dye her hair. I could tell. Her blonde roots were an inch long.

"They're nice, but I have to wear white." I set the ivory shoes on the shelf. "Thanks anyhow."

"If they're too expensive, you might check back. We get new inventory every Monday."

The sign on the door said they opened at nine during

the week. If I scraped up another seven dollars, I could buy them before going to work.

"I need them by tomorrow. Can you hold them? I'll come by in the morning."

The woman fidgeted. "Sorry, I'm not allowed."

****

When I got home, I walked into a hornet's nest. My mere presence stirred up trouble.

The queen wasp, Priscilla, displayed her crabby face. "Where've you been all day?"

"At work, why?" Her tone warned me to stop before I reached the living room. I knew this. Mom questioned me this way when she presumed I had done something wrong.

Dick, Priscilla's live-in boyfriend, stepped out of the kitchen with a glass of milk. He acknowledged me with a wave, but his eyes held concern.

Priscilla continued. "Your list is still sitting on the kitchen table."

What was she talking about? What, a note for me? I didn't see it, but then again, I left in a rush.

I shrugged and glanced at Dick.

"Don't look at him. Look at me when I'm talking. This house is a pig pen, or maybe they call it a pigsty in Arkansas. We're not hogs."

I took a deep breath.

No one here will hit me. It's just words, only words.

"I'm sorry, I didn't see the list. I've been at my second job."

"You stay gone all day. Banking your money. I know what you've done. You took another job to avoid the housework."

"That's not it—"

"You'll wait 'til I'm finished before speaking. I have clients in the morning. You'll have the basement and the rest of the house spotless by seven tomorrow. Understand?"

I couldn't work tonight and clean the house by morning. And since Cal grew more distant, she piled on the chores. Still, I needed to get along with Priscilla. If I moved out, I wouldn't be able to save money for a ticket home. Heck, I didn't even earn my Sprinkles paycheck yet. But as soon as I did, I'd have my butt on a bus.

"You can talk now," Priscilla said, satisfied with her rant.

Dick swallowed the last of his milk and gazed at the floor as if embarrassed by his girlfriend's behavior.

I could use this to my advantage since her anger simmered below the surface. I'd expose her little by little, while appearing humble.

"I'm sorry I haven't been here to help you, but I'll clean the house. By the way, where is everyone?"

Dick went to the kitchen and returned without the glass. He lingered at the edge of the dining room.

"Logan's dad came for him. Cal is at the hospital with Kimmie. She's in labor."

"Labor? The baby isn't due until July," I said.

Priscilla hesitated. "Yes, she'll lose the baby. It's for the best."

Dick cleared his throat. "Priscilla, that's a terrible thing to wish on the girl."

I stepped closer, into the living room, to get a better look at him. He folded his arms over his chest, and his eyes held stern. It was the first time I saw him stand up to Priscilla.

"Why not? The kids are back together again, no

thanks to you, Tracie. My bleeding-heart son thinks he has to save every stray on his doorstep."

Oh, please. Cal had showed up on Debby's doorstep. I never asked him to come to my rescue. Rhode Island was his idea. And Priscilla's attitude about teenage mothers reminded me of my dad's comment about a neighborhood girl. 'Lucy went out and got herself pregnant.' It was all Lucy's fault. In his mind Lucy had hopped bed to bed, tempting the boys. She was a shameless slut, and the boys couldn't resist.

The door sighed open, bringing in a breath of fresh air. I turned to see Bess coming in while carrying a Hello Kitty backpack. Behind her trailed another teenage girl, also lugging a colorful book bag.

"Hey, Mom, me and Katie are going to study in my room," Bess said and smiled at Dick and me.

"Katie and I." Priscilla corrected her like a snobby English teacher.

"Katie and I… This way." Bess ushered her friend to her bedroom, and her door clicked shut.

Inside, I fumed. How dare Priscilla say Cal had rescued me like a stray? I wasn't an animal, though she kicked me around like a mangy dog. If I held two jobs, I might get out here, rent a room from someone. But I had to save money to make it happen. It couldn't cost much for a bus ticket. I'd find the station number and call them.

Priscilla turned back to Dick. "Why don't we have dinner at The Lobster Palace?"

"Again? We ate there two nights ago," Dick said.

"Yes, I'd like the king crab salad tonight. Let me change my clothes."

Priscilla settled down, and I was able to hold my tongue, so I took a chance.

"I need a favor," I said to Priscilla.

"You can ask."

An agreeable person would say *sure*.

"Can I borrow a few dollars? Just 'til I get paid on Friday."

"No, the Russo bank is closed."

I didn't dare to push her. I was in enough trouble for not cleaning the house.

Dick took a few steps toward us. "Lend the girl a few bucks. Didn't you say you kept her last paycheck?"

"You heard me. It's not up for discussion." Priscilla stomped away, leaving me standing in the living room like a dummy.

I sat on the sofa and swallowed hard. I didn't want to look at Dick with tears in my eyes, so I checked the wall clock. Damn. My shift started in less than an hour, and I stunk like sweat. Since I had to walk to work, I didn't have time for a shower.

Dick strolled over and sat on the end of the couch. "How much money do you need?"

I sniffled to keep the snot in my nose. "Seven dollars for shoes at the thrift store. My boss said I have to wear white ones. I don't have any."

He looked down at my raggedy gray sneakers. The threadbare material gave way to a hole over my little toe. My dirty sock peeked through. I understood how homeless people felt. They had nothing new. Everything was old and tattered.

Dick opened his wallet and pulled out a fifty. "Here. Keep this between us."

I took the money and folded it in half. "I'll bring you the change tomorrow and pay you the rest on Friday."

"No, it's yours. Spend it on new shoes. Kiddo, you

shouldn't buy used shoes. That's how people get foot fungus and other nasties."

He probably had a daughter my age and didn't let her shop at second-hand stores.

The water in my eyes spilled out, and I blinked several times. Dick didn't have to be nice to me. I didn't belong in Priscilla's house. With her lists of chores, she never let me forget I wasn't equal to her kids. But this man treated me like a human being. He understood my challenges.

"Thank you." I rechecked the clock. There was no way I'd make it to Sprinkles in time for my shift. Not if I had to walk.

"You're worried about getting to work, aren't you? I'll give you a lift."

I didn't want to kick the hornet's nest and face Priscilla's wrath. If her boyfriend treated me better than she did, it wouldn't sit well with her. Was it worth the risk? Could Dick handle her?

"What about your dinner at The Lobster Palace?" I asked.

"It doesn't close 'til nine. Besides, we're not going there. I'm in the mood for a cheeseburger." He cut his eyes toward the hallway. "Go get ready for work."

"Okay, I'll hurry."

His generosity allowed me to take a quick shower. After lathering up and changing into my Sprinkles uniform, I smelled like Irish Spring soap. Dick waited upstairs, while Priscilla dolled up to go out. I'd give anything to see her reaction when he parked at a fast-food joint.

When I got upstairs, he was playing with his cellphone.

"I'm ready."

He pulled his keys from his pocket.

Priscilla pushed an earring through her lobe. "I called ahead. Someone canceled, so we have a table at seven."

Dick turned to her. "I'm taking Tracie to work first."

"You don't have time. It's a quarter 'til seven," Priscilla said.

Here we go again.

"This young lady needs a ride. You won't starve in the meantime." He moved closer to the door, and I opened it, thankful to escape Priscilla's glare.

"No, you're cutting it too close," Priscilla called after us.

"Cancel the reservation," Dick said. "I'm tired of fancy food. I'd like a burger, dripping with grease. And french fries. The kind with too much salt, crispy on the outside, soft and hot on the inside. And I'm dying for a chocolate shake."

"Oh, you're impossible." Priscilla trailed after us and stood in the doorway, scowling at us. Dick hit his key fob. His car chirped. He never flinched as he slid into his Cadillac. I hopped in, happy to accept the ride even if I'd walk into a firestorm later.

Chapter 26

Yay, Dee was back, a bonus for me. Beyond Sprinkles' glass door, she arranged fresh donuts in the display case, spacing them an inch apart. The tension in my muscles eased now that I was no longer worried about Tammy. As my job skills improved, the customers grumbled less. It was a good thing. My tolerance for complaints hit its limit for the week. I gave Priscilla all the credit.

When I entered, the fragrance of sweet yeast and vanilla made the air sticky and pleasant. I inhaled, taking it in the way someone sniffed a rose. The plastic phone in my pocket pressed against my hip bone as my reminder. Later, I'd call Debby. She'd have news about my family.

Maybe my parents didn't move away without me. Mom might be in the kitchen, frying up a skillet of corned beef hash. She'd ask Jason to set the table. His clumsy fingers would grab the dishes. The forks would clank and scrape against the plates as he carried them. He'd lay them on brown woven mats, placing the silverware on paper napkins like he always did.

"We got a new filling," Dee said, snapping me back into reality.

"What?"

"Blueberry inside." She held up an overstuffed long-john with indigo goo oozing from its blunt end. Berries weren't that color. It was the shade of a soap pod used in automatic dishwashers.

As an experiment, Sprinkles featured a new pastry, donut, or muffin. They should stick with the tried and true. They might've believed they'd get a few customers to eat them if they advertised enough. The last ad I saw on television aired wide-eyed kids licking the pineapple glaze like a Popsicle. I imagined few brave souls came asking for it.

"Want to try one?" Dee asked.

"No thanks." The thought of swallowing colored corn syrup made my throat clog. Sickening sweet sludge had that effect on me.

A drink, I needed a drink.

"Are you okay?" Dee bit into the pastry, stuffed it into her mouth, and the filling gushed like thick blue snot.

I sauntered to the soda fountain and filled a cup with ice water. "As okay as I can be, why?"

"What's wrong?"

Watching her eat the fat bomb bothered me, but more important things crossed my mind. She was the first person to show an interest in me and ask. Talking about my problems might make me feel better. But how much should I say? I couldn't decide if Dee was a true friend or not. So far, I hadn't been a good judge of character. The frustration I held inside gurgled like bad gas. I wanted to belch, but you only burped around the best of friends.

"I'm homesick. I haven't seen my family in Arkansas since I moved here." What I wanted to say was I missed Jason, my adorable younger brother. I missed his puppy-dog eyes and his silly giggles. But Dee would never understand if I only mentioned Jason. I couldn't exclude my parents.

She took the last bite and wiped the sticky glaze from her lip. "Oh, I bet. I could never leave my mom. We're too close."

At twenty-two, Dee still lived at her parents' house. On slow nights, she talked and talked. Her dad had repainted her bedroom from bubble-gum pink to a more mature aqua blue on Dee's nineteenth birthday. She slept in a white-washed canopy bed with wispy ivory drapes. I had seen the curtains made of sheer organza in old movies. Fancy.

Dee and her mother ate lunch together every Saturday at Rochelle's Bistro. The word bistro sounded snobbish to me. It was a place that sold small plates of food with big prices. They'd order three appetizers to share. They loved the New England crab cakes with a side of homemade red pepper aioli, a gourmet mayonnaise. No one in Arkansas ate aioli. Or if they did, I didn't know about it.

Her dad managed a department store. He bought her dozens of stuffed animals. Dee kept them in a sheer net, anchored to her ceiling. Her Muppets hung in one corner of the room. A girl like her never flinched when her dad removed his belt. Her dad didn't fly into a blind fury and hit her. She and her mother never looked into the mirror with black eyes staring back. What did Dee know about abuse?

Envy shot through me when she told me her dad bought her a car for her fifteenth birthday. I didn't even have my driver's license.

"It was his old Camry," she said. "A hand-me-down until he bought me a better one."

"He gave you a second car?" I asked, uncertain if I heard correctly.

"Yes, when I graduated high school. I went to college, but I blew it. Too many parties. I'm not a morning person, and I had no choice but to sign up for early classes. I dropped out."

Dee landed a job here at Sprinkles where she worked the night shift and went home to her mommy, daddy, Fozzie Bear, and Kermit the Frog. Her daddy let her keep the red BMW with chrome wheels, a souvenir from her college days. Loving parents made all the difference. For her, life was grand.

Rectangular lights pierced the dark parking lot. Customers. They came for coffee, and we had steaming pots brewed. The canisters of creamer stood tall on the counter. I was ready to pump it into paper cups. This time, I'd be careful not to topple the drinks over.

Within a minute, the patrons jostled in and surrounded the counter. We served them.

I took a deep breath and punched the vintage cash register buttons. It was easy tonight. My fingers were hot knives slicing through butter. I made the correct change. Dee made the correct change. We cheated no one. I never mentioned Tammy's stunt. Why should I? We were getting along, and I didn't want to ruin our night.

When the rush ended, I took a short break. The restroom, several doors down the hallway, gave me the privacy to call Debby. After the third ring, Bobby picked up.

"Is Debby there?" I asked.

"No," he said, in a clipped voice.

"Bobby, it's me, Tracie. When will she be back?"

Why was he answering Debby's cellphone?

"You haven't heard?" He grew silent as if the news would drift through the phone line.

"No, I'm not in Arkansas." Possibilities ran through my mind like cats chasing mice. Thoughts went astray every direction without answers. Gone. Where was she? Was she dead?

"What did you say to my wife when you called?"

"Nothing, other than I wanted her to check on my family. Why? What happened?"

Oh, sweet Jesus. Debby did something horrible. I saw a report once on the news. The lady drowned her baby. Some women went crazy after giving birth. Did Debby kill Junior, or herself?

"She took off with our baby. Moved in with her mother." He spewed it along with his breath which he recaptured during our pause. Relieved that Debby didn't hurt anyone, I sat on the hard tile floor in this semi-public restroom. His harsh tone had my back stiffened against the wall.

Bobby blamed me. Debby had problems, but heck, we all had issues. When I lived there, I saw it. She'd push against her chair, wobbling, struggling to stand with the weight of a pregnant belly. She had to go to the toilet. And before she waddled to the bathroom, he'd have her serving him. 'Get me a beer, chips and bring me a pillow.' Oh, his tender head must rest on something soft while he binged on ESPN. Debby took care of him first, though the baby she carried, his baby, pressed on her bladder. Bobby didn't care if she peed her pants. She didn't leave because of anything I said.

"She never told me she was leaving you... Can you give me her mother's number?" I asked, hoping he didn't detect my lie.

"No."

"Why not? Please?"

A knock came on the bathroom door, and I prayed the walls absorbed my words.

"Tracie, are you okay in there?" Dee asked.

I covered the phone's receiver. "No...I have an upset stomach. Sorry, I'll be out as soon as I can."

"Make it quick. We have a parking lot full of customers. They're coming."

I had to help Dee. But this was my chance to find Debby. As soon as I got my first paycheck, I'd buy a bus ticket and ride as far west as it took me. I'd hitchhike to Arkansas if I had to.

I covered the receiver so Bobby wouldn't hear my lame excuse. "I'm sorry, Dee. It might be a while. I have stomach cramps—"

"Eww, don't tell me," Dee said. "Take your time."

Diarrhea to the rescue. Mentioning it made people run away. Dee left in a hurry. No one wanted to hang around for details.

With her gone, I continued. "Bobby, I swear Debby never told me she was leaving. Please give me the number." I had a pen in my pocket and clicked it, ready to jot it down on my arm.

"Why should I? You're always filling my wife's head with crap."

"I can't reach my mom. She said she'd check on her."

Customer's voices drifted through the building. I had to get back to work. Otherwise, Dee would have thirty people screaming at her.

"Oh, yeah, she drove over there," he said.

"Tell me what she said."

"I'll tell you, but do something for me."

What a pain. I understood why Debby wanted to divorce him. But I would've promised him anything he wanted to get the phone number. I didn't remember her mom's last name. It wasn't like I could look her up. Besides, most people had cellphones.

"Sure, anything you want," I said.

"Convince Debby to come home." He breathed even heavier now. "Tell her I'm sorry for taking her for granted. Tell her I miss her and the baby. Every time I call, her mother hangs up on me. I'm going crazy without my wife."

He did believe I could influence Debby. Me, a teenager. And for once, he cared about her. I didn't want her to end up living as a single mom on welfare.

"You got it. Now, will you please tell me what she said?"

"Your parents moved. She tried to find out where. She talked to their neighbors, but no one knows where they went."

How would I find them? I didn't even have my aunt Martha's phone number. This couldn't be happening. I should be heading to Arkansas today.

"Are you still there?" he asked.

"Yes." I gasped for air. Why didn't my parents tell someone where they were going? In a second, everything changed. With my parents gone and Debby at her mother's house, I had no lifeline. I was at the mercy of strangers.

"Got a pen and paper?"

I did. Bobby's news hit me so hard that I squeezed the pen into my palm. "I'm ready."

Bobby rattled off his mother-in-law's number. I

scrawled it in blue ink on my forearm, thanked him, and disconnected. I'd call on the next break. The chatter in the lobby escalated into shouts. We had an angry mob screaming for their coffee.

Chapter 27

Working two jobs made me dog-tired. By midnight, when my shift was over, I couldn't will my legs to carry me home. And I hadn't even left Sprinkles' parking lot. With every step, the hard, rectangular phone pressed into my hip.

I called Cal, and he answered on the third ring. "Hey, how's Kimmie?" Kimmie's early labor had me concerned, but only ten percent. It was a long walk to Priscilla's house.

"She's not well. The baby died."

"Oh… I'm sorry she lost it." And I was. The poor baby didn't get to live one day. It made me sad like when I found a cracked robin's egg on the ground with a dead hatchling inside. Only this was worse because I knew Kimmie. Even though we weren't friends, I wanted her to have a healthy child.

"We weren't expecting this," Cal said.

I wasn't sure how to ask for a favor, but I needed his help. "Where are you?"

"At the hospital… Kimmie's mom is here. She doesn't like me, so I'm leaving."

"I'm done at work. It sounds like you need someone to talk to. Any chance you can pick me up on your way home?"

He hesitated. "Sure, give me a few minutes." He disconnected.

I was a leech, a user, a burden to Cal and his family. His mother knew it. It terrified me when she peered down into my face with those squinty eyes. The tone she took with me gave me the chills. 'Tracie, you are responsible for cleaning my house. Logan is off-limits. You are an adult. You will act like an adult.'

I had crossed the boundary with her boyfriend, Dick. No doubt they fought after he drove me to work. Priscilla didn't get her lobster salad. It didn't matter if Dick wanted a cheeseburger. The blame showered onto me. And she'd make it stick.

I was pathetic. Dutiful Cal was driving the streets after midnight. After hours of drama and fluorescent lights, he was willing to give me a ride. He'd shield me from his mother's wrath. I'd cling to him like a piece of lint on a shirt. Eventually, he'd pick me off and discard me forever. They all would.

While I waited for Cal, I sat on the cement walkway leading into Sprinkles. A listless Dee stood at the pink bar beyond spotless glass windows playing with her iPhone. The disposable phone I carried lacked internet ability. We lived in a world of haves and have nots. Someday, I'd have things. I'd have an iPhone, my own car, and a safe place to live.

The curb under me was numbing my butt when the truck tires broke the silence. The gleam of white threw a spotlight on me. With sore feet, I pushed myself up and hurried to Cal's truck.

Cal didn't wait for me to close the door before hitting reverse. I could smell his sweat and lingering oily body odor. He hadn't showered.

"Thanks for giving me a lift." I cupped my hand over my nose, pretending to scratch an itch. "Your mom said Kimmie went into early labor. Tell me what happened."

"They had to give her a blood transfusion," he said. "She almost died."

"I'm glad she pulled through."

Poor Kimmie. I was rooting for her. She had been through too much. All the stress did this to her health.

He turned right onto the sleepy road. "I feel terrible. Telling her lies to break off our engagement. She got upset. Lost the baby."

What do you say? It was true. The fights stressed Kimmie until the baby couldn't take it anymore. I had done things to rile her up, too. We were immature, all of us. The baby didn't stand a chance.

"Cal, it might've happened anyway. My mom lost her first baby."

His grip on the steering wheel was as tense as the silence between us, and I almost preferred to be at Priscilla's house rather than in the cab of his truck.

"I feel like it's my fault," he said. "I wish I could take it all back."

The streetlamps cast an eerie glow onto the little homes we passed. Within a few minutes, Cal parked in Priscilla's driveway.

Dick's Cadillac wasn't here. We stood a fifty-fifty chance he and Priscilla went somewhere versus Dick had enough of her.

Cal had the house key on his key chain. Thank goodness we didn't have to stand on the doorstep and knock until Bess answered.

Inside the quiet house, nothing seemed unusual until something crunched under my shoe. The kitchen shed light onto the broken glass. Hundreds of pieces were scattered on the floor.

"Watch out." I stopped him before he stepped in it.

A clatter in the kitchen had us sidestepping the mess. More shards littered the floor. Bess, in her Hello Kitty nightgown, swept a cracked English teacup into a pile.

"You missed the drama," Bess said.

I didn't dare talk and rouse Priscilla from whatever self-pitying state she wallowed in nearby.

Cal frowned at a busted dish. "Let me guess. Mom had a meltdown."

"Not just a meltdown. I think she and Dick broke up," Bess said.

Cal picked up a teacup with half a handle and tossed it into the trash. "These came from London. What a waste."

"You know how Mom acts when she doesn't get her way."

Cal found the dustpan and steadied it for his sister, while she swept the shattered plates into it.

I pulled the trashcan from under the sink and leaned it toward Bess. She dumped the glass into the container. "We need to wear shoes for a while. We'll never find all the pieces."

Bess set the broom down. "There's something else."

"What?" I asked, though I suspected the part about me was coming.

She looked at me. "Mom said you have to leave."

Cal didn't say a word.

Homeless. I'd be homeless if he didn't intervene. After I found out about Logan and Stephanie, I moved my valuables. I hid my money in the basement, under the loose carpet. Dick gave me fifty dollars for shoes, and I added it to my meager savings. I still had my own phone and Debby's number. Did I have Cal's loyalty? Though I wanted to leave, where would I go? Living in Rhode Island wasn't cheap.

"Do you think she meant it?" I asked, in a whisper though they spoke in normal voices.

"Oh, she meant it. They got into a fight over you. Dick was in big trouble after he took you to work. So much, they didn't go to dinner. You made Mom break her best china."

What? She had to be kidding. Priscilla chose to fling her dishes against the wall. I wasn't even here. I wasn't responsible for her childish outburst. Holy crap, she's a licensed therapist. She never lets Cal forget she's the great Priscilla Russo of Queenstown.

Bess set the trashcan in its spot. "Good enough. I don't want Mom to catch me out of bed when she comes home." She scurried to her room.

A weight lifted off me, and I could breathe a little better. The old bat took off after the spat. She was chasing her boyfriend. Trying to track him, trap him, and drag him home again.

I needed to spritz off before going to bed. It might be my last night sleeping here.

"Don't look so worried. I'll talk to Mom," Cal said. "I've had a helluva day. I'd like a smoke. Join me?"

He flipped off the light and padded toward the basement. I followed his lead to where I left my fifty-dollar bill under the loose carpet. The solar nightlight shed enough light to see the steps. Once on the lower level, Cal went to the pipe, ignoring the oversized pillows Priscilla ordered me to stack. Instead of the usual fruit air freshener, the place reeked of damp mold. No wonder Priscilla masked it with the scent of artificial strawberries. Cal pulled the end cap from the PCV pipe. He crammed his fingers inside and poked around.

"Did you smoke my weed?"

"No." It didn't bother me that he asked. Another worry entered my mind. "Is it empty?"

"Yeah… If you didn't, I guess Logan could've. But wait, I remember seeing it after Dad picked him up."

"It wasn't me. I don't even like it." I hurried to the corner of the main room and yanked the corner of the carpet.

Cal followed me.

My stash was gone.

"Someone took my money," I said.

Cal stood speechless, scratching his head. He pulled his wallet from his back pocket. "How much did you lose?"

"Fifty-three dollars."

He opened his billfold. Under a leather flap, he pried out a half-smoked joint. He slid the wallet into his back pocket and flicked his lighter. A flame jumped onto the joint. It burned while he sucked the other end.

This turned out worse than I thought. My cash disappeared. I needed it to buy work shoes. Who took it? People didn't go around lifting the rugs unless they're looking for something. With my money missing, even thrift-store shoes were out of reach.

"Cal, can I borrow ten dollars? I'll pay you back."

He strolled over to the therapy pillow and sat down. "You could've, except I spent my last dollar on lunch. I was going to ask Mom for money to pay my auto insurance."

Of course, Cal never worked for a living. Why should he when the Russo bank opened its purse for him?

He benefited from Priscilla's job and her alimony checks.

The joint glowed brighter when Cal sucked it. Marijuana made his life better. Too bad my head throbbed when I smoked.

"Sure you don't want some?" He pinched the tiny, rolled piece between his thumb and finger, avoiding the lit end.

"No, I'm okay. I'll take a shower and dress for bed." I left him sprawled on the pillow, and I went into the bathroom door a few feet away.

The warm water and soap washed away the sweet scent of donuts. Too bad it couldn't rinse away my worries.

With Cal on the floor, I'd find the spare room upstairs available. By now he drifted into a sleepy high, courtesy of what my grandmother used to call Mary Jane. Good ole weed to the rescue. Until it wasn't.

The latch to the front door turned over upstairs.

Click, click, click of shoes…heels. "Who's down there?" Priscilla called from afar. "Who's smoking weed in my house?"

I held my breath, still naked. Quiet and careful as if walking through a minefield, I slipped into my pajamas.

"Answer me, damn you."

"It's me," Cal croaked out beyond my closed door.

Her footfalls grew closer, and so did her voice. "I thought I got all the drugs out of this place. I searched every nook and cranny."

He cleared his throat like he had cobwebs in it. "You were the one who took my stash?"

"It's my house. You have no right to smoke here. And where's Tracie? This place is filthy like an Arkansas pigsty. I want her out. Gone."

"You don't have a right to take my stuff," he said.

"I have a right to anything I find in my home."

Here I was shivering with a towel wrapped around my wet hair, standing in pajamas. Would he tell her I hid behind the door? Oh, the light seeped under the threshold. I turned it off and held my breath. If she didn't see it, she'd still recognize the Apple Pectin fragrance from the shampoo. Unless the cloud of weed smoke masked the scent.

Priscilla moved around. Her shoes no longer clicked, but they rubbed on the carpet. Closer...closer. She jiggled the doorknob.

"Tracie, you've overstayed your welcome. I want both you and Cal out tonight. Understand? Gather your things and go."

"All my money was hidden under the carpet. Can I have it?"

"No, it's mine. It doesn't even cover what you owe me for keeping you. You should've paid me rent. I want you out, tonight."

I changed into my jeans and a T-shirt. I knew this day would come, but I wasn't ready. This was unbelievable.

"Mom, you can't be serious. It's one o'clock in the morning. Where do you expect us to sleep?"

"I don't give a flying banana. Get out!"

Chapter 28

Priscilla paced the floor upstairs, her heels clicking like a clock ticking down the seconds. "Hurry up. I can't go to bed until you're gone."

Cal and I scrambled, gathered our jeans, raggedy T-shirts, and my work uniforms while Priscilla ranted. She didn't even let us get bags before booting us out into the yard.

As we walked past Priscilla's car, Cal leaned over it, made a hock-up-a-loogie sound, and offered up a disgusting blob. With a splat it hit the windshield.

Classy. It was so Cal-like. Of course, Priscilla would give credit to the birds.

I got into the truck, holding my belongings. Cal hopped in and slammed the door.

"Where're we going?" I asked.

In four hours, a new sun would break the sky. It seemed useless to even think about renting a motel room. Neither of us had any money.

"We'll crash at Dad's house. It's not far." He drove us past a few sleepy neighborhoods before we rolled up a hill to the large colonial home perched at the top. We parked, and Cal activated his cellphone flashlight. On the way to the door, he kicked over a rock in the flowerbed and retrieved a key.

With my clothes in hand, I followed him to the door. No one expected us.

"Hey, shouldn't you call your dad? Tell him we're here."

I imagined tripping a sensor and sirens screaming.

"Nope." He shoved the key into the lock and in a second got us inside.

A dog barked.

"Shhh, Buddy, it's okay."

I stepped into the home that smelled like pine. The wood floors beneath our feet creaked, but no one other than the pup stirred. A stairwell curved upward. We tiptoed past it and around a kitchen to another door. Beyond it, steps descended. Cal's phone light helped us navigate to the basement.

Someone snored nearby. Cal took my arm and guided me the opposite direction. When we reached the room, he flipped the switch on a floor lamp. A double bed occupied the bedroom.

"There's only one bed, but it's the best I can do on short notice," he said.

****

I woke to the sound of a girl's giggles. My vision adjusted. Cal slept with his back to me, still reeking of weed and body odor.

There was laughter beyond our closed door, Logan, and someone else.

Nosy as I was, I peeked at him, but only caught a glimpse of him climbing the stairs. The girl he entertained, Stephanie, sat in a chair looking at her cellphone. Thank goodness for electronic distractions.

I had the full picture. Logan and Stephanie spent the nights together. Not just last night...often. She looked comfortable in the recliner, too comfortable. Her bare legs were sticking in the air spread apart, her oversized

T-shirt barely covering her crotch. The stink of sex hung around like a barrel of dead fish. Logan had been inside her. I shouldn't care. He wasn't my boyfriend. He was just a guy who kissed and groped me, while he left his girlfriend fantasizing about their next date. What if I told her his penis stiffened like a Coke bottle when he pressed against me? Wouldn't she love to hear it?

"Tracie," Cal whispered.

I closed the door and spun around. Cal propped himself up against the pillows.

"What? I have to pee," I said.

He gestured to another door behind me. "Don't go out yet. I'll let Dad know we're here before he sees my truck."

On the other side of the wall, the fully-stocked bathroom gave me a private retreat. And it supplied new soap and clean towels. I even found a shopping bag for my clothes. After relieving myself and taking a quick shower, I dressed in my Flavors uniform. Work started at ten. Shoes, I needed white shoes.

Cal left me alone. Rather than roam a strange house, I sat on the unmade bed, waiting. The door creaked open.

"Excuse me. I didn't know Cal had company." Stephanie stood before me, in a Wonder Woman T-shirt. The hem of her nighty skimmed her upper thigh, barely covering her.

Her long brown hair draped over her shoulders in soft bouncy curls. She looked almost as good as on her prom night when I last saw her. It didn't seem fair someone could wake up gorgeous.

"It's okay. I didn't mean to scare you," I said.

"I got to go to the bathroom. It's the only one downstairs."

"No problem, you can use it," I said.

What you need is a shower. You smell fishy. Gross.

Footsteps came down the stairs. I headed to meet him with my crumpled bag of clothes.

Logan stopped on the steps with a tray and stared at me with the *you-caught-me* look. "Hey, Tracie."

"Hey…what's wrong?"

Wicked me. Busted you, didn't I?

"Not a thing." He cleared his throat. "Is anyone else here?" He came downstairs and set the tray on a small coffee table.

"Oh, yummy." He brought two plates with scrambled eggs, home fries, and bacon meant for him and his girlfriend. "Cal is around. Have you seen him?"

"Yes, did you see anyone else?" He raked a hand through his hair as if combing it helped him keep a step ahead of me.

"You mean the girl? She's in the bathroom," I said without malice.

"Did she talk to you?"

"Not really. I mean, she wanted to use the toilet."

He let out a heavy breath. "Oh, she's shy. She's my stepsister. She has a stomach bug, so she's staying down here. Go upstairs and meet the family. They're having breakfast."

Liar. Did he think I was stupid?

My body tensed, and I took a calming breath, while I debated what to do next. I should go. Cal was upstairs, piling eggs and bacon onto his plate. He didn't care if I was starving. Neither did Logan. He wanted to shoo me away before Stephanie came skipping out of the bathroom. But it was time he paid for his lies.

"Oh, I'm not hungry yet." I searched for a place to

sit. I didn't want to plop down on the recliner where Stephanie's butt touched it. Even if she wore panties, she had stained the cloth.

"Well, you can't stay here. The virus my stepsister has is contagious."

"She didn't look sick," I said.

"She's been ill for a few days. Her fever broke, but you can still catch it."

The lies shot out of his mouth. Smooth like a basketball swooshing the hoop. If I didn't know better, I would've believed him.

Stephanie breezed into the room wearing a bath towel. "Oh, sorry. I thought you left." She headed for a large canvas bag in the corner.

Logan turned as white as a new fallen snow. "C'mon, let's give her some privacy. I'll take you to Cal."

Stephanie squat down and rummaged through the bag. "Logan, I forgot my hair tie. Could you ask Lacie if she has one?"

I played the scenarios through my mind. Should I tell Stephanie he called her his stepsister? Should I ask her name with him in the room?

I liked the subtle approach. Let Logan squirm.

"Okay, I'm getting hungry. Hey, I hope you get *well* soon."

Stephanie looked up, questioning me with soft brown eyes. "I'm not sick."

"Good, I'm glad…" I turned to Logan. "See, your *stepsister* is better already."

"Stepsister?" Stephanie puffed her cheeks and blew out the air.

She acted like this wasn't the first time it happened.

It had to be the reason for their breakups. He chased other girls. She knew, but she was hopelessly addicted to him. He pulled her strings. He tried to pull mine, only I cut the strings. I didn't want a puppet master, not even Logan.

Logan beckoned me toward the stairs. When I didn't move, he came back for me. "Let's go."

"No, wait. Why did you tell her I'm your stepsister?" Fire danced in her eyes.

"Calm down, it's a misunderstanding."

I wanted to expose Logan. I wanted to strip him of every lie until he stood naked in a puddle of truth.

She turned to me. "I'm Stephanie, his girlfriend."

"I'm Tracie. I've been living with Logan's mom."

Stephanie's jaw dropped.

She must've realized he and I spent the nights under the same roof.

Logan said nothing.

It was the quiet before the hell storm. Satisfied to have ruined their happy morning, I stopped myself from saying more. Stephanie would nag him all day, if they didn't break up first.

I picked up my bag of clothes, not certain if Cal and I would stay here another night. "Nice to meet you, Stephanie. Excuse me, I'm joining my *friend* Cal for breakfast."

****

It sucked to be penniless. Neither Cal nor I had cash or credit for my work shoes when he drove me to Celia's Attic.

"Stay here, I won't be long," I said.

"Hurry, I have a job interview in an hour." He had to find work. Daddy didn't lend him any money.

Past the glass door, the same gothic lady with milky skin, dressed in black, worked the thrift store. A few customers picked through overstuffed racks of blouses marked half-price.

I dropped my gaze and pretended I didn't notice her. With a little luck, she might not remember me.

The shoe selection had doubled, but the ones I preferred still had a ten-dollar tag dangling from the shoestring.

Goth girl dashed toward a woman balancing a heap of vintage jeans. I had to work fast.

I pulled off my shoes and slipped on the white ones. They fit well. My feet sank into the soft padded arch support.

It's not right to steal. But I'm broke, and it's not a bracelet or a ring. I need work shoes.

My heart beat into my ears.

Goth girl faced the dressing rooms.

What do I do?

Like a thief, I moved my old shoes into the empty spot.

Goth girl unlocked a dressing room. While her back was turned, I vanished out the door.

I hopped into Cal's truck. "Go, drive."

He looked up from his cellphone. "You didn't buy anything?"

"Nope, there's no credit here." I made a trade—not quite stealing. But I got the better deal.

Some desperate soul might pay a nickel for my tattered shoes. My dishonesty was only temporary. Later, I'd make good on the debt. I'd walk inside the store and drop ten bucks on the counter, then leave without admitting what I had done.

"Tracie, I have to tell you something." We rolled onto a street humming with traffic.

"I have something to say too. Thank you for taking me to your dad's last night." It felt good to thank Cal, let him know I appreciated his efforts. He saved me from sleeping under a bridge or someplace worse.

"You're not making this easy," he said. "If I get the job, I'll be working nights."

The wheels in my mind started turning. What did he mean? Wouldn't he talk to Priscilla so we could move back into her house?

"So people work nights," I said.

"Dad arranged this interview. It's in *his* factory. He said I must work my way up like everyone else. Imagine me working the floor, a common laborer." His jaw tensed.

Sure you will. Daddy has bigger plans for you.

"You'll get promoted before I will," I said.

We rolled up to a stoplight. "What I'm saying is I won't be able to drive you to work. Also, Dad said I can stay at his house, but *you* can't live there… I'm sorry."

Ouch. It stung. The day I dreaded came. How could he do this to me? He said I couldn't count on him anymore? He and his family left me to fend for myself? How would I get along? I still had Debby's mother's number. I had to get in touch with Aunt Martha. I needed to hop on a bus and leave this horrible state. I was in a mess, and no one here cared.

"Are you okay?" he asked.

What a silly question. Who's okay when they're sixteen, homeless, and broke? And miles upon miles from the nearest relative. Kermit the Frog's song popped into my head. I changed the lyrics to *'It's not easy being sixteen.'*

"No, I'm not okay." I'd be less okay when my Flavors shift ended, and I went to my second job. The gloom would hit worst when my Sprinkles shift ended. Where the heck would I sleep tonight?

"I'm really sorry about this."

Chapter 29

Cal dropped me off at the park. It was the logical place, located between both of my jobs. Inside, my stomach slipped into a knot I couldn't undo. I sat down on a weathered bench and held my sack of clothes. He left me here the way someone might abandon an unwanted dog. But this wasn't a nice neighborhood where a friendly family would take pity on me.

The trees surrounded me as if to hide me, and I wanted to disappear. My shift at Flavors didn't begin until ten. If I showed up early, the questions would start. 'Tracie, why are you carrying a bag? What's in it?'

At least Flavors had lockers in the break room. I'd slip in and stuff my belongings in one. No one needed to know about my homelessness. I didn't have a roof over my head, but I had my dignity. And this dignified girl needed to find Debby. She was my best chance of getting back to Arkansas. Last I heard, she was living with her mother. And I called.

On the third ring, her mother answered. "Hello, I don't want any." She disconnected.

The strange number must've looked like a telemarketer's. But her dismissive tone didn't keep me from trying again.

"Is Debby there?" I asked without hesitation.

"No, you missed her," she said, competing with the dog barking in the background. "Hold on...quit barking."

It wasn't like Debby to roll out of bed this early. Where did she go?

"Ma'am, I'm sorry I don't remember your last name. Where's Debby?"

The yipping dog blended with her voice. "It's Kippler, and Debby has gone home. Call her there." The line went dead.

Great. At least I had Debby's old number. Something told me she ran back to her husband. Bobby let her stew before begging forgiveness. It was typical. I imagined her baby screamed half the night. Her mom probably encouraged Debby to leave and tend to little Junior. Good mothers took care of their babies.

Cigarette smoke drifted from two raggedy men. They looked homeless and were walking my direction. Other than them, no one else hung around the park.

I collected my bag and scurried nearer the road. I sighed with relief when they sat on the bench instead of stalking me. Homeless men were always looking for easy money, but I didn't have a red cent in my pocket.

Remembering what I needed to do, I tapped Debby's number into my phone. Five rings later, Debby's line went to a message that said the mailbox was full.

Of course, plenty of her friends must've called to congratulate her when she gave birth. She didn't delete their well wishes. Her voicemail was the least of her worries.

A few blocks separated me from Sprinkles. It was my first payday. I stayed on the sidewalk, avoiding a stream of cars moving as slow as parade floats. When I arrived, Sprinkles buzzed with customers. I held my bag low and behind me.

The employees ran circles around Tammy, and a new girl poured coffee, while another woman worked the register. Our manager sent me to Wendy's office.

I walked into the bookkeeper's office and stopped in front of her desk. "Gloria said you have my paycheck."

"Yes, but you never brought me your social security card or state ID. I'm supposed to verify you," she said. Her wire-framed glasses were angled on her nose.

"I'm sorry. I came by once, but you were out. Since I work nights, we keep missing each other."

Her eyes disapproved, but she handed me my paycheck. "Bring it Monday. Don't forget."

"Yes, ma'am," I said, though I knew I couldn't. It was miles away, tucked inside Mom's drawer. And I couldn't find Mom.

When I had my paycheck in hand, I stuffed it into my pocket. Rather than fret any longer, I returned to the dining room and ate a hot glazed donut. The ice-cold milk helped to wash it down along with my concerns. Was it possible to cash my check without a state identification card or a bank account?

I hurried to the bank, three blocks away, dodging cars between street crossings. The employees had just unlocked the lobby. The place smelled like wet ink and new plastic.

A lady, with the name tag *Nancy*, called me to the counter. Nancy drummed her cherry-red manicured nails on the desk. If she stared upward during a thunderstorm with her funnel nose, she'd drown.

"Cash this please." I passed the rectangular paper, still stiff from the bookkeeper's printer.

Nancy eyed the bag I carried. "Do you have an account with us?"

"No."

Nosy. Something told me she'd stick her big nose into my business. Her type always did.

Nancy's lips lifted at the edges with the *we don't serve your type* smile. "You must open one to deposit this, then withdraw the money."

My heart sank. Couldn't she make an exception? It was my first paycheck, and I needed the cash. I didn't even have a library card.

Please don't make me search for one of those check-cashing businesses where undocumented workers go.

"Miss, do you understand?" She set my check on the cool marble countertop.

Bluff, when things get rough.

"I'd like to open an account, but I don't have my driver's license with me. Can't you cash it, anyway? I'll come back later to set it up." I straightened my spine and pulled my shoulders high and wide the way my aunt Martha told me to. She said, 'When in doubt, act confident.'

Nancy pinched her lips into a tight line, shook her head, and set her wavy hair to bouncing.

I took back my check, turned, and slammed straight into the lady who stood behind me. "Oops, excuse me," I said as I stepped on her toe and stumbled.

"Ouch, you klutz." She smirked when I dropped the bag and a pair of panties fell out.

I snatched the underwear and shoved it under my jeans. "I'm sorry."

If only someone I knew would walk in here, they might help me. But no one was here but the grouch I tripped over. She pushed past me and was already at the counter.

"Nancy, were you giving the bag lady a hard time?" the woman said, teasing her.

"Shut the front door…" Nancy took the woman's check and keyed the numbers into the computer. "Didn't you move to Maine?"

"Yeah, but I'm back for good this time…" The grouch went on to tell her news, but I blocked it out.

Bag lady? She called me a bag lady. I had to get this check cashed.

An elderly woman came through the door. I stopped her before she made it to Nancy's desk.

"Ma'am, would you cash this for me?" I held the paper.

The woman sidestepped me and shook her head.

A man in a suit approached. "Miss, you can't solicit here."

"I'm not selling anything. Do you know where I can get this cashed?"

"Not around here, but there are check-cashing businesses in Providence."

Of course, he'd tell me to go to another town.

He walked behind, ushering me toward the door. Once I was outside, he stood at the window.

No doubt if I bothered someone coming into the building, he'd call the law. I best get to Flavors and ask Jill for help.

****

I had earned over three hundred dollars. It should buy a bus ticket to Arkansas. I'd have to call and check prices. Hopefully, Greyhound didn't sell tickets online by credit card. I needed to use a computer to find out. Jill had an iPhone. While I was at it, I needed to read my email, too.

216

My shoes put a spring in my step as I walked to Flavors Ice Cream Shop. Though not new, these cushioned my feet better than the crappy sneakers I abandoned at Celia's Attic. If someone cashed my check, I'd sneak into the thrift shop and pay my debt. I'd leave the money on the counter. It felt good to know I could pay.

The bell tinkled when I opened the door at Flavors. It was too early for ice cream, and we didn't have customers yet. Jill and Rae's voices filtered from behind an office door. Jill sobbed, and Rae spoke soft enough their words muffled as if they spoke through a cloth.

"It's me, Tracie," I said, as I moved like a prowling leopard when passing them. Once inside the break room, I stuffed my bag in a locker and returned to the front.

Jill had time to talk to her boyfriend. If she wasn't crying over a breakup, maybe he'd let me crash at their place tonight. If I didn't have enough money for a trip, Rae could pay me early. I'd hop a bus to Arkansas tomorrow. If I could reach Debby, she could visit Aunt Martha, Mom's older sister. Maybe Aunt Martha would take me in.

When Jill and Rae finished, sniffles replaced the sobs. The ajar door swung open, and they joined me. Jill looked down at me with a bright-pink face and black streaks of mascara. She dabbed her nose with a crumpled tissue and excused herself to the bathroom.

"Bad news," Rae said.

Don't tell me this place is closing. We lost our jobs? You haven't even paid me yet.

"What happened?" I asked, trying to stay calm.

"Jill's grandmother died."

How awful. She's close to her family. She won't

work this week with the funeral and all. Or cash my check.

Rae looked at me as if she read my selfish mind. My skin burned with shame. Embarrassed, I raised my hand to my face, turned away, and fake coughed.

Jill returned with her purse and keys. "I'll call next week."

Rae nodded, but her expression hinted a hamster wheel spun in her brain. She watched Jill go to her car. With a heavy sigh, Rae turned to me. "You and I are working the store until Jill comes back."

Extra hours for me. But I needed to leave Rhode Island.

Flavors opened at ten, but someone had to come in earlier. Jill was here before me. After Jill sent me home on work days, I assumed Rae returned and closed the shop.

"So am I opening the store?" I asked.

"Yes." Rae led me to her personal office. Within a minute, I signed a form, and she handed me the silver key.

It was my first key to anything since I left home. I had access to the whole store. Bins of ice cream, air conditioning, bathrooms, and a place to clean up before work were all mine. And if I didn't find a place to stay the night, I could sleep here.

Rae filed the paper away. "I'm glad I hired you. I like new employees with experience."

She buttered me up. People praised me when they planned to dump more work on me. In my case, I needed the money. But if I could leave tomorrow, I would.

"Yes, I haven't opened at Sprinkles yet, but I'm getting good at serving customers."

She locked the cabinet. "I'm sure that's great experience too. What I'm referring to is your old job at your aunt's donut shop. People apply for work here, and none of them are useful."

I had forgotten about the lie. Tammy and Gloria hired me on the spot at Sprinkles. In fact, it worked so well, I lied on my Flavor's application too. My aunt never had a donut shop.

"Oh, I only worked there after school and during the summer." I looked past the windows to the empty parking lot. Cars flashed by the shop, waving at us in a ribbon of red, white, blue, and gray. None of them stopped.

Please, quit talking. Won't someone please buy an ice cream?

I put the key in my pocket and picked up the broom and dustpan.

"Another thing I like about you, you stay busy." Rae trailed me, while I swept around the chairs, searching for crumbs.

"Got it," I said, as the broom bristles freed a small piece of waffle cone stuck against a chair leg. With a brisk swipe, it flew into the dustpan. "My aunt insisted on having a spotless floor." I set the broom and dustpan back in their places and washed my hands.

"Good, I knew I could count on you. I'm going to share the security code with you. Don't tell anyone. Keep the number in your head."

Gee, she did trust me. I didn't know they had a security system since I was so new. Rae had faith in me. This morning, I stole a pair of shoes...not good...but to my credit I planned to settle the debt.

We walked past the break room, toward the back

door. She pushed four numbers, 2, 4, 6, 8, on a panel which ticked off a timer.

"You have sixty seconds to get out and lock the front door."

"What happens if I don't make it in time?"

She reentered the numbers, and the countdown stopped. "The bell will blast, and the police will come."

Good to know.

"Wait, I'll be coming in the front door and turning off the alarm in the mornings."

"You'll do it mornings and nights. You're opening and closing the store, starting today." Rae walked back to her office and snapped up her purse.

"Rae, I'm scheduled to work at Sprinkles at seven p.m. I have to talk to you about something, too." I still had the Sprinkles check in my pocket.

To my disbelief, she didn't root through her bag for a stick of gum or mints. She slung it onto her shoulder and charged toward the front door. "I don't have time to talk right now. You can close the store earlier on the days you work there. Come in early and finish cleaning before reopening. Don't worry about the cash drawer. I'll deal with it tomorrow morning when I get here."

"You're leaving me in charge, by myself?"

"Yes, the Providence store is unmanned. I'm needed there." She stopped and scribbled on a sticky note. "Here's my cellphone number. If you have a question, call."

I straightened my spine and drew back my shoulders. "You can count on me."

Chapter 30

Haste made Rae forget. In her rush to leave Flavors Ice Cream Shop, she failed to lock her office. The opportunity lay before me. Beyond the doorway, her computer was up and running. With a few keystrokes, Google showed me where to buy a bus ticket and directions to the station in Providence. The best part—I didn't need a credit card. And the check in my pocket was enough to buy my way to Arkansas.

First, I had to find a home, a safe place. Aunt Martha was my favorite aunt, Mom's only sister. The last time I saw her, when I was twelve, I asked for help. I had the feeling she wanted to, but something stopped her.

Between serving double dips of chocolate ice cream and wiping tabletops, I slipped behind Rae's sleek desk. My fingers shook as I typed. No new addresses came up for Mom and Dad, but I found Aunt Martha's and her landline number. Thank goodness. Most people didn't have clunky phones hanging on walls or sitting on a side table, but my auntie did. Heck, she believed in driving a car until it lost its muffler in the street. When I asked her about her boxy television, she said, "I'm not buying a flat screen until this one blows up. This one will last for years."

I wondered if it still claimed the space in her living room.

It seemed silly I didn't know where my auntie lived.

Daffodil Lane was not more than five miles from Debby's house. When you don't drive or visit, memories frost over like a windshield in January. Funny how I didn't remember my auntie's eye color, but I remembered her home smelled like brownies. She used to stir pink lemonade in a crystal pitcher. It tasted tangy, yet sweet. Aunt Martha's hugs covered me like a big warm blanket—except for the one time.

One July morning, when I was twelve, Dad told me to mow the lawn. We had a thunderstorm the previous night, leaving the grass high and soggy. With the air thick and humid, I mowed before the sun rose too high— before the temperature soared to ninety degrees. The combination of wet grass and a dull lawnmower blade ensured it clipped the lawn like a bad haircut.

Dad returned to find clumps and ruts in his precious yard and me sitting on the sofa, drinking Coca Cola.

His face flushed a fire-truck red. "Get up, you lazy girl. Look, look what you did to the lawn." He snatched the Coke away and yanked me to my feet. Before I could get my balance, he dragged me to the window.

"Ow, you're hurting me." I tried to escape the big fingers, but he had a tight grip. "I couldn't help it. It's muddy."

"Exactly. Too early to mow. When I told you to cut it, I meant later today. You know better." He let me loose only to unfasten his belt. The rub of leather against belt loops followed.

With his shove, I stumbled toward the sofa. I knew what came next. I regained my footing and ran behind the couch, wedging it between us.

"Get over here," he said. "And bend over."

My eyes swelled with tears. My arm throbbed where

he pinched. He had his belt doubled over the way he did every time I pissed him off. I was sick of this. A few muddy bald patches in the yard shouldn't get me a beating. But he snapped.

"No, don't whip me. I didn't mean to tear up the grass."

He ignored my begging and moved squarely in front of the sofa. "Julie, get your ass in here. Control your daughter."

Her obedient steps came from the utility room where the urgent sound of water filled the washing machine.

"Mom, I cut the grass like he said. I can't help that it rained last night."

She stood in socked feet, somber, the way she always did before when he raged. "Honey, I'm sure Tracie did the best she could. She's only twelve."

He flicked the belt straight, and the popping leather made me cringe. "Yes, twelve. Stop making excuses. When I was twelve, I did ten times the work these kids do. She's old enough to know better."

If I ran fast, I might beat him to the back door, jump the chain-link fence before he caught me. The purple welts he gave me two weeks ago faded. He planned to replace them. I didn't want to feel the sting of the strap again. But where would I go? If only I could run away, Dad could never hit me again.

I looked at Mom. She met my gaze and gave me a slight shake of her head as if to say, 'Don't try it.' She was right. He'd whip me even harder later. While I was gone, he'd take his anger out on her. He'd smack her. Shove her against the wall and punch her face until her lip split and bled. Later she'd blame me. For the days after, I'd have reminders, her bruises and mine.

Mom stood by, ready to tackle me. God forbid Dad would have to exert himself. He must save his energy for swinging the belt. He'd never ground me the way my friends' parents punished my friends. Dad like to teach lessons his way.

The front door slammed.

Jason, my brother.

I bolted toward the back door.

Mom lunged toward me. "No! Come back."

Fingernails clawed my bare arm.

Stinging scratches leaked red. She ripped my skin, and it was under her nails.

I sprinted across the yard.

Over the fence I went.

A wire spike ripped my T-shirt as I tumbled to the ground.

Behind me, Dad's voice blasted like a gunshot.

I never looked back. Like a hunted doe, I fled.

Aunt Martha lived a few blocks from us that year. I leaped behind her backyard hedges. Terrified, I huddled down and bawled. My heart thumped in my ears louder than Dad's screams and Aunt Martha's humming air conditioner. After a few deep breaths, the purring steel box comforted me. It reminded me a cool refuge waited beyond her back door. Inside, my aunt would console me with loving hugs.

But I had to hurry. Dad would be here soon. He'd flush me out. I had one chance. I stepped into the open yard, away from the safety of trees and bushes and ran to my auntie's back door. A few knocks later, it creaked open.

"Tracie?" Aunt Martha's smile disappeared when she saw my torn T-shirt and damp hair.

"Can I come in?" I expected Dad to show up any second.

"Tracieeee." Dad's voice grew louder and angrier.

"He's after me," I said, gasping for air.

Aunt Martha knew what I meant. She had seen Mom's eyes, red streaks in the whites, black-and-blue circles under them. She let me in and locked him out.

I was safe, while Dad prowled the neighborhood.

The blood on my arm clotted into little red beads where Mom's fingernails scraped. I had forgotten about it until Aunt Martha asked, "Who hurt you?"

"Mom tried to stop me from leaving."

Aunt Martha didn't say anything nasty about her younger sister, but I read the disgust on her face. It was the way she frowned when she didn't approve. She didn't approve of dogs chained to trees or the declawing of cats. She'd rather scrub a toilet than watch another movie showing the *Ku Klux Klan* burning crosses to terrorize people of color.

Determined knocks came at the front door. It wasn't the knock of a kid selling Girl Scout cookies or the timid rapping of a lady recruiting church members. Big fists banged on the wood which separated me from the devil.

"Martha, it's me, Brent." He restrained himself and spoke like a civilized man. He was good at fooling people. So charming, Mom's friends and acquaintances repeatedly told her how nice a man he was. 'It must be wonderful being married to Brent. He's so witty and sweet. And he's always laughing.' They told her this between beatings when her cuts and bruises had healed.

"Aunt Martha, can I live with you and Uncle Chuck?"

She cupped my cheeks like she cradled a ripe peach.

It seemed like she'd say yes, but Dad banged on the door again, and she dropped her hands.

"Martha, please answer the door. We have to talk."

"What did you do to upset him?" Aunt Martha whispered.

"I messed up the lawn. I didn't mean to. Please let me live with you."

More bangs came. Dad didn't budge.

"I have to talk to him. We can't hide forever," Aunt Martha said.

I stepped back, keeping one eye on the back door, just in case. Aunt Martha went to answer.

The lock that kept the devil at bay clicked open.

"Hi, Brent. What's going on?" She didn't invite him in, making him stand on the porch like a stranger.

"I'm looking for Tracie. She's missing. Is she here?"

"Yes."

Dread bubbled up from my stomach. Oh God, he'd make me come home unless she convinced him to let me stay. But she never said I could.

"Can you get her? She must come home."

"She's afraid. Frankly, I think she has good reason." Aunt Martha kept a relaxed hand on the door. She probably didn't believe Dad would barge in, but I did. He stood a few inches outside—almost inside the house.

"Martha, this is none of your business. I have the right to raise my kids without interference. If you don't send her home, I'll call the cops. Don't make me do it."

"She's my niece. Go ahead, call. I have a story to tell, too."

"She has fifteen minutes to get her ass home. I'm not playing," Dad said.

Aunt Martha shut the door, and the lock turned over.

I exhaled.

Before we had a chance to talk again, the phone rang. It was Mom. Mom did all the talking. Aunt Martha didn't tell me what she said, but it was brief.

"Aunt Martha, can I live with you?" I asked.

"I'm sorry, honey, you can't."

I didn't see Aunt Martha much after that day. And I never knew what Mom said to her to convince her to send me home. By fall, Aunt Martha and Uncle Chuck had a for sale sign in her front yard.

More than four years had passed. Dad wasn't here to stop me from calling my auntie. I'd be seventeen in July. Maybe she'd let me move in with her and Uncle Chuck. I could buy a bus ticket and leave Rhode Island.

The clock in Rae's office said six. I'd be closing the store soon and heading to Sprinkles to work the night shift. Later, I had to find a place to sleep—somewhere besides the park. Thank goodness I had a key to stay here. Rapists, thieves, and pedophiles stalked the grounds at night for prey. They preferred teenage girls who had nowhere to go, no one to call.

I was one decision away from a different life. One successful conversation with Aunt Martha could change everything. I tapped my auntie's number into the phone, held my breath, and listened to twenty rings. Typical.

When Aunt Martha didn't answer, I logged into my email. MyDNA sent me several messages. The bright blue DNA packages were in Jason's room when I ran away. He must've mailed them.

Once inside the program, I opened the section to the relative list. Uncle Chuck and Jason popped up first on the list. We shared fifty percent of our genes. How could it be? Uncle Chuck was my uncle by marriage. Or was he? No. According to this, he was either my brother or biological father.

Wow! He's my real father.

Chapter 31

The pitter-patter of rain hit Sprinkles around eleven forty-five p.m., the same time the wind started howling. Guttural moans like the mourners at my grandfather's funeral, elderly women wailing into handkerchiefs. Except instead of dripping noses, rain fell in sheets. A muddy river hosed the street. I didn't own an umbrella. I clocked out and didn't have a ride.

Before leaving, I snuck into the bathroom and put my belongings in a trash bag. With a knot tied at the top, it would stay dry. I tried calling Cal. He didn't answer. Heading back to Flavors was my best option. I could shut off the alarms and lock myself inside for the night.

Dee paid me no mind at first. "Set it there. I'll take the garbage out when the storm lets up."

The bundle I carried looked like the other piles we collected from the trash cans. Mine didn't bulge as much as the ones stacked in the corner. My face flushed when she offered. I'd die of embarrassment if she found out I was homeless. Everything I owned, except my guitar, fit inside the plastic bag. I forgot my beautiful Fender.

"I'll take it out before Cal picks me up." She didn't need to know he wasn't coming. I lifted my sack of clothes and held it away, pretending it was dirty paper cups, chocolate smeared napkins, and half-eaten donuts. I grabbed two other sacks of trash and headed for the outside dumpster at the back door.

"Leave it. There's no reason to get soaked. If it's raining when my shift is over, the baker will take it out."

Dee had crossed the line from being considerate to annoying. Each comment felt as if she was one step closer to exposing my secret.

She eyed the bag with suspicion. "What's so urgent about taking out the trash? The bag isn't full."

Right...it wasn't. I didn't have a full wardrobe like Dee. I had work uniforms, jeans, a few tops, and necessities hidden away. I could survive a few days. A girl who slept in a canopy bed and lunched with her mother at bistros wouldn't understand my situation. I might spend the night at Flavors. If I didn't make it there, I'd huddle in dark doorways, shrouded by shadows. At daylight, I'd have to move along before someone shooed me away.

I wrinkled my nose. "Well, I was going to spare you the details, but since you're interested... Can you believe someone left two dirty diapers in the bathroom? Not the pee-pee type either. From the looks of it, a couple of toddlers had blowouts. We need to talk to the dayshift girls. They're slacking. It's not the first time I found nasty diapers after they clocked out."

Dee's repulsed expression made it hard to keep a straight face. "Oh gross. If I ever say I want kids, slap me. There's nothing worse than wiping someone else's butt."

"Yeah, I know. I only babysit potty-trained kids for that reason. Since I'm leaving, I'll take this one out. Next time I'll let you do the honors."

"Deal."

"Well, I better get going. My husband will be here any minute." Two cars threw light onto the parking lot.

"There he is."

At least one of them was a customer. When they came in asking for coffee, I slipped away.

****

My mother should've hit me in the head with a rock years ago. It seemed I made one wrong decision after another. I didn't even walk two blocks after leaving Sprinkles before the storm drenched me head to toe. Ahead on the left, fluorescent lights beckoned from the twenty-four-hour laundromat. They were bright and welcoming in contrast to the night shadows.

I ran toward the shelter with cold rain pelting me. When I got there, my hair dripped like I went swimming. It was after midnight. No one did their laundry this late. On the ceiling, bulbs buzzed while the sky thundered.

Inside a dryer, someone forgot a tattered towel. Goody, goody. I patted the wetness away with soft cotton loops. The scent of baby powder was comforting like Aunt Martha and her warm hugs.

I was safe. A couple of dozen washers and dryers lined the white walls. Red fire extinguishers hung here and there and added a splash of color to the bleached room. It made sense. Dryers could catch fire if no one cleaned the lint screens. I should check the traps for money.

A soap center and vending machines sat in one corner. Formica tables were set up in the center to serve for folding stations. Outside, the wind ripped between the buildings and the rain beat the windows. If Cal were here, I'd strangle him. Because of him, I'd wander from place to place. I needed to get to Flavors.

I dug inside my pocket. My soaking wet paycheck was folded into a square. Without a driver's license, the bank would never cash my check. I had heard about check-cashing businesses. For a fee, illegal immigrants used those places back home. But how much of a fee? Cal might cash it for me. It was the least he could do since he moved me here.

I called Cal again.

No answer.

A sign pointed to a unisex restroom. Good to know. I might have to stay awhile. With nothing else to do, I set down my bag and opened a dryer door.

Someone neglected the lint screen. Commercial dryers were bigger than regular dryers. Jason, Mom, and I used to visit a laundromat like this. While the clothes tumbled for an hour, we checked the machines. Inside, we found a twenty-dollar bill, along with several single dollar bills stuck in the fuzz. One day we found thirty dollars in all. Lazy people forgot to empty their pockets. They were the same lazy people who didn't check the machines.

I inspected each trap, scraping the lint off the screens and dropping it on the floor. In all, I found three stiff dollar bills—folded squares like the paycheck in my pocket. Once finished, I inspected the washers and took a trip to the restroom.

Male voices bellowed like lions claiming their territory.

No one did their laundry at this late hour. Who were they?

With no other doors to escape through, I was stuck. Two guys talked while the sound of metal on metal banged. The visitors weren't leaving. They were probably homeless people looking for cash. The storm must've had them running like rats searching for high ground. I stood still and held my breath when the squeaky footsteps approached.

Wet sneakers chirped louder. Then stopped.

A jiggle of the doorknob sent my heart racing.

"Hurry up. I gotta go," a male said.

As I touched the knob, the door unlocked and slammed into me.

The older man in a muddy T-shirt and moth-eaten pants stood over me grinning. "Les, we got us a girl."

Crapola, I wasn't someone to be gotten. Not by them or anyone. Not if I could help it.

Another guy, a younger one, peered down at me. "One of those chicks from Sprinkles."

"You know, they threw me out of there even though I had *money*. The snooty bitch refused to serve me 'cause I wasn't wearing shoes."

"Mister, I would've served you. Tell you what, come by when I'm working, and I'll make it up to you. All the free coffee and donuts you want."

The taller man eyed my plastic bag. "What were you doing in here besides taking a piss?"

"Nothing," I said.

"You've been treasure hunting, haven't you?" I didn't doubt he came by weekly or nightly to search for money.

"I don't know what you're talking about."

"We saw the lint bunnies you threw on the floor," he said. "They weren't there earlier."

"It wasn't me. I was walking home from work and stopped here when it started raining."

Les's lips stretched, exposing yellow teeth. "No, you weren't. It's been pouring for hours. Rich, I bet you my last dollar Miss Sprinkles filled her pockets."

Rich took a forward step.

Stepping back, I hit the wall.

"We don't have to bet. I know she did." He stood close enough for me to get a whiff of his foul breath. It smelled like a dead animal, one run over three days ago.

He planned to suffocate me. It must be true that stinky people got used to their own odor. And the longer they lived like wild beasts, the more they behaved like them. These two traveled in a pack and stalked their prey. They were ready to tear me apart.

Bluff when things get rough.

"Sir, you're crowding me. Do you mind?" I tried to sidestep him, but he latched onto my arm. "Don't." I smacked him with my bag, but it only thumped him like a pillow in a pillow fight.

I writhed from his grip and yanked him along beside me.

Les closed in and seized my other arm. He shoved one hand into my pocket. "Miss Sprinkles, you ain't leaving with our money." He pulled out the cash I had pilfered from the dryers.

Rich dove into my other pocket and dug out my key, paycheck, and cellphone. "Well, well. It's been a while since I had a telephone." He threw my key and check on the floor.

"No, please give it back."

Rich ignored my plea and confiscated my trash bag. "What else you got?" He ripped a hole in the plastic and dumped my clothes.

"If you're on your way home, why are you carrying your clothes around? Huh, Miss Sprinkles?" Les kicked my Flavor's uniform, leaving a muddy smudge on the pristine white top.

"I stayed the night with a friend." I stooped and gathered my garments, stuffing them into the torn bag.

They flipped off the light and laughed as they returned to the main part of the building.

They could hurt me before the night ended. Three dollars didn't mean much, but the cellphone was my lifeline. Without it, I couldn't call Debby or my relatives. I had to get it back. Those assholes weren't going to pick on me. Not anymore.

I grabbed my bag and opened the door. The red cylinder hanging on the wall could do more than put out fires. And I knew how to use it. The firefighters came to my school one day. 'Everyone needs to know how to put out flames,' they said.

Quietly, I plucked it from the wall and pulled the pin. The torn sack concealed my new gun. With one hand on the trigger and one gripping the hose under the bag, I headed for the bums.

Les and Rich sat on chairs, playing with my phone.

I hung my head, as if defeated, when I approached them. "Hey, guys, I'm sorry my co-workers didn't serve you at the donut shop. And I'm sorry I invaded your territory. You won't see me around here no more," I said in my most convincing voice and squeezed the trigger.

Hiss.

Their necks snapped back. White powder blasted their faces. Hands slapped furiously. My phone bounced across the floor. Screams, curses, and coughing followed. They scratched at their eyes.

Too bad.

The chemical spray stuck like wet flour.

I launched the cylinder, a torpedo, smacking Rich in the head. I picked up my phone. As I ran, I yanked the lever on the fire alarm. It rang loud enough to wake Massachusetts. "Good morning!"

Chapter 32

The only light to guide me flashed in silver streaks across the sky. It was after two a.m., and the storm raged.

Sirens screamed. 'Move, move, get out of here before someone catches you,' it said.

Cool water splashed under my feet, while I hauled my trash bag toward Flavors Ice Cream Shop. When the sidewalk ended, I trudged on the grass instead of the street. The drunks were leaving the bars. If I walked on the road, an intoxicated driver might slide across the pavement and slam into me.

I thought staying beside the street was safer until I stepped into a hole and tumbled downhill. My face landed in a puddle. When I rolled through the mud, I lost my sack of clothes. But that wasn't the worst of it. A sharp pain shot through my ankle. I sat up, and my fingers traced the skin. It throbbed, but I could still move the joint.

Thunder rumbled. Lightning popped in the sky and gave me a glimpse of the knotted bag. It had washed in a ditch where the current pulled it. Water spilled over the street, sweeping everything in its path. On my hands and knees, I crawled closer to the trench I could no longer see.

Okay, Mother Nature, help me. It's dark, and my uniforms are floating down the stream. The stream wasn't here yesterday. All the crap in the street, the glass, trash, dead animals are down here.

Mother Nature got the wrong idea. Instead of more light, she turned off heaven's faucet. The wind dwindled to a breeze, and I would've welcomed it during the day. But it was nighttime. Dark clouds shrouded the moon as if to put it to bed. I wanted someone to tuck me in bed with clean sheets.

Completely soaked, I stood in the mud and listened to the trickle of nearby water. One misstep and I risked breaking a bone.

After a long while, cars drove by. Night workers cast headlights in my direction. The drivers answered my prayers. Wedged between rocks, my bag poked out above the water. The knot was like the hand of a drowning swimmer. If it rained five more minutes, my possessions would've sunk.

I took slow steps toward the ditch and fished out the bag. The water got into it. It weighed what felt like a ton. Lugging it uphill had my ankle throbbing more.

Once I climbed to the street, a car drove by, and I glimpsed my Sprinkles uniform. Mud covered it. I had to get to Flavors. It was a good thing I didn't have to clock in until ten this morning. It gave me time to wash my clothes in the sink and to explore the ice cream shop. Maybe there was an extra bathroom—one with a shower, blow-dryer, and towels.

Gusts of cool air replaced the calm, and I shivered. My ankle screamed with each step. I had to change into dry clothes. Hopefully, I'd find something to wear at Flavors. Within ten minutes, I was there.

The streetlight cast a shadow onto the empty parking lot. It felt wrong to enter the ghosted place.

I dropped my bag. My arm ached from carrying the

load.

What was the alarm code? 2, 4, 6, 8. Rae warned me to move fast once inside the building and punch in the number. If I didn't, the deafening ring would have every police officer here within minutes.

Probing my pocket, my fingers rubbed against damp polyester. I checked my other pocket and pulled out my cellphone and a wet crumpled paycheck.

Where's the key?

I dumped my bag and ran my hands over all the clothes. Great…I probably lost it when I fell.

Cal never called to say if he got the night shift job. I phoned him, but he didn't answer. No matter how bad things got, I'd never call Logan. With limited choices, there was only one other option. Priscilla. I rang her landline.

After three rings, Dick answered in a raspy voice.

"Dick, it's Tracie. I'm in big trouble," I said, unaware that Priscilla must've had another phone in her bedroom.

"What's wrong?" he whispered.

"I'm at Flavors Ice Cream Shop. I'm hurt, and I need help."

"What happened?"

"I sprained my ankle. My clothes are wet, and I have nowhere to go."

"Dick, are you on the phone?" Priscilla croaked.

A queasy feeling hit my stomach. Priscilla wouldn't like me asking her boyfriend for a favor.

"No, baby, you had a dream. Go back to sleep," he said. We both stayed quiet until she did, and he whispered, "See you in a few minutes."

****

Dick pulled up in his Cadillac and lowered his window. "You look like you lost a mud-wrestling match."

It wasn't funny. Mud caked my eyebrows and hair. It covered me, and my feet were soaked.

He passed a folded towel from the passenger seat and got out but left the door ajar to supply extra light. "Here, dry off."

I wiped my face with the soft cloth. "Thank you for coming. Priscilla kicked me and Cal out."

"She told me. Let's see the ankle."

I lifted my pants leg. My ankle was the size of a small grapefruit. I kept my weight on my toes for balance. Any weight on my heel brought tears to my eyes.

"You should see a doctor."

"It's not too bad. Besides, my parents would have to take me. They're in Arkansas, I think."

"In Arkansas? Tracie, how old are you?"

"Sixteen." I gave him the short version of my story.

"Let's get you to Priscilla's." Dick wrapped an arm around my waist. "Lean on me, kiddo."

"I need my bag." I pointed to the ripped plastic sack with my clothes spilling out. I had tried to pack them inside, but once wet, my garments swelled like sponges.

He frowned at the mess. The city dump had tidier bags of garbage.

With an arm around Dick's neck, I hopped to the passenger side of the car. He had wisely covered the seat and floorboard with towels. My dirty clothes would stain Priscilla's linens. No doubt when she saw the mud, she'd scream and stomp her feet like I had burned her bacon.

After Dick buckled me in, he went for my bag. He

opened the trunk and removed a tarp. He unfolded it. With care, as if he cradled a precious baby, he laid my bundle of clothes on the waterproof sheathing and shut the trunk.

Dick slid into the car and started it. "Do you have any other clothes?"

"No." My face warmed with the shame of admitting I had lived sixteen years and everything I owned was stuffed into a grimy trash bag.

"Don't worry. I'm sure I can find pajamas in Bess's room." He shifted the car in gear and hit the gas.

My life came full circle. The night Cal brought me here, I borrowed Bess's clothes. I had arrived at Priscilla's house stinky, hungry, and tired—déjà vu.

"I'm sorry I woke you," I said.

He turned left into a quiet neighborhood. "I'm glad you did."

"Why?"

"I had a sixteen-year-old daughter. She got into trouble, and no one helped her."

Had? He spoke like a man with a guilty conscience. He was married, and he moved in with Priscilla. Had he discovered lobster wasn't better than hamburgers? And nagging was nagging whether the words came from Priscilla's mouth or his wife's. Even though he was helping me, the thought of him abandoning his child pissed me off. It seemed all dads were bad in their own way.

"What happened to your daughter? What's her name?"

"Her name was Amy. She passed away two years ago."

"Oh, I'm sorry."

Open mouth and shove a foot and leg inside as Aunt Martha used to say.

"Amy and her best friend left a party. They'd been drinking. Her friend was driving when…" His voice cracked, and he swallowed the pain that gurgled up with knowing his little girl was gone.

"I'm sorry. You don't have to say it."

"Nothing's been the same since. My family never recovered. I went to therapy…to Priscilla… I shouldn't burden you."

I understood. Therapists weren't supposed to sleep with their clients any more than teachers with their students. Priscilla lured this broken man downstairs into the basement for his session. It was a dark and seedy place where weed burned as casually as incense, hands slathered in cocoa butter stroked penises, and semen stained the therapy pillows. Underfoot, the odor of sex rose from the carpet as we trudged across it. The Russo basement was the temptation station.

Dick's problems were none of my business, but I was too nosy for my own good.

"Do you miss your wife?"

"Terribly. I made an awful mistake. If only I could go home and make amends. But my wife isn't talking to me. My other daughter, Tammy, hasn't spoken to me either…since I moved out."

Dick and I wanted happy homes, but we didn't have any place to go home to.

"What does Tammy do?" I asked.

We were turning onto Priscilla's street, and her driveway was ahead on the left.

"She works at Sprinkles. Do you know her?"

No, not money-grubbing Tammy. Dick drove a

Cadillac. He had plenty of cash. I was sure he didn't raise a vodka-drinking thief. After all, the name Tammy was as common as Michelle or Jennifer. Maybe there was another Tammy working at Sprinkles. It's strange he never mentioned Tammy before now. But maybe they were talking then.

"What does she look like?"

"She's a little taller than you, has dark shoulder-length hair, and has freckles on her cheeks."

I had never guessed they were related.

He cut the headlights and rolled into the driveway. "Do you know who I'm talking about?"

"Yes, I know her. She works the day shift."

He looked at me like he had a favor to ask but didn't know how. At least he cared about his daughters. Dick wasn't a bad guy. We both got mixed up with the Russos. If I helped him reconcile with Tammy, maybe he would keep helping me.

Chapter 33

I wrapped a towel around my naked body and cracked the bathroom door. Dick handed off Bess's clean pajamas. The Tweety Bird pajamas were warm and soft in comparison to the grimy work uniform I had removed.

My dirty clothes were still damp when Dick took them. "Be careful when you go upstairs. Don't let Priscilla catch you. I'll put your clothes in the washer. If she asks, I'll say they're mine." He left me and headed for the laundry room around the corner.

With my partner in crime gone, my heart beat into my throat. I felt like a burglar who avoided a trip wire.

When I showered, I stood on my good foot. The ace wrap in the medicine cabinet was handy to bandage my sprained ankle. An ibuprofen relieved some of the pain which came in merciless throbbing waves. After picking through my few belongings, I combed my tangled hair. It was too risky to use a blow-dryer, so I toweled it dry, then spot-mopped the floor, wiping up the telltale signs that I had been here.

Water rushed into the washing machine. I hobbled that way to check on it. I was tempted to shut it off and stop the chamber from filling. When Dick started the washer, it seemed to scream 'I'm awake and running.' Priscilla was too smart to believe Dick laundered his clothes after midnight. If she heard the swishing and spinning, she'd come down here and see for herself. But

I was a risk-taker who needed clean clothes.

Priscilla's favorite sundress, the yellow one with bright-blue trim, hung on a rod between the washer and dryer. It fit her tight. The sight of it made me cringe as if she stood there with a judging smirk. The smirk said, 'What's wrong? You couldn't hack it out there in the cruel world?'

But the dress hung harmless and lifeless next to the white shawl Priscilla wrapped around her shoulders when she went on a shopping errand. It could hurt me no more than my filthy uniform in the washing machine.

I hobbled upstairs and tiptoed to the guest bedroom on the main level. After locking the door, I slipped between clean sheets. I breathed in the fresh scent of fabric softener and let my head sink into the pillow.

Morning came too soon along with passionate moans. Dick made sure Priscilla had a good start to her day. My aunt Martha used to say, 'When mama's happy, everyone's happy.' The *swoosh* of water running through pipes followed.

I waited, unsure what to do since my uniforms were in the basement. I needed to change out of Bess's Tweety Bird pajamas. A gentle knock came at the door.

I opened it to find Dick on the other side.

"Stay here until I take Priscilla out to breakfast. Then go." He handed me a piece of paper with his cellphone number scribbled on it. "Oh, your clothes are in the dryer. They should be ready soon."

"What about Bess?" Priscilla's daughter might wake up and tell on me.

"She spent the night with a friend." He looked down at my ankle. "If you can, go to the park. Call me. I'll pick you up there. You shouldn't be walking far."

I'd have the house to myself for a few minutes. Risky. If someone came home, they might accuse me of breaking in. In the worst-case scenario, my presence here would cause more headaches for Dick.

"Dick, where are you? Aren't you going to shower?" Priscilla yelled.

I shut my door before she opened hers.

"What are you doing in the hall?" Priscilla said.

"I thought I left my cellphone in the kitchen."

"You did, but I moved it. It's charging on the nightstand."

"Thank you…the battery was almost dead… We're going to Ethan's for breakfast."

Awesome. Priscilla loved the place. She liked eating her meal under the crystal chandeliers.

"I don't mind cooking," Priscilla said.

"You deserve a break. I know how much you love their spinach eggs benedict, and if I could cook, I'd make you breakfast in bed. Today, I want to pamper you."

"Oh, Dick, you're so good to me. While you shower, I'll put on my yellow sundress, the one you like, and I'll make us mimosas to celebrate this glorious morning."

No, not the yellow one. Dick either didn't hear her or didn't realize where she'd go to find her beloved dress. It hung on the rod downstairs next to the dryer filled with my clothes.

Priscilla's footfalls lightened as she walked the hall. I needed to empty my full bladder in the worst way. If I hurried, I'd have time to go to the main bathroom down the hall.

Once I relieved myself, I tiptoed back to the guestroom and closed the door. Five minutes passed, and I made the bed. I couldn't find a bag or anything to put my clean clothes in. My guitar leaned in the corner. My other belongings were stacked neatly on the dresser or still in the basement. As soon as Priscilla and Dick left, I'd find a new trash bag and be on my way.

It didn't take long for Priscilla to return within earshot. "Dick, are you done showering?" The hiss of her bedroom door swinging open followed.

"What's wrong?" he said, but I already had an idea what happened downstairs.

"There are work uniforms in the dryer. Tracie's stuff. You said you were washing your laundry. Why are you doing hers?"

"Her clothes were dirty," he said.

Dick didn't lie. But would he fess up?

"I'm sure her clothes were filthy. You owe me an explanation. What *is* your *relationship* with my son's friend? Tell me why a grown man who is in a *relationship* with *me* would be doing *her* laundry."

"Priscilla, don't use the therapy lingo on me. You're no longer my therapist. If you were, I wouldn't have ended up in your bed."

"Dammit, you're changing the subject. We're talking about you, not me."

"No, we're talking about us. I can have more than one type of relationship. Tracie needed my help."

The wooden door between us was all that kept me safe.

"You have no business washing Tracie's clothes in my washer. If you thought it was okay with me, you wouldn't be hiding it. Where is she? Is she in this house?"

Dick got quiet. He might have nodded. I prayed he shook his head. But Dick wasn't a liar. I was in trouble.

Even if he lied, she'd sniff around until she tracked me down. Hunting. She'd hunt me.

"Tracie! Are you here?" Her footsteps came closer. The sucking and blowing of air beyond the wall grew louder. "I'll find you if you are."

I held my breath and opened the door. The creaky hinges made me queasy. The gap widened until she showed me her scowl.

She was a sneering witch, with twisted lips and teeth clamped together.

"Well, well." She barged into the room as I sidestepped her. "I thought I made myself clear. You no longer live here. You might have manipulated Cal, but Dick is off-limits."

Oh, the off-limits speech again. Please.

Dick stood in the doorway. "Tracie didn't manipulate me."

"She sure did. And now she's got you defending her. How convenient." Priscilla gave me a wicked grin. "Get out of my house before I call the police. They'll know what to do with a teenage runaway."

Holy crap, I had plowed up the wrong plot and unearthed the rot of jealousy. And it stunk.

"Can I please get my clothes out of the dryer?"

"No, you can't. Leave now." She took a swipe at a lamp, and it flew across the room. The bulb shattered, glass skidding over the wood floor.

"But I need my uniforms and shoes."

"You should've thought of that before sneaking in here."

Dick took a step forward. "Priscilla, be reasonable. Let the kid have her clothes."

"It's not negotiable. Go before I lose my temper."

"Why can't I have my clothes and my guitar?" I pointed to it and hopped on one foot while she shooed me along. "My ankle hurts."

"I don't care about your ankle. Don't you get it? Your problems are not my problems." She clapped beside my ear. "Go, out of my house."

"Quit it, Priscilla." He came toward us, reaching for Priscilla.

Hopping along, I lost my balance and stumbled.

Again, she clapped, closer to my face this time. A threat.

Dick reached for my hand and put an arm around my waist. "Stop it. Leave the girl alone."

She slapped him.

He let go of me. Confusion spread across his face.

"Get out of my house before I have you arrested," she said.

I hobbled down the hallway, out the front door, to the street. When the door slammed, Dick wasn't behind me. A car turned onto the road and passed the house. My face burned when the woman driving a Lexus saw me in the Tweety Bird pajamas.

Oh no. My cellphone was still in Priscilla's guest room along with Dick's scrap paper, the one with his number scribbled on it. I didn't have a phone, shoes, or clothes. Every step on my right foot ached, despite the tight ace bandage wrap. If I stayed here, Priscilla might call the police. I waited for Dick. Minutes passed, and he didn't come.

Lead clouds gathered in splotchy gray patches, and it promised more rain. Rae expected me to open Flavors Ice Cream shop at ten. I didn't have a key, a uniform, or even her phone number. The number was in the phone I left behind. With no one to help me, I limped toward the park. In a few blocks, I could rest on the bench.

My ankle throbbed. When I got there, I tried to stay on the grass but sank into the soft earth. Cool mud squished between my toes.

Ahead, two guys sat on my bench. The bigger one wore moth-eaten clothes, a scarecrow of a man. I knew the men from the laundromat. Last time they saw me, they got a face full of fire-extinguisher spray. They'd never forgive me.

Fat rain drops fell. Spheres of water plopped and splattered against me full force. I moved behind an oak tree. It was tall and strong—strong enough to shelter and hide me. It was all I had in the world. The two bums on the bench stood and turned.

Thunder rumbled.

They strolled my way, while I hugged the scratchy tree bark.

If only I could blend in.

"Hey, it's Miss Sprinkles," one of them yelled.

A spiderweb of lightning flashed through the clouds. It could've struck the tree. I scanned the park for a safe place. There was nowhere to go. The homeless men and I were almost alone. Almost.

Chapter 34

A horn blasted, and a white Cadillac pulled up to the curb.

That didn't stop the homeless men. They ambled toward me.

I limped toward Dick's car. Over my shoulder, the guys jogged across the wet grass. They were coming for me. Raindrops plummeted from the sky.

As I dodged the puddles, my ankle burned with each step. "Leave me alone."

"Miss Sprinkles, we have a score to settle."

I waved my arms, hoping Dick would come before they nabbed me. "There's my dad. He's a cop. If you don't go away, he'll arrest you."

Wicked laughter followed.

Mud coated my feet while endless rain washed it away. The wet Tweety Bird pajamas stuck to me.

"You hear her, Rich? Ms. Sprinkles either is lying, or she's crazy. Either way, we owe her one."

They were probably going to throw me into the swan creek or hold me facedown in a puddle as payback. Maybe something worse.

Dick opened his door and stepped out. "Is there a problem, fellas?"

"It's none of your beeswax. Why don't you get back in that nice caddie of yours and drive on?"

"Arrest them, Daddy. They're after me."

Dick rushed to my side. "Don't make me take you fellas into the station. It's my day off, and I get pissed when punks like you make me go back to work."

The guys stopped. Their jaws dropped when Dick wrapped an arm around me. I leaned on him, while he guided me to the car. Inside, the Cadillac was clean and dry. Dick brought my clothes, and my guitar sat on the back seat.

He hurried to the other side and got in. "Good bluff. But it could've gone either way."

"Those guys robbed me last night. I got even with them. And got my phone back," I said.

Dick handed me my cellphone. "You almost lost it again."

Rain cascaded over the windshield. He started the engine and began to drive away when he changed his mind. Instead, he let the car idle.

"I can't drive in this. The storm will let up in a bit. Then we'll go."

"What happened after I left Priscilla's?" I asked, knowing it didn't go well since he was here with my clothes. She would never let him leave without a fight.

"It's over between us. This time for good."

A rock crashed into the windshield and bounced off the hood. It left a star-shaped crack that rippled across the glass. The homeless guys stood several feet away, grinning.

"Are you okay?" Dick asked.

"Yeah. I guess they want to test you."

He hit the gas and sped away.

"You're not going to do anything to them?" I asked.

"I could report them, but how would this look to the police? I have a teenage runaway in my car. You're wet, barefoot, and in pajamas. What do you think they're going to say?"

My dad would've whipped the homeless guys' butts. He would've punched them, broken their noses, legs, and any other body parts. He'd never call the police.

"What time is it?" I asked.

He glanced down at my muddy feet. "It's time for you to take another shower." He turned onto a curvy street, winding into town. "You're going to get sick wearing those damp clothes."

"Where are we going?"

"Someplace safe."

****

When Dick and I arrived in Wakefield, the rain fizzled to a light mist. He drove down a desolate street that ran parallel to the sea. As he turned into a circle driveway, the red door of the colonial house opened.

A lady with long silver hair stood smiling and waving at us.

"She's my mom." His serious face eased into that of a son who missed and needed his mother. The jitterbugs in my stomach stopped kicking and punching me. I took a deep slow breath. After what happened at Priscilla's, he wouldn't bring me here if his mom was a troll.

Dick parked the car. "She's a great lady who makes friends with everyone in five minutes. You'll love her."

"But look at me. I'm a mess." I brushed back my tangled hair and sighed.

"Trust me, she won't care."

If she took a hard look at me, she'd take me behind the house and hose me down. Dick will need to detail his car after I sat in it. No way this woman was letting me into her home.

I opened my door when he did and slid out. He picked up the laundry basket with my clothes.

"Hey, Mom, I brought a visitor. Her name is Tracie."

"Hi, Tracie. All the kids call me Grandma Mirna. Come on up here."

It was a lovely gray house with white columns flanking the rosy door. It seemed as warm and inviting as the woman who lived here.

I limped closer to the steps, and Mirna continued to smile despite my wet pajamas and dirty feet. She must be a saint. It felt awkward just the same. I might as well be walking into church this way.

Dick set the basket down and hugged her.

"We have blueberry pancakes, coffee, and hot chocolate," Mirna said.

"I'm starving. I bet Tracie's hungry, too."

"I am." It had been two days since I had a decent meal. The thought of sitting down at a table and eating a pancake smothered in butter and maple syrup made me want to jump for joy.

"There's enough food for everyone."

Mirna whispered something to Dick, then disappeared into the house. She returned with a pail of water and towels. Within a few minutes, my feet were clean and dry. She gave me another dry towel to wrap around my waist until I could change my clothes.

"Your ankle looks swollen. Does it hurt?" Mirna asked.

"Yes, ma'am."

We stepped inside the entryway which opened into a spacious living room. A stone fireplace anchored one wall. It extended from the wood floor to a lofty ceiling.

The skylight brightened the room despite the rain clouds. Beautiful antique tables, lamps, plush sofas, and chairs were everywhere.

"Come into the kitchen." She led us to a room with mint-green walls and quickly set the wooden table with plates, forks, and cups. "Sit down. Don't be shy."

I hovered in front of a chair. "Can I help?"

"You're sweet, but it's under control." She lifted a ceramic platter and set the pancakes on the table. "I'm so pleased Dick called and you're here. I love to cook, but I hate eating alone. Too often I end up doing that."

Dick poured the coffee and cocoa while Mirna retrieved a bottle of maple syrup. The fluffy pancakes were made with fresh blueberries, not the rehydrated kind. When we finished eating, the doorbell chimed.

Mirna stood. "I'll be right back." She left us alone in the kitchen.

"You're right. I love your mom." A warmth spread through me as I said it. I hoped he could work out his problems. I'd help anyway possible.

"You know what? Mom raised me and my sister all by herself. My dad died when I was four. She's retired but volunteers part time at the hospital."

Mirna was the type of lady to sit at someone's deathbed and hold their hand while they passed.

Through the open plantation shutters, we had an ocean view. The turquoise sea settled into a peaceful calm despite the earlier storm. Playful sunrays danced on the waves lapping to shore.

"This is a beautiful place," I said.

"Thanks, my sister and I bought the house for Mom after we started making money. Mom worked two jobs to put us through college. She deserves this."

Wow, Mirna was a supermom. My mother didn't care if I went to school. When I asked my father about going to college, he had said, 'Girls don't need to go to college. Even if you did, you'll never make as much money as a man. Find a good husband to support you.'

His words hit me as hard as his belt. 'But, Dad, I want to do something more with my life. I don't want to be stuck at home, cooking and cleaning.'

He shook his head. 'That's too bad. You should appreciate the life you're given. Study hard, and you'll graduate high school. Your mother doesn't have a high school diploma, and she gets along fine.'

The rattling plates interrupted my thoughts. I should be helping Dick clean the kitchen. I hobbled to the sink when Mirna popped into the room.

"Look who's here."

It was Tammy from Sprinkles. "Tracie, what are you doing here?" she asked with wide eyes.

"Just visiting."

Dick set down a cup and went to Tammy. When he hugged her, she shirked away.

"It's okay, sweetheart. We have a lot to discuss," he said.

Mirna patted my arm. "Tracie, let's get you settled. Come with me."

We left them alone. I picked up my laundry basket and walked the hallway to a bedroom with peach-colored walls. The mattress was set on a sleigh-bed frame and made up with a white comforter and frilly pillow shams. On one end, there was an adjoining bathroom.

"I thought you might like to freshen up," Mirna said.

"May I shower?"

"Absolutely. And if you need to call someone, you

can use the phone." She pointed to the vintage telephone sitting on the nightstand. "You can use anything you find in here."

"Thank you."

"I have something else for you, too." She opened the closet and pulled out a medical boot with Velcro straps. "The doctor gave it to me when I twisted my ankle. If it fits, you can have it." She handed me the walking boot.

"Thank you."

Mirna disappeared into the hallway.

The well-stocked bathroom had soap, shampoo, conditioner, new toothbrushes, and everything a girl could want. There was even a blow-dryer and curling iron in the drawer.

I took a hot shower and washed away the grime. My scalp tingled when I lathered it with the tea-tree shampoo. It felt so clean and fresh. I even forgot about my swollen ankle.

The linen closet had a first-aid kit. I re-wrapped my ankle though it didn't hurt anymore and dressed in my Flavors uniform. Rae might fire me for losing the key.

There was no guarantee Dick would cart me to work. I had already put the man through hell. Because he protected me, the thugs broke his windshield. On the flip side, I showed him the real Priscilla. Maybe he'd fix his marriage and his relationship with Tammy. She was on a fast track to alcoholism. She needed her dad before she ended up dead like her sister, Amy.

The clock on the nightstand said it was nine fifteen. I had to call Rae.

I opened my phone and scrolled for the number. Instead of using all my minutes, I called on Mirna's phone. Rae answered on the third ring.

"Good morning, Rae, it's Tracie."

"Hi, Tracie, is everything okay?" Rae sounded stressed like something was terribly wrong.

"No. I lost the key to the store."

"Already? Don't tell me you left the shop unlocked all night. I can't deal with any more bad news."

"No, the store doors are locked. I lost the key after I finished working last night. It's probably in a ditch, covered in mud. Can you give me another one?"

"I can't. My son's sick, and we're on our way to the hospital."

"Oh, I hope he'll be okay… Can I have Jill's number? She has a key."

"No, I tried calling her all morning. She's not answering."

Of course, Jill and her family were busy with funeral arrangements. The poor girl was probably bawling her eyes out since her grandmother died. She didn't want to hear from Rae. I didn't want to go to work anyhow, not with my bad ankle.

"I can't talk now, but thanks for the heads up. When corporate calls and screams at me because we didn't sell any ice cream, I'll know why."

"Rae, I'm sorry. It was an accident."

"Accident or not, you let me down."

This wasn't going well. But I had to ask. "So do I still have a job?"

"I can't talk now. Call me later." She disconnected.

I set the phone on its hook. Part of me was relieved. I didn't have to stand on my ankle all day. Would Rae lose her job because of me? I didn't want it to happen. There was no doubt in my mind she had to fire me. When she reported what I did, corporate would say I was just another irresponsible employee. They'd let her keep her job. If she fired me, it was for the best.

I had a more important call to make.

Chapter 35

Mom's lie had caught up with her. When growing up, I never questioned her. On long road trips, she said if we closed our eyes, we'd get there faster. Jason and I shut our eyes and fell asleep. When we woke, we were there.

Mom used to say the windshield wipers knew when it was raining. It seemed they did as they whipped back and forth at the first sprinkle. It wasn't until I turned nine that I learned about the sensors.

Those were white lies. But what about the things that mattered?

According to a talk show, one third of the fathers raised other men's kids, unknowingly. It seemed like it had to be someone else, not me. It was the red-haired boy who lived two doors down. His dad's hair was brown and straight. The blue-eyed children I babysat had parents with brown eyes. Their mothers might've lied to their husbands. I didn't doubt Dad was Dad until MyDNA sent the results.

While sitting on the bed in Mirna's guest bedroom, I called Aunt Martha's house again. It was strange my auntie and uncle weren't home. Leaving messages didn't seem like a good idea. You don't leave a message saying, 'Hey, Uncle Chuck, I'm your daughter.'

The MyDNA test didn't lie. Uncle Chuck and I shared fifty percent of our DNA. Did he even know we were on the same relative list? How often did he check his email alerts?

If Brent knew Uncle Chuck was my real father when Mom was pregnant, he would've beaten her until she miscarried. Then again, there was always the possibility Mom didn't know for sure.

I picked up the receiver and pressed the numbers. On the fourth ring, Uncle Chuck answered.

"Hi, Uncle Chuck, it's me, Tracie—"

"Tracie, we've been worried sick. Where are you?"

My heart beat faster now. But it was good to hear his voice.

"Out east. I've been calling, but no one answers."

"Martha got in a car accident. But she's okay."

Oh my, she could've died.

"Are you there?" he asked.

"Yes. Is she home?"

"No, your auntie is in a rehab facility. She's coming home tomorrow. The doctors and therapists have done a great job with her."

I need to leave Rhode Island today. She needs me.

"Have you talked to your mother?" He sounded as if he knew something I didn't.

"No, her phone was disconnected."

"Something happened. She and Brent aren't together. Your mom moved to Missouri, to your grandmother's house. Jason is here, with us."

How odd.

"Tracie, we want you to move back to Arkansas. Don't you want to?"

The words were sweet. If only he'd let me live with him, I'd agree. There was no way I'd live with Brent again. I'd call him Brent since he wasn't my real dad.

"I want to. But I don't want trouble. I can't get along with my parents."

"Ever since we heard you ran away with an older boy, we've been going out of our minds. If you could live with me and Martha, would you come?"

All I had to do was cash my Sprinkles paycheck and hop on a bus. I didn't belong here. I belonged in Arkansas with my people. People who loved and understood me.

"Yes. I'd like that... Will Jason still be there? Uncle Chuck, there's something else." It was time to tell him he wasn't just my uncle by marriage. This gave him the power to become my guardian.

"Good, I'm glad you're coming. Jason will be here for a while. And yes, you need money. I can send you whatever you need. Western Union is everywhere."

If I told him what he wasn't prepared to hear, would he change his mind? Taking in a runaway niece is different from finding out the girl is your daughter. It was a bomb, and once I lit the fuse, it would blow. If the news upset Aunt Martha, they might send me away.

"I've been working and saving my money. I got paid yesterday. It's enough to buy a bus ticket."

"It's not safe for a teenager to travel alone."

What did he expect me to do? Cal wouldn't drive me home. Aunt Martha and Jason needed Uncle Chuck there. It was time to put someone else ahead of myself. I'd make the trip alone. By golly, I was almost seventeen.

"Uncle Chuck, I'll be okay. It's not like hitchhiking. There's lots of good people on the bus."

"There's something else I want to tell you." His voice was deep and thoughtful.

I shifted on the bed and leaned on the frilly pillow.

"Dad beat Mom again?"

Above me the ceiling fan spun. Round and round it went in circles. Dad went round and round in circles. Dad slapped Mom if he found his favorite shirt wrinkled in the dryer. When Mom neglected to pay the bills, the thirty dollars in late fees cost her a black eye.

"Brent broke her jaw. A neighbor called the police, and they arrested him. This time she pressed charges."

Good for her. A busted jaw wouldn't heal fast. She'd flinch when she chewed or brushed her teeth. It must've been one heck of a fight. As far as I knew, Brent never broke her bones before.

"Is he in jail?" I asked.

"Yes, the judge sentenced him."

With Brent locked up, we were safe. Maybe Mom would piece her life together. Grandma would help her. She never liked her son-in-law.

"Wow, I'm glad he can't hurt her anymore," I said. Mom failed at mothering me, but with Brent in prison, she'd be a better mother to Jason.

"No, he can't hurt her or anyone else. At least no one outside the iron bars."

"Do you know why they fought?"

He cleared his throat. "Are you sitting down?"

I fluffed the pillow under my head. "I'm lying down."

"You took a DNA test, didn't you? The one your grandmother sent to you? She sent me one, too."

Oh, did he know?

"Yes, Mom threw it away, but I found it in the trash."

"Did you see the results?"

"Yes, did you?"

"Yes, I did. I took the test. Brent saw the results. You had the passwords saved on your computer, and he logged into your email. Your mother was as shocked as he was to learn he's not your father, but he accused her of knowing all along. I suspected but didn't know for sure until your test results came back."

Oh no, My DNA results stirred up all this trouble. It didn't surprise me Brent got into my email. He was always spying on me, trying to catch me doing something wrong. This time he dug up something he couldn't control.

"Does Aunt Martha know?"

"Yes…but I want to explain something to you. Your mom was pregnant before I married your aunt. Julie was dating both me and Brent. She made her choice clear."

It was hard to believe Mom picked Brent over Uncle Chuck. No doubt she regretted it over the years. That's why she was bitter toward Aunt Martha. Mom was jealous.

"How's Aunt Martha taking the news?"

"It surprised her in a good way. She said you were like a daughter to her. She wants you here."

"I'd like that."

A knock came at the door. "Are you okay in there?" Tammy asked.

"Yes, I'll be right out."

"Good, I need your help with something important."

Chapter 36

The next twenty-four hours sped by like an Amtrak Train. Tammy took my check to the bank, while I worked her shift at Sprinkles. It freed her up. She and her dad spent their afternoon sitting on her grandmother's deck overlooking the sea. What better place to have a heart-to-heart talk?

Outside Sprinkles' windows, the sun streamed in, the last hurrah before it faded into dusk. I organized the fancy pastries, brownies and lined up cinnamon rolls in the display case when Tammy dropped by.

"Here's your money." Tammy set a bulging bank envelope on the counter.

I moved the last peanut butter brownie into its spot. "Thank you. I'll buy a ticket home tomorrow. Sprinkles can send the rest to my auntie's address next payday."

Tammy smiled. "No problem. Thanks for covering. My mom and dad are going to dinner tonight."

Maybe Dick's wife would give him another chance. I hoped so.

"I'm happy for him and you." I was happy for myself too. By the weekend, I'd see my own family. With a little luck, Mom would let Jason live at my aunt's house permanently.

Tammy slung her purse, which looked more like luggage, onto her shoulder. "I've got to go, but I'll pick you up after your shift. Grandma Mirna invited you to stay with us until you leave. I'll take you to the bus station in the morning."

"You guys are the best."

"You're all right yourself. Dad said because of you and what happened with that Russo woman, he came to his senses. It's funny how things worked out."

Cars pulled into the Sprinkles parking lot, and the patrons ambled toward the door. Tammy stepped aside, letting them in before going.

Between pouring coffee and fetching donuts, I phoned Cal. He picked up on the second ring. "Hi, it's Tracie. I called to say goodbye."

"Where are you going?" he asked, but didn't sound interested.

"Arkansas. I've decided to stay with relatives and graduate with my high school class. I'm leaving tomorrow."

Though I found my birth father, I didn't care to explain it to Cal. I wanted him to know I survived Rhode Island.

The lull in our conversation had me clenching my teeth, and I cleared my throat.

"Well…have a safe trip," he said.

My onetime friend didn't have anything else for me. He didn't offer to meet one last time. It occurred to me that it was my fault. I had milked the goodwill cow dry. I should've acted grateful when Cal looked after me. If I had, maybe he wouldn't have left me to fend for myself. But his weak goodbye in this final exchange stirred my bitterness. A frog wedged itself in my throat, and nothing I wanted to say would croak out.

"Okay. Bye," I said and cut him loose.

****

Mirna packed me an assortment of food. Inside the brown paper bag, baggies held peanut-butter-jelly sandwiches and potato chips. She also gave me an apple, a banana, and two water bottles. Dick spent the night with his wife, but he left a hundred dollars in small bills for my trip. He also gifted me a carry-on suitcase with wheels. It was nice not to have to haul my clothes around in a trash bag.

Mirna handed me the cash. "Use this money for vending machines and anything else you need. Don't let anyone see how much you have."

A happy tear slid down my cheek. I loved Mirna and her son. They were the best. As for the money, well, it was a sweet bonus. I would've had to work several hours to earn so much.

Tammy waited in the car while I said goodbye to Mirna.

The gray-haired woman with the soft round face hugged me and patted my cheeks. "You take care of yourself, honey. Call us if there's trouble."

"I will." I hugged her. "Thank you for everything."

Once inside Tammy's car, I remembered something.

"Hey, can you take me to Celia's Attic?"

"Why?"

"I have an old debt to pay."

Ten minutes later, she rolled into the thrift-store parking lot.

A black cape fluttered above the floor as the goth woman walked toward a customer across the floor. No one stood near the counter, so I dashed to it.

Thumbing through my money, I pulled out twelve dollars, two more than I owed, and placed it next to the register. Somehow by leaving more, it eased my conscience a little, but wrong was wrong.

I returned to Tammy's car and slid in.

"You owed someone money?" Tammy asked.

"Yeah, I stole a pair of shoes. But I feel better after paying for them."

"I'm changing my ways, too. Since my sister died, I couldn't stop drinking. I'm ashamed of how I've been stealing to support my habit. Dad said I need to go to rehab. I agreed."

"Good."

The trip to the bus station flew by. Tammy zigzagged through the traffic. Slow cars we passed blurred into red, gray, and blue flashes. At the bus station, pedestrians flooded the sidewalk. A bus stopped with a screech. The people lined up and showed their tickets to the attendant as they climbed the steps into the massive vehicle.

Tammy parked and flipped on her hazard lights. "I'll see you off."

The jitterbugs kicked inside my stomach. Soon I'd have a ticket in my hand, and Tammy would drive away, leaving me with strangers. Busses loaded, unloaded, and rolled away in different directions. Overwhelming.

Tammy's car idled in an illegal zone, so we rushed to the counter. Five minutes later, a station employee sold me the ticket, and I stood among the sea of unwashed travelers. I called Uncle Chuck and gave him the news.

"Your brother is excited to see you," he said.

I wanted to ask about Jason, but the phone minutes were running out. In two days, we'd talk again, and he'd pick me up at the final station.

****

The journey home was an endless cycle of sleeping, stretching my legs, bathroom breaks, and eating tiny meals. My sticky skin smelled like bus seats and sweat. By day two, I ate all the goodies Mirna packed. Each stop, in new cities, created an influx of weary travelers. People came, people went. The bus was never full, making it possible for me to have two seats for myself.

Short stops allowed me to brush up on my guitar. Playing songs broke up the boredom. People gathered around for a sing-along, including three jolly ex-convicts. They enjoyed music so much they sang on the bus.

I missed them after they left. The trip droned on like the humming engine. After several layovers in Midwestern towns, I arrived in Arkansas.

I picked up my luggage, guitar, and stepped off the bus.

"Tracie." A woman's voice called to me.

Aunt Martha, Uncle Chuck, and Jason stood on the sidewalk, smiling. Jason had Tigger on a leash.

I ran to them, lugging the suitcase. They met me halfway, and Aunt Martha's soft arms embraced me.

"We're glad you're here," Uncle Chuck said.

Happy tears tracked down my cheeks as each family member hugged me. Tigger jumped on me and licked my face.

"Wow, you got our dog back." I scratched behind his ears.

"I sure did. I asked Mr. Thompson, and he let me have him. Tigger went to obedience school. He's even house-trained."

I was safe. Seeing Jason made me realize how much I missed him. They were all here, and it was a dream come true.

We loaded the car. While Uncle Chuck drove us to their newest place, I told them about the trip. We pulled into the circular driveway of a two-story red, brick house.

White roses bloomed in the flower beds. Elephant ears and lavender lined the sidewalk to the door.

"Let me help." Jason hopped out and rolled my suitcase to the door. "I can't wait to show you your room. I helped paint it."

"He sure did. And he painted his room too," Aunt Martha said.

Was it possible? Mom let Jason move here? Fantastic. And how did they manage to fix up a room for me? I called three days ago.

We entered the grand entryway where a rustic chandelier dangled from the ceiling.

"I made it myself," Uncle Chuck said, pointing at the beautiful overhead light.

Jason smiled. "Dad can make furniture, too."

Did I hear him right? Did he call Uncle Chuck his dad?

"What did you call him?"

"Dad," Jason said, removing Tigger's leash and letting him roam free in the house.

"We learned I'm Jason's father too," Uncle Chuck said.

In the excitement of finding my real dad, I forgot to check the rest of the DNA report.

"But you said Mom made her choice and married Brent. After that, you married Aunt Martha."

"Yes, but not right away. Your parents broke up and almost divorced. You were too young to remember. I

270

saw your mother then. Later, she never said anything about the baby, and I thought Jason was Brent's son."

Aunt Martha smiled. "I always wanted a couple kids whether they're his or mine. I'm your aunt and your stepmother. I know I can't replace Julie, but you can call me Mama Martha."

My head spun. It was exciting news, but Mom never let Jason out of her sight. She didn't just hand him over.

"Where's Mom? What did she say about this?"

Uncle Chuck glanced at Aunt Martha, and his expression grew serious. "She's in Missouri. She's been going to therapy. I petitioned to keep Jason, and the judge agreed."

There had to be more to the story. Mothers didn't lose their children easily. But I just got here and didn't want to ask too many questions, not yet.

Jason beckoned me to follow him upstairs. "C'mon, I want you to see the bedroom." When we climbed to the second level, he opened the door to the first room which had a queen-sized canopy bed with billowy white drapes. Under it, a golden looped rug warmed the hardwood floor.

"Wow," I said.

He pointed to the walls. "The color is sea spray blue." The shade was as vibrant as the ocean in Rhode Island. The light streamed through the open blinds, making it seem magical. It was a bedroom like Dee's.

"It's beautiful. Thank you." I hugged him. He didn't know how much I loved him, but I had an idea how much he loved me.

****

In early September, the doorbell chimed.

Jason and I looked up from the kitchen table where

we sat quietly and did our homework. Mama Martha stopped dicing potatoes, wiped her hands on her apron, and answered the door.

Who was it? We weren't expecting company on a school day.

"What are you doing here?" Mama Martha said from the other room.

"I came to see my children." It was Mom's voice.

"You're not supposed to be here."

Jason and I exchanged glances and closed our books.

Mom has come for us? No, this can't be.

Jason hopped off his chair. "I don't want to see her. She just stood there and let Dad hit me." He ran through a door, bypassing our mom's view. It led to an alternate stairwell going to our rooms. His feet pounded the steps on his way up.

It explained why Dad and Mama Martha were able to get custody. Jason took my beatings after I left. My heart sank. My poor little brother. I couldn't look at her knowing she failed to protect him. And the last time we spoke, she forced me to stay in Rhode Island. She was a terrible mom.

I edged to the kitchen doorway where I could sneak a peek at Mom. Part of me still wanted to see her despite our problems.

My aunt blocked the door, but Mom pushed her aside and came into the living room.

I ducked into the kitchen.

If she spotted me, would she try to drag me to the car?

"No, you can't see them," Mama Martha said.

"It's not fair to punish me for what Brent did. Why

did you slap a restraining order on me?"

"You never gave a damn about those kids. If I would've known the whole story earlier, you would've lost them sooner. Besides, we don't know the man you're living with."

This was the first I heard Mom had a boyfriend. She didn't waste time replacing Brent. She restarted the cycle. She'd never be a mother to me or Jason. But Mama Martha would protect us.

"They're my kids, not yours. Chuck isn't their father. He was a sperm donor."

"Don't you ever say that to me again. Leave before I call the police."

"Please give this to Tracie," Mom said.

I snuck another peek. She held a piece of paper.

"What is it?"

"My phone number. If I can't see her, at least let her call me."

"I'll do no such thing. It's time for you to go."

"I have a right to talk to her." Mom set the pink Post-it on the coffee table.

"Someday, but not today. When you straighten out your life, you can ask Chuck."

"This isn't fair. He was nothing more than a sperm donor."

"Go, or I'll call the cops." Mama Martha picked up the paper and crumpled it.

"Sperm donor, sperm donor, sperm donor," Mom screamed on her way out.

The door slammed, and Mama Martha turned the lock. She looked over her shoulder at me. "I'm sorry you had to hear that rubbish."

Mom was crazy. Not just a little crazy. Insane. But

she was still my mother.

I joined Mama Martha in the living room. From the window, I spied Mom standing in the driveway, and she caught my stare. She brought her hand up to her mouth and made the call-me hand gesture.

If I could get the number, I would.

Chapter 37

I found the crumpled slip of pink paper in the kitchen trash can and held it to my chest.

It was Mom's number in her own handwriting. Guilt washed over me. I should've interfered when Mama Martha told her to leave. I had plenty of questions only Mom could answer. Why did it take her so long to come after Jason? Why didn't she let me come home when I was stranded? Why did she stay with Brent so long?

Saturday came, and I mustered the courage to pick up the phone and tap in the numbers.

She answered after three rings.

"Mom, it's me."

"Tracie, baby, are you okay?"

"I'm fine. How are you?"

"I'd be better if I could see you."

Could I trust her? So far, I liked living with Mama Martha. Would meeting her mess up my arrangement? My seventeenth birthday had passed, but I was still a minor. The restraining order didn't cover me, only Jason.

"I want to talk," Mom said.

"We are talking."

"Please, this is awkward. If it makes you feel better, we can meet in a public place. Anywhere."

An hour later, we met at Canter Park, not far from Mama Martha's house in case our conversation soured.

Mom hugged me, and I sank into her warm arms.

I couldn't remember the last time she was happy to see me. Even when I was a child, Mom didn't hold me often. When I ventured near her, she shooed me away.

We settled for a private gazebo far from the busy picnic pavilions. Most of the screeching and laughter came from children on the swings.

"I don't know where to begin," Mom said.

"Why didn't you want me home?"

"I did. Your dad and I were having problems. I protected you."

"By cutting me off?"

"You survived."

"What if I hadn't?" I said, realizing I was lucky and not smart.

"You've always been a survivor. You were better off without us."

"How can you say that? You had no idea what I went through—"

"You chose Cal over us."

"You didn't protect me from Brent."

"Watch your mouth. He raised you as his own."

"And you're still defending him. I had to leave. He was going to beat me, and you didn't care."

"I did the best I could, but you broke the rules. You were always pigheaded."

Her words hit hard, and the pain came rushing back. Nothing had changed between us.

A weighty silence followed, while I fought the tears. No matter what she said, I refused to cry in front of her.

"I have a favor to ask," she said.

"What?"

"Convince Martha and Chuck to let me have Jason on the weekends. They might listen to you."

"I have to go… Mama Martha is probably wondering where I am."

Her jaw dropped. "Mama Martha? You call her Mama?"

"She is my stepmother."

Chapter 38

Five years had passed when we got the news. Up until then, we didn't hear from Mom. I sent her invitations to both my high school and college graduation, but she didn't respond. I wondered if she planned to go to Jason's ceremony when he finished.

"Dad, it looks like twister weather," I said.

"We get a lot of them in May."

Jason stood by the window. "Are we still eating on the patio?"

Gusts whipped the tree branches, and they waved frantically as if the day was darker for more than one reason. Black clouds loomed like they were ready to burst.

"Babe, I better barbecue before the storm hits," Dad said.

Mama Martha toted a big platter of raw, seasoned chicken from the kitchen and handed it to him.

My family intended to have the picnic anyway, even if it meant bringing the food indoors. Dad grilled the meat, while Mama Martha and I chopped boiled potatoes and onions for our potato salad. We mixed in the pickle relish, mustard, and mayonnaise. Jason brewed the tea.

Thirty minutes passed when the telephone rang.

Mama Martha wiped her hands on a dishtowel and picked up her cellphone. "Yes, you have the right Martha... Oh...when did she pass?" A stony expression replaced Mama's smile. Her eyes widened as she struggled to process the caller's words.

I set the bowl aside on the counter.

Someone died. Who?

Mama Martha listened to the caller and turned her back to me.

Whatever happened wasn't any of my business. She knew lots of people. The caller could've been a well-meaning friend who let her know someone departed as a courtesy to their family.

Dad yelled from the patio, "Can someone get me a clean plate?" He swabbed the chicken thighs with a generous blob of sweet hickory sauce, and the fire dried it quickly into a shiny, rich glaze. The grillmaster knew the difference between perfect barbecue and a burned dinner, which amounted to minutes.

I ran to a cabinet and found a platter. Dad piled the meat onto it and carried it inside. Jason placed the drinks on the table and set the plates and silverware. By the time we had everything arranged for our indoor picnic, the sky split wide open, showering the lawn. High wind ripped the trees naked, sending branches sailing over the fence. Thunder boomed, and silver flashes etched the sky.

Mama Martha finished the phone call. We sat down, ready for the feast.

"Something terrible has happened. I hate to say it during dinner, but if I don't, you'll hear it on the news," Mama Martha said.

"What?" Dad asked.

We all froze, six eyes piercing her.

Mama Martha drew in a breath. "Julie is gone. Brent killed everyone, including the man she lived with and most of his children."

"Oh my gosh." Her words shot through my heart, and it bled sorrow. It seeped into my bones. I never expected Brent to attack Mom after he made parole. The parole board was supposed to guarantee he was rehabilitated before they turned him loose.

Jason covered his face, and even at seventeen he appeared small and vulnerable. Somewhere in the cavern of our hearts, a soft spot remained. Once we dug out the resentment and anger, we still loved Mom. And she was gone, forever.

Brent will come. He has bullets with our names on them.

"Brent's still out there," I said.

Mama Martha shook her head. "No, he'll never hurt anyone again. He blew a hole in his own head."

The barbecued meat and fixings on the table no longer interested me. The similarity between dead chicken and dead people lying in the morgue made me queasy.

"I can't eat right now," I said.

Dad's face was somber. Jason stood, still hiding his from us.

****

Mama Martha was right. It didn't take long before the whole nation heard about the murders. The news blared on every major network the way it did when a creep blew up a federal building.

Mom belonged to us. With heavy hearts, we made the arrangements. The cemetery on the edge of town had a peaceful spot. We buried Mom under a big oak tree. She would've liked her granite headstone with a lamb carved into it. We gave her a quiet funeral. Other than us, only a few of her neighbors and her boyfriend's grown daughter, Callie, attended.

As for Brent, his elderly mother claimed his body. She had him cremated and planned to bury the urn in her casket when she died someday.

Callie had her father and her siblings laid to rest in Newton County. We attended. Dad contributed what he could to help pay for the funeral.

On the day of the service, Callie called me over. "I was cleaning out Julie's things and came across letters addressed to you and Jason." She passed the sealed envelopes to me.

Our names were scrawled in the center, in Mom's handwriting. My heart pounded. Mom had something to say. I had no idea how long ago she wrote them, and I itched to read mine, but the formalities weren't over. I wanted to read it in private, at home.

We attended the wake at Callie's home where her father's friends and neighbors trickled in with trays of food. They piled finger sandwiches, tuna noodle casseroles, macaroni salads, and platters of carrots, celery, and cheese wedges on the table. It sat there, untouched as the people milled around. It was a pity that food ended up in the garbage, uneaten after these events. No one had an appetite, including me. I wanted nothing more than to escape and open Mom's letter.

****

Two hours passed, a respectable amount of time to leave the wake. Dad drove us home. Thirty minutes seemed like an eternity as we rolled by my old school and neighborhood. My dress pocket held the sealed secrets. Jitterbugs kicked my stomach.

What did the letters say?

Once inside, I waved at Jason. "Let's go upstairs."

With him on my heels, I trudged upward and stopped on the landing.

"What are we doing?" he asked.

I gave him his letter. "Callie found letters from Mom." I hurried to my room and locked the door. With a fingernail, I ripped it open and unfolded the paper.

Dear Tracie,

If you're reading this, I have missed my opportunity to tell you in person how I much I love you. I planned to tear up this letter if we ever talked again. I made mistakes I can't fix.

When you called me from Rhode Island, I should've found a way to help. I said no, even though it broke my heart to push you away. It was hard not to have my baby girl with me. But I still believe you were better off without us. I failed. Even mothers are afraid of monsters. I had to let you go. I knew you'd find your way out of the darkness, somehow.

I found my way too. Since Brent went to prison, I found a real man who never raised a fist against me. I had hoped you'd call me again. I'm not allowed to call you. Besides, I can see you're happy at Martha's house.

I always knew Chuck was your biological father. Brent always suspected. He didn't know Chuck was also Jason's father. I was wrong to throw away the DNA kits. I'm glad you and Jason found out the truth.

Since you moved in with Martha and Chuck, I've watched you from afar. I even went to your graduation. Tracie, I'm proud of you and Jason. I always have been.

I'm sorry I was a bad mother. I should've done more for you and Jason. I hope you can forgive me and Brent. Forgiveness isn't for us. It doesn't excuse the horrible things that happened or minimize them. It's about letting

your anger go before it kills you. It's a gift for yourself.
I hope you understand.

Love Always
Mom

As I read the letter, the hot tears slid down my cheeks. It was the first time I cried since her death. All these years I blamed her for what Brent did. But like she said, even mothers were afraid of monsters.

I sobbed into my pillow. When I finished, I heard Jason bawling in his room.

At first, Jason and I buried the secrets with the tragedy. Over time, we talked about it. Mom was still our mom. Our hearts would never be whole without her, but we leaned on each other. Jason and I lived through the good, the bad, and the ugly.

Two years passed, and the murders seemed like a bad dream. Memories of Rhode Island faded, too. In a way, Mom saved me by not letting me come home. And after Jason took the beatings, Mom let him go, too. She couldn't save herself. Brent would never let her have peace.

I took Mom's advice and forgave everyone. Forgiveness was for me, not for them. It didn't mean I accepted the abuse. It meant I set them free. Resentment was my heart's prison, so I set myself free.

Jason and I stayed on at Dad's and Mama Martha's big house even after we were no longer teenagers. 'Stay with us. There's plenty of room,' they said. 'We have a huge house to hold all the love we have for you.'

A word about the author...

Ellen Y. Mueller enjoys writing YA novels, dark fantasy novels, poetry, short stories as well as nonfiction pieces. She is a member of Arkansas Ridge Writers and Oklahoma Writers' Federation Inc. She is an avid reader and lives in Arkansas with her husband, two dogs, and three cats.

Find Ellen online at:
Website: Ellenymueller.com
Instagram: @ellenymuellerwrites
Twitter: @EllenYMueller

Thank you for purchasing
this publication of The Wild Rose Press, Inc.

For questions or more information
contact us at
info@thewildrosepress.com.

The Wild Rose Press, Inc.
www.thewildrosepress.com

CPSIA information can be obtained
at www.ICGtesting.com
Printed in the USA
LVHW020947251122
733911LV00014B/379